The King's Jockey

For my dear brother Mike.

The King's Jockey

Lesley Gray

 Solis Press

First published by Solis Press, 2013

Although *The King's Jockey* was inspired by real people and actual events, it is a work of fiction. Events, characters, timelines and situations have been changed. Certain characters are composites or entirely fictitious.

ISBN: 978-1-907947-61-2

Published by Solis Press, PO Box 482, Tunbridge Wells TN2 9QT, Kent, England

Web: www.solispress.com | *Twitter*: @SolisPress

Contents

Prelude: The Derby Stakes, Epsom, June 1913   7

PART I THE EARLY YEARS

1 Epsom, June 1891   12
2 A new home, June 1892   24
3 Back to Epsom, October 1892   40
4 Flora, November 1893   45

PART II THE YEAR OF THE DIAMOND

5 Egerton, April 1900   52
6 2000 Guineas, Newmarket, 1900   65
7 Derby Day, Epsom, 1900   77
8 Newmarket, July 1900   89
9 St Leger, Doncaster, September 1900   93
10 Egerton, September 1900   96
11 Jockey Club Stakes, Newmarket, September 1900   102
12 End of the season, November 1900   106

PART III CELEBRITY

13 Paradise in the Strand, London, May 1902   112
14 Reg: Newmarket, 1906   117
15 Derby Stakes, Epsom, June 1909   124
16 A day out in London, November 1909   127
17 The end of an era, May 1910   138

18 Lily in Cambridge, November 1912   143
19 Morning of Derby Day, Epsom, 1913   146

PART IV AFTER THE FALL

20 Going home, June 1913   154
21 Royal Ascot, July 1913   179
22 Loss, July 1913   195
23 A dry spell, September 1913   199
24 Snowy's wedding, Newmarket, November 1913   206
25 Northumberland, November 1913   209
26 Christmas, December 1913   213
27 London, February 1914   219

PART V RESURRECTION

28 Report of a death, February 1914   234
29 The Derby, Epsom, June 1914   241
    Postscript   251
    Author's note   252

Prelude
The Derby Stakes,
Epsom, June 1913

A T THE TOP OF the hill the course drops away and the horses fly. The beat gets faster; hooves and hearts. The people shout up a gale fierce enough to burst an eardrum, whipping up the air until it drips greasy with fairgrounds and food stalls. Pulling away, the front runners barge and bump. Bertie holds Anmer steady. He leans forward. Come on boy, just one nice long run now. Swinging his head, Anmer gives a short shudder. Spots of spittle flick back on to the rich brocade of the royal silks.

Down and round at the Corner. Anmer is tiring. Bertie curbs the colt's urge to roll out with the camber. His own muscles ache. The screams and calls of the crowd close in. Tildy's words flash into his mind. He pushes them away and locks back into the race, checking the field and finding a line as the home stretch comes into sight. Up ahead the thrashing and jostling are frenzied. Hard pellets of mud pepper back. Bertie's face stings. Grit gathers on his tongue. He tries once more. Come on boy, let's go now, we can still put on a good show. Anmer responds and thrusts his head forward for the final gallop.

Up ahead something moves by the barrier. Black, flapping, darting out on to the course. A figure. It dodges the two horses in front. It's a woman. She pauses and turns. Her gaze is fixed on him, on him and Anmer. There is something almost familiar. Then she runs at them, right at them. As fast as she can, she runs. No room to swerve. No time. Bertie tries to pull up.

As they collide, the woman's face gapes open, all mouth and eyes. Anmer screams one long high-pitched cry, rising up, and they are caught in a dream. The woman's head hits Anmer's breast with the sharp crack of a spoon on a soft-boiled egg. Her body sags and twists like a sawdust doll. Spinning. White petticoats. Her hat sweeps away, taking red hair with it.

Anmer hovers in the air and topples. A writhing weight smothers Bertie as the grass comes up to meet him. Crushed ribs, empty lungs. A jolt wrenches his leg and his body follows, bumping over the unsteady ground. Then a release with just the sky for company. And then nothing.

A stream of light far away and his father's voice.

"Stay down, Bertie, two more to come."

"Dad? What are you doing here?" The words echo in his head but make no sound.

"Lie still lad, don't move."

"But the horse … "

"He's fine. He's gone off."

"There was a lady … "

Bertie's breath disappears. Darkness is all around. He rocks in an invisible cradle.

"Ring of light. Keep inside the ring of light," another voice.

"Tildy?"

"Stay still, Bertie."

From far away, someone touches him.

Thudding.

The ground throbs. Stampede. Voices, loud.

The shouting, close by. "Give us a hand. Poor bloody jockey. He's out cold."

"Prop him up."

"Let him have some air."

There is a pressure under his back. The darkness shifts, falling all around. His shoulder twists and the pain makes him open his eyes. Air rushes in, warm and earthy. Sitting up, wobbly top. Rattled brain won't think. Faces look down at him, waving. Sea-sick, his lids sink. Words bob up and down.

"Stand back. Stand back now."

8

"Mr Jones. Mr Jones, sir. Can you hear me?"

Light. A midsummer sunbeam widens into a tunnel of gold. It is warm and safe. He tumbles in long slow somersaults through the sparkling air. A familiar note calls. It is home. A skylark sings. Hooves clatter along the lane.

PART I
THE EARLY YEARS

I

Epsom, June 1891

STEPPING OUT OF THE morning mist, the horses trailed in from the gallops. Steam puffed from their coats and melted into the early blue of the sky. Bertie stood straight against the open gate leading into the yard. He lined up his spine against the wooden bars, flattening himself out as best he could. Swaying past, some of horses turned their heads to him and he greeted them each by name. He smiled at the riders. Most of the lads lodged at the house, so Bertie came across them every day as he went about his chores.

The new black colt, Ossian, looked particularly fine. There was now no trace of the nervousness that the horse had shown at first. But that wasn't surprising given who was riding him. Bertie squinted up at the great jockey sitting so straight and commanding in the saddle, just like King Arthur himself riding down from Camelot.

A commotion shook the thicket at the side of the lane. Whirring and clucking, a young pheasant half-ran, half-flew across the path of the colt. Bertie saw the startled glint in the horse's eye and made himself as still as could be. He watched as the great jockey took up the slack in the reins, ready but without fuss. The animal started to move backwards, jumbling his steps and stiffening his neck. But Mr Watts calmed the colt, so that soon they stood still and steady in the early sunshine.

"Perfection of nature," that was it. Bertie couldn't remember where he'd heard the words, maybe at school, maybe at church. Fancy words, but just right. Dad said horses were never born bad, it was just that sometimes the wrong treatment could turn them that way.

"Young Bertie, eh?" Mr Watts looked right at him. "Good lad. You didn't run."

"No, sir." Bertie's voice came out piping thin. He swallowed and tried again. "Dad said you shouldn't. It spooks them more."

"Your dad is quite right. Quite right."

Mr Watts guided the black colt towards the stables. Bertie wanted to follow and talk to him some more, but his legs had other ideas. They shook so much he couldn't move. It probably wasn't a good idea anyway, such a fine man would not want to be bothered by a stupid schoolboy.

"Catching flies, our Bert?" Reg ran up and snatched his little brother's cap, swatting it around his head. "You shouldn't be standing round here, you're supposed to be warning mother. She'll be mad if everyone turns up and things aren't ready."

But Bertie took no notice. "Did you see who that was?" he stammered and lifted his arm to point at the dismounting figure in the distance. "And he knew my name."

"Blimey," Reg whistled through his teeth as he followed Bertie's gaze.

ʊ ʊ ʊ

Bertie ran into the house, hot and hungry. Inside it felt very cool. His mother was glaring at the downcast form of his younger brother Percy. There was no smell of food.

"Just get the little sod out of my sight, Bertie. Look what he's done now!"

His mother pointed to the far corner of the kitchen. A chalky mush slopped over the edges of two enamel buckets. One of the kittens was already hunched over the pool that had formed. Its pink tongue slipped in and out with a fury as the milk seeped down into the gaps between the flagstones.

"I was making bread pudding to sell at the fair," Percy protested, only to receive another clip round the ear. He started to howl.

"Just five minutes. I turn my back for five minutes. He's used all the bread in the house and most of the sugar. Your sisters have disappeared; the little ones have been bawling their eyes out." His mother paused for breath. "Now you're back, and then your father, your brother and the others will be here, all wanting breakfast."

"Perhaps we can give Perce's pudding to the horses?" Bertie suggested, trying to be helpful. But his mother wasn't listening.

"And you know how your father is, just as likely to offer a meal to every passing tinker, trainer and stable hand." She tried to gather herself. "Now then, Bertie, run down to the bakery, there's a good boy. Bring back a couple of cottage loaves and two large tins."

She took down her housekeeping chest from the dresser. The chest was an old tea caddy displaying scenes from the life of Queen Victoria, but it was one of his mother's most treasured possessions. Bertie noticed that it didn't rattle much as she opened it and took out a shilling.

"There you go, and don't lose the change."

Bertie took the coin, carefully knotting it in his handkerchief and placing the bundle deep into his pocket.

"And don't forget to take that little sod with you," she called as he shot towards the door.

Bertie stopped and ran backwards lightly on his feet, sliding his step like the performer from Egypt that he'd seen at the fair. His mother shook her head at him, but grinned despite herself.

"Go on with you," she smiled, turning her head and glaring at Percy. "And don't you dare let him out of your sight!"

Bertie grabbed Percy's hand. The 'little sod' sniffed, smearing his nose across the shirtsleeve of his free arm.

"Cheer up, Perce. The sooner we go, the quicker we'll see our breakfast." Bertie paused to try and brush down his milk-streaked brother, but he just made the stains worse. "You're going to smell lovely when that lot dries."

ᴗ ᴗ ᴗ

Outside again, Bertie squinted. The morning shadows were already shrinking to nothing. Even though it was early, the roads were crammed with carts brimming with barrels, boxes, strips of wood and large coloured signs. Bertie always liked Show Sunday. It was easier to see the horses than on Derby Day itself. The town would be full of day-trippers, although not everyone welcomed them. Many of the houses had their fronts closed, making sure that the light, the noise and the general goings-on were all kept out. The shopkeepers grumbled to one another and let down their awnings.

Up ahead there was a commotion at the crossroads. Screams that made Bertie's scalp shiver cut across the chatter and clatter of the street. People rippled back along the road trying to pull away, but the trouble followed them. Through the dust, the front legs of a horse flayed out, back legs kicking: a lovely bright bay, young, probably only in its second year, all saddled up and with its reins hanging loose. Even from where he stood, Bertie could see the whites of the animal's eyes stark against the midnight brown iris. The colt's veins, full and pounding, snaked along the damp skin that clung to the thick muscle. As the animal twisted and turned, blood sprayed from cuts in its neck and hindquarters, spattering those close by and setting them off in a panic.

Bertie knew that the horse would keep hitting out, and it would only get worse as the fright took hold. He looked about for anyone from the stables, but there was no one. Round and round went the colt, becoming more frantic in its search for an escape route. People swarmed one way then the other. Bertie chewed his lip for a moment, then dragged Percy off into a side lane.

"Perce, you duck down there. Don't you dare move, you hear me?" he said, tucking his brother behind the chocked wheels of a cart that stood against a wall.

"Can I have a sweet if I don't move?" Percy sniffed.

"Just stay there!" snapped Bertie.

Behind him, the noise was getting louder. He turned to look. People scattered and screamed. The men kept as far back as the women. It was only a small horse but it was creating pandemonium in the High Street, and getting far too close to Mr Higg's grocery shop.

Bertie took a deep breath and walked into the space that had been left around the horse. He stood still, gauging the rhythm of the animal, waiting until he could feel the fear and the unease of its mind, until he could see the flashing shadows that flicked across the horse's eyes, smell the acrid odour of human sweat that fouled its nostrils, until he could taste the bitter metal thick between its teeth and feel the scorch of sore skin pricked raw by the burning air.

Slowly, Bertie moved towards the horse. Approaching alongside with his arms loosely outstretched, he kept his eyes down and talked quietly in a low gentle tone. The animal knew and beat its right hoof on the path, snorting and flicking its tail; but it didn't lash out. Bertie stood his ground and then moved a bit closer. The horse stopped. Bertie did the same again, and again, until the horse followed his movement and came towards him. Once the reins were within reach, Bertie smoothly and quickly caught them. He felt the people watching, but he couldn't worry about that just now.

Securing his grip and keeping the animal close to him, Bertie stretched up his left hand and stroked the colt's neck, pausing as he felt a rough line of scar tissue and the open wounds. The horse still flicked its tail and grunted, but its breathing became less hard and furious. Bertie kept on talking and stroking. The horse let him. The crowd came together, but drew back as Bertie walked the horse around. The bristling mouth of the colt twitched and blew gently into Bertie's ear.

Someone started to clap, but was shushed by the others. A murmuring started behind him. A man with a red face and tight clothes elbowed his way towards them. The colt tugged and cried as the red-faced man came close, blocking out the sun.

"What are you doing to my horse, you stupid brat? Give him here." The man lurched at Bertie and snatched the reins. The horse tried to move his head back, but the man was strong and grabbed the bridle hard, so hard that blood leaked from the soft skin of the animal's mouth. The red-faced man pulled the colt away.

Bertie stood there, unsure of what to do. He tried to speak, but an awkward croak was the only sound he could make.

The red-faced man turned and raised his whip at him.

"You waiting around for a thrashing too, are you?"

"Leave the boy alone." An older man wearing a brown apron stepped between them. He took Bertie's arm. "Come on, lad. Best leave it now."

Cursing and swaying, the red-faced man staggered off, dragging the colt after him. People muttered and drew nearer. Bertie tightened his lips to hold back the shakiness he felt inside. He wanted his dad to come and sort things out. He wanted his family, even Percy. Percy?

He remembered his brother and rushed over to the cart. Percy was still crouching where he had left him, his eyes peering out from under his milk-matted copper hair.

"Can I move now, Bertie?"

"Yes, Perce. Out you come."

Percy held out his arms. Bertie picked him up.

"I watched you, Bert," Percy whispered in his ear and clung on tight. For once Bertie didn't shrug him off. "Were you scared, Bert? Were you scared when you went over to that mad horse?"

" 'Course not, he was just a little horse who needed a friendly face." Bertie felt his throat go tight again. "Now, we'd better get a move on or we'll really be in for it."

"Hey, you! Just a minute." A voice called from behind.

"What now?" Bertie muttered to himself, but stopped and turned. It was Mr Higg, the grocer.

"You saved my shop just now, you did. Thought that horse was going to come right at the window." The man paused. "You're one of Jones's lot, aren't you?"

Bertie nodded.

"Well, you take after your dad then. Anyhow, here's something for your trouble." Mr Higg put a sixpenny piece and a weighty paper bag into Bertie's hand, then patted him awkwardly on the shoulder.

Bertie looked at him, then at the sixpence and the bag.

"Hold that for me, Perce." He gave the bag to Percy, so he could take out his handkerchief and put the sixpence with his mother's shilling. By the time the money had been tucked away, Percy had his nose in the paper bag.

"Look, Bertie, sweets! You said I could have a sweet if I stayed still and I did."

Bertie peeped in. "Crikey, bullseyes." He looked up to thank Mr Higg, but he'd already gone.

ʊ ʊ ʊ

Percy lolloped around Bertie and little Jack as they lay on the grass watching the people down at the fair.

"I bet you a bag of bullies that you'll be riding in the Derby one day," Percy shouted.

17

Bertie turned and looked up at his brother. "Oh shut up, Perce. Why can't you be good like little Jack?"

Percy took no notice. Light glinted in and out around his body as he grabbed a long bunch of dried grass from the scorched clumps and whipped his imaginary mount into a gallop. Bertie rolled over and turned his attention to the activities over at the Hill.

Tildy had set up her booth in a prime spot, displaying her sign 'Real Romany fortune-teller'. He and Reg had made it for her. There were all sorts of folk queuing up. Tildy had quite a following. People would return every year and ask her advice on marriage, family matters and business opportunities. Tildy always made things better. She'd often come over to the house and help Mother with medicines and potions. Sometimes Mother would send him and Reg over to her on errands. He liked that best. Tildy would toast honey cake on her fire and tell stories of the open road and far-off places where horses roamed wild and people rode bareback.

"Look, down there," little Jack pointed. "They've won a coconut. I like coconut."

"Bah, you've never had it," said Percy.

"Yes, I have, Dad won one. Didn't he, Bertie?"

Bertie decided not to comment. There was quite a crowd already at the beer tents, but nothing to what it would be like next week when the racing started. The sunshine would bring them all out, especially if the good weather lasted until the big day itself. That would make Mother happy.

"There you are, speeding along on a fine horse. The crowd are cheering 'Come on Bertie!' " Percy carried on with his game, his voice was thick with excitement. "You slip in front of the favourite and past the post."

Bertie shook his head and heaved himself up on to his elbows. Balancing on one arm, he pulled the wrinkled paper bag from his pocket and waved it in front of the hot frenzied figure as he circled them once again.

"Come on, have a bullseye, Perce, and calm down."

"I'd bet on you to win, Bertie," little Jack piped up from his side, eyeing the sweets and moving closer.

Bertie sat up. "I know you would, pipsqueak. Expect you'd like a bullseye too, wouldn't you?"

Bertie pulled out one of the fat sticky black and white sweets. "Open up, then. Those mitts are too mucky to go near food."

Jack did as he was told and was soon slurping away.

"You want one, Perce?"

Percy flopped down in front of him and opened his mouth. Bertie held the sweet out at arm's length.

"You can feed yourself. There's enough rubbish coming out of your cakehole, so a bit more going in won't hurt."

Percy grinned and took the sweet.

Bertie looked in the bag. There was just one left. That would be for Reg.

"Dad says you're a better rider than our Reg. I heard him." Percy was off again, sucking the bullseye into his left cheek so that he could make his point. "Don't know why you always get so funny about it."

"For goodness sake, Percy, can't you shut up for a second?" Bertie was losing patience. "And our Reg is miles better than me, so don't you go saying anything different. You hear me, Perce?"

Percy didn't answer, but sprang up and remounted his imaginary steed. "Now I'm going to be Dad winning the National." And he was off, squawking into the distance.

Bertie watched Percy flying down into the crowd, causing havoc by suddenly leaping in front of first one person, then another. There was Reg cutting through behind the tents. Reg always stood out from everyone else, especially in the sunlight. Percy had also spotted Reg and ran like a mad thing, jumping from side to side. Bertie laughed as he watched Reg try to swat him away, but Percy was not one to give up.

"Oi, Reg!" Bertie called. "You alright?"

"Yeah, fine. They're all having a break, so thought I'd come away and fetch you lot. Good job you took these two out of the way. Mother's in a bit of a state."

"Kept this for you, thought you could do with it." Bertie passed over the bag.

Reg popped the last of the sweets into his mouth. "That's lovely, but better not let Dad know you gave me this; he already thinks I'm turning into a giant."

"It's just the one, Reg. That can't make much difference."

"Well, you know Dad when it comes to racing," Reg said. "Once you reach fourteen, you have to mean business."

Bertie thought for a moment, then turned out his legs so they were rickety, pulled his jacket over into a hunchback, and contorted his mouth to look gummy and toothless.

"Come on, master Reg. Give us a smile."

Reg pulled a gargoyle face back. Bertie replied with a somersault and bowed. Percy and Jack ran round them, giggling and getting in the way.

"Play horses with us, Reg." Percy pulled at his hand.

"Come on then," Reg bent down at the knees and held his arms out behind him. "Jump up, Perce."

Percy clambered on to his back.

"You take Jack. We'd better head home." Reg stood up and looked over at Percy who was now trying to gee him up. "Or Mother'll start worrying that the city folk have got you."

"It would be the city folk you'd have to worry about, not our Perce." Bertie pulled little Jack over his shoulders like a sack of potatoes. "They'd soon bring him back, wouldn't they Jackie?"

ʊ ʊ ʊ

At his mother's request, Bertie had gone into the training yard to find his father. Tea would be ready at five o'clock, she said, and not before. Percy came too, as he was still full of energy despite all the efforts to tire him out.

Late afternoon in the stables was a peaceful time. The horses felt it too as they were generally quieter and calmer. The warm air softened the clank of metal from the tack and the horseshoes into a dull lazy thud. The baked manure mingled with fresh straw gave the stables a whiff of sweetness that almost covered the sharp tang of sweat and ammonia.

Bertie saw his father standing in the middle of the yard, giving directions to some of the lads. Next to him stood Richard Marsh.

"Look, it's Uncle Dick," squealed Percy.

Bertie noticed that Dad looked small and shrunken next to the dapper but well-rounded form of his father's old friend.

"No, Perce, no," hissed Bertie. "Mr Marsh, you have to call him Mr Marsh here."

But Percy let out a piercing whinny that made the nervous horses flinch and the lads stop in their tracks.

"Perce, be quiet." Bertie tried to grab at him but he was off in mock canter across the yard.

"Uncle Dick! Dad! Guess what? Guess what Bertie did today when we were in the town? He caught this horse that was going wild. And he got given bullseyes and we ate them."

"Oh give it a rest, Percy." Bertie caught hold of his brother and held him fast. He wanted to shake him. "And, I told you, Uncle Dick is Mr Marsh at the yard."

Bertie tightened his grip on the wriggling Percy. To be fair, though, it was hard to think of Uncle Dick as anyone else, but he was an important person now.

"Sorry, sir, he gets carried away."

Richard Marsh laughed. "Well, young Bertie, what you been up to now?"

Bertie's father intervened. "It's alright, boy, we've already heard."

"I had to do something, Dad. That poor horse, it was in such a state, a lovely little colt too. The bloke who owned it, he was … " Bertie's throat tightened and his face felt all hot again. He struggled to stop his voice cracking. "He was a real idiot, Dad. People like that shouldn't be allowed near animals."

"I know lad. But they said you did well. You stopped people getting hurt, saved the horse from harm. You did what you could and that's all you can do. In any case, sometimes things have a way of sorting themselves out." Dad stopped abruptly. His breath caught in his throat, so that he struggled for air. Then the coughing started, so violent that his body trembled from the effort.

Bertie went to help, but Uncle Dick held him back.

"Run and fetch your dad some water, Bertie. You help him, Perce, nice and quietly now." Uncle Dick took his friend by the arm and sat him down on a low wall. "Come on Jack, have a bit of a rest here."

Bertie walked away, keeping half an ear on what they were saying. Perhaps Dad would listen to Uncle Dick.

"I'm alright, Dick, it's just so hot today."

"But you have to take it a bit easier, Jack. Those lungs of yours aren't as young as they used to be. We have to face it, none of us are." Uncle Dick paused. "And, you must think of Annie and your little ones."

The cough came back, this time thick and choking. Bertie rushed over with the water, unable to stop it sloshing over the edge of the cup. He saw the blood on the handkerchief.

ʊ ʊ ʊ

"You off now, Tildy?" Bertie ran over to her wagon.

"Just finishing loading up. Come in and give me a hand, Bertie, if you like. I've something for you to give to your mother."

Bertie walked up the green and red wooden steps, touching the silver horseshoe for luck as he entered. Inside it was an exotic palace. Crockery of all colours packed the dresser that was built into one side of the wagon. Pots and pans clattered on their hooks from the ceiling, bundles of herbs tied with string fanned the air with their musty sharp smells. Mysterious dark-glass bottles holding Tildy's potions were shut away in the cabinets that lined the walls.

The sleeping quarters were partially hidden by a brocade curtain. A rich red patterned rug covered the floor. There was one big chest in the corner where Tildy kept her treasures, and a basin set in a washstand with a large pitcher of water next to it. The way that everything fitted in, all tidy and neat, never failed to amaze Bertie.

Painted wood-carvings covered the walls. Bertie's favourite was the bird on the door: a dove clasping an olive branch in its beak, returning to Noah after the flood. Golden and set on a green background, it was like an altarpiece. The carvings had all been made by Tildy's father, a master craftsman.

"I think this must be the nicest place in the world," Bertie said.

"It'll do for me and it has everything I need." Tildy padded over. "It was built for our wedding, mine and Reuben's. Newlyweds should always have their own vardo."

Bertie didn't like to ask where Reuben was now. He'd once over-heard his mother talking about it being a sorry business.

"Well, Bertie love, fetch me the old horse and help me harness him up. I'd better go with the others."

He went out on to the common and took up Patch, Tildy's old dray. The men from the camp were fixing up their horses. Two colts on long ropes chased each other in the sun. The young bright bay, its body etched with scars, stopped when he saw Bertie, stretched out his neck and called to him. Bertie never forgot a horse and recognized the colt straight away, but how could it be?

One of the men caught Bertie's eye, and gave him a wink.

2

A new home, June 1892

"EXPLAIN TO YOUR BROTHER, Jess, for heaven's sake; he listens to you. I'm all done with trying."

Bertie's mother turned away from him and slipped into the big wooden armchair in the corner of the kitchen. She pulled a handkerchief from her sleeve, tugging the cuff so hard that a button flew off. It dropped, chinking against the stone floor. Bertie's thoughts twisted this way and that. He didn't like to make a fuss.

Jess came forward in her official capacity of oldest sister. Her jaw was tilted up and her hands were clasped tightly in front of her. It was the Joan of Arc stance she'd seen in one of her books. The story of the soldier saint who died for her beliefs was one of Jess's favourites. Bertie had heard the story many times and, as Jess had always fancied herself as a bit of an actress, there were often dramatic interpretations to accompany her readings, no matter how much they all protested.

"Come on now, Bertie. It's very kind of Uncle Dick to take you and Reg on. You were looking forward to going yesterday."

Bertie's five younger brothers stood side by side in the middle of the room, grubby skittles arranged in order of size, biggest first. Their eyes were fixed on him.

"We'll be alright here. The boys'll help look after things, won't you, boys?" Jess kept trying.

They moved their heads up and down, but without enthusiasm.

Bertie had his arms folded, but watched them back. Bill, the fifth and littlest, tried hard to stay upright, unable to stop wobbling even when he hung on to the brother next to him. Jack, second from the top, broke rank and ran to his mother, burying his face in her lap. Mark and Cyril followed. Bill kept up well with the scuttling crawl that was his speciality. Percy, despite being bigger than the others, flung himself across Mother's chair and started an almighty racket; tears dripping, nose running.

"Don't let our Bertie go. You can't let him go." The words shook as he sobbed. The others joined him, baying and howling; baby Lily in her cradle started to wail.

Bertie knelt by his mother, rummaging through the heap of siblings for her hand.

"But why can't I stay? Reg can go and I can look after things here. I can help."

Reg walked in and put his case by the door.

"You wouldn't let me go on my own, Bert, would you?" He ruffled Bertie's hair and settled down next to him. "You know how difficult it is for Mum now Dad's not well. She can't train horses. But you, you want to stay with horses, don't you?"

It was suddenly quiet.

" 'Course I do, you know that."

"You're twelve years old now, Bertie, and you have to grow up. Uncle Dick is offering you a job in the finest yard in the world. If you are good and work hard, you might even get to ride one day."

Jess put her hand on Bertie's shoulder, trying a softer approach this time. "Reg is right, you know."

"But it's so far from home, Jess."

The others started up again. Bertie knew he was just making things harder for them all.

There was the sound of a cart outside.

Reg looked out of the window. "It's Old Ben come to collect us."

Richard Marsh's head stable lad, Old Ben, was the oldest stable lad Bertie had ever known. He had always seemed to be old, which was how he got his name, although there must have been a time when he was Young Ben. Bertie had often wondered how he had made the change from young to old. Had it been gradual process or was it sudden, overnight? Old Ben had worked for Dad for a long time but had gone off to Newmarket with Uncle Dick when things got a bit tight. No one was quite sure when he was born but he had come down from one of the big cities in the north many years ago. Old Ben didn't ride much now, but he was still pretty agile when he wanted to be, and there wasn't much he didn't know about horses; he was happy to talk about them for hours on end. Bertie liked him.

"Uncle Ned's brought the big carriage too, so we can all get in," said Reg.

Jess sprang into action.

"Boys, get up. If we're going to go with them to the station we'll have to be quick now. Shall I take your apron, Mother? Your dress needs smoothing, you go and see to it. I'll tidy up."

"Bertie, you alright now?" Jess gave him an affectionate chuck under the chin.

"Yes, I'm fine, Jess, honest," he said, but crossed his fingers behind his back.

"Now, where's your new bag? Have you put all your things in there?"

Bertie pointed towards the door.

"You know, it's what all the young gentlemen take with them for travelling, that's what the man in the shop said. Reg has got Dad's old case as he's the eldest, but we wanted you to have something special too."

Bertie sat back on his heels and took a deep breath of home. He lightly jumped to standing.

"Now, you lot, you heard what Jess said. Up, up, up!" He grabbed the two youngest round the waist, lifting them up and twirling them round. They shrieked and kicked out.

"Watch my china!" called Mother as she picked up the baby and went upstairs.

Bertie gathered his brothers close to him. "Well, you boys will have twice as much bossiness from our Jess with me and Reg out of the way. So you'll have to watch it." He ducked as Jess went to flip him around the ear with Mother's apron.

Bertie heard his father's slow step on the staircase. Dad came into the kitchen. A spot of dried blood clung to his chin where he had cut himself shaving. Odd lines of missed stubble made a strange tattoo on one cheek. Dad wore his good shirt and collar. His trousers needed both the belt and the braces.

"You look very smart this morning, Dad." Jess smoothed his hair; it had lost most of its colour and the golden down that peaked from his cuffs was the only reminder of his auburn youth. Jess fetched his cap and helped him into his jacket.

"I think you'll need a scarf too though, there's a chilly wind out of the sun."

"Hurry your mother up too, there's a good girl, Jess," Dad called. "You know what she's like."

Although Jess was out of earshot, Bertie knew she'd do it anyway.

Jess returned with Dad's grey check woollen scarf. It was a present from the Christmas before last. She tucked it around him. Mother followed soon after, a muslin cloth across her shoulder and Lily asleep in her arms.

Dad picked up Bertie's bag. His muscles had lost their hold on his crumpled, freckled skin, but he was still stronger than most.

At the station, Dad stood wrapped up in the sunshine, beads of sweat on his face, the breeze threatening to snap him in two. Bertie stayed close, breathing in the baccy smoke that clung to his jacket.

"You should go home now, Dad, you look tired," Jess said as she grabbed little Jack by the hand and held Percy by the collar.

"I'll be fine. We can't not see our boys off, can we, Annie?" Dad said, staying firmly put. "Ben, you'll look after them for me, won't you?"

"Just like they were my own, Jack, I will." Old Ben stood to attention. Bertie almost expected him to salute. "And Master Dick will see them alright too, that you can be sure of."

Nobody could think of anything to say.

"Are you sure you don't need me around to help, Dad?" Bertie asked eventually.

"Thank you, son, but we'll manage. You go and do us proud," said Dad. "Anyway, it will do young Percy good to roll up his sleeves for once."

Perce looked up from Jess's grip and frowned.

Any other time Bertie would have been excited about the journey, but as the train drew up to the platform, all he could see was just a grimy old lump of metal. Reg kissed Mother, Jess and the baby in a proper grown-up way, then shook hands with Dad and the boys.

Bertie followed his lead, but ran back to hug Dad. The little ones started to cry, they abandoned Jess and clung to Mother's skirt.

Jess reached into her wicker basket. She pulled out some large brown paper bags. "Some sandwiches. Ham and pickle, Bertie, your favourite, and some cake. It's fruit cake just as you like it."

"And mind you make sure Ben has some too. Do you hear that, Ben? They'll eat the lot given half a chance." Mother's voice broke and her eyes were wet.

"Don't you worry, Mrs Jones." Old Ben tapped his temple. "I'll watch 'em."

It was only the third time that Bertie had been on a train. In fact, it was only the third time he had been out of Epsom. The journey hadn't even started and he'd already nearly lost his cap down the gap between the platform and the train, tried to climb into the First Class carriage and trapped his jacket in the compartment door. Reg had stepped in and saved him every time, but Bertie still felt a fool.

With his new bag stowed in the luggage net, Bertie sat between Reg and Old Ben. They had their backs to the engine. The carriages creaked as the locomotive pulled on them. Bertie kept his eyes on the platform and, as the train drew away, he watched the family grow smaller and smaller, huddled together, arms waving. Bertie looked over at his brother. Reg sat with his head in his racing paper. That was Reg though; he just took things in his stride.

The dry-grassy hills were soon replaced by row upon row of houses with neat rectangular gardens, shops and factories. Smoke was everywhere: it trailed back from the engine, it poured out from the big chimneys, it puffed from Old Ben's pipe.

The sun on the glass and the bodies in the compartment made the air hot and heavy. Bertie closed his eyes. The rocking of the train carried him home and he was back in his bed, Reg on his left and little Jack by the wall; Percy, Cyril and Mark asleep in the bed across the way. Jess would be along in a minute to wake them to do their chores. Dad was well again and out on the Downs. Mother was cooking bacon and eggs for breakfast, even though she rarely did. The babies, Lily and William, were playing on the floor.

The train braked sharply as they pulled into a station. Bertie woke up but tried to keep his eyes closed so that he could hold on to his dream a little longer. The roughness of a prickly material rubbed his cheek and the odour of old tobacco was very close. Bertie realized that his head had slipped down and was buried in Old Ben's jacket. Old Ben was still snoring away to himself, as were the two young chaps in the far corner. Reg still had his nose in his paper. The tall, slim woman sitting opposite smiled at him. She looked a bit like his mother. Bertie's mouth was dry and his stomach felt hot and heavy.

"I know you, don't I?" she asked.

"Umm?" Bertie tried to think.

"Of course, you're that young lad from the stables. Saw you with that runaway horse last year. Terrible business. You know, we were talking about it only the other day."

Bertie shuffled in his seat.

"Would you like a strawberry?" Pushing her basket towards him, she picked up a corner of the striped linen tea cloth that covered it. A sweet smell of summer teatime filled the carriage.

"I picked them from the garden myself this morning. Good crop this year. Taking them to my sister."

Bertie would have loved a strawberry, but didn't think he should.

"Go on. The others won't see, look at them."

Bertie still shook his head.

"Well, please yourself. But, if I see you on the way back, perhaps you'll take a small pot of jam home?"

"I won't be going back," Bertie muttered. "But thank you."

"Oh no? Where are you off to then?" she asked.

Old Ben twitched and opened an eye.

"He's off to live at Newmarket, aren't you, young Bert? He is going to be working in the stables of royalty. And his brother too." Old Ben puffed out his chest.

"Oooh, you don't say." One of the two young chaps had just woken up. He elbowed his friend in the ribs. "Hear that?"

Bertie didn't much like the look of the pair. They reminded him of the sorts that hung around the racecourse, the ones always causing trouble, and about as welcome as rats in a granary.

"A little goblin, that's what you look like," said the other rat chap to Old Ben and sniggered.

"Cheeky young devils," Old Ben sniffed and straightened his waist-coat. "Think you should have stayed at home until you sobered up."

"Think so, old man? Think so, do you?"

The carriage door clicked open. A young lady with freckles and a yellow dress poked her head into the compartment. Her sandy hair was all tidy like a smooth cornfield and her hat was studded with meadow daisies and poppies. Behind her was an older woman dressed in black.

"Come back, Miss Louisa!" said the woman, looking left and right along the platform. "What would her ladyship say?"

But the yellow lady was too quick for her and had already jumped inside. Everything in the carriage went very quiet.

"Hello," she said, smiling at them all as if she knew them. "We are campaigning for women's suffrage, our right to vote. May I offer you one of our leaflets?"

She peeled a sheet from the string-tied bundle. Bertie leaned forward to take one, but she ignored him and thrust one in the direction of Old Ben. The print left dark smudges on her cream leather gloves.

"No use to me, miss, save it for someone a bit more educated." Old Ben shook his head and gave it back.

Undeterred, she turned to Reg, waving the piece of paper under his nose until he grinned and took it. Then she moved on to the woman with the basket of strawberries.

"Now you *must* have one. We are the cause for all women, even married ones." The young lady sounded quite fierce.

"Oh no, dear, I don't think so. My husband can't vote, so don't think he would like it much if I could." The woman with the strawberries looked nervously at the two rat chaps who were whispering and nudging one another, edging as far away from them as she could. "And I really don't think you should, well, I think you'd best go back to your proper carriage."

"You haven't asked us yet, miss," one of the rat chaps called out.

The lady smiled and walked towards them.

"Yeah, we'll take your leaflets." The other one stifled a laugh. "But we'll expect something for our trouble."

Whistles sounded along the platform, pillows of smoke smothered the windows in an oily fog. The companion in black bustled into the carriage, catching the yellow lady's arm.

"Miss Louisa, please come away now. The train is pulling out."

At that moment the guard slammed the door shut, shunting the woman in black further into the carriage. The yellow lady and her companion looked at one another.

"Come and sit with us, love," the second rat boy laughed and started to move towards them, "but call off the old bulldog, it'll spoil our fun."

The whistle went again. The train lurched forward.

Old Ben sprang up. "I'm afraid, ladies, it looks as if you'll have to stay here until the next station. Now Reg, budge along."

Reg put his paper down and shooed Bertie over. The yellow lady sat down by the window and her companion took the place next to her. Old Ben stood perfectly still in the middle of the carriage as it jerked backwards and forwards. He seem to grow until he towered over the two rat boys.

"Now, you show some respect when there are ladies present, or get out."

"Ha, we can't, it's moving now." The other rat chap darted his head round his friend's shoulder and moved back quickly.

The metal of the wheels shrieked. Old Ben's face had lost its usual friendly smile. When he spoke, it was almost a growl.

"Not that fast, it's not, and not so fast as my boot will move you, so I should run along quick."

Bertie's heart was thumping and he felt a bit sick. If only people were like horses, it would be much easier. The yellow lady shrank back against the seat. She clutched the hand of her companion, who held her parasol in front of them like a sword.

"Oh, enough of this." Old Ben darted towards the two chaps and caught them by the scruff of their shirts. They looked like a couple of dunked puppies.

Reg opened the door and tried to shield the ladies, nearly getting speared by the parasol in the process. With much cursing and swearing, the rat chaps tumbled out just as the train reached the end of the platform.

"Take no notice of those two. They wouldn't know the front end of an 'orse," Old Ben swung out and slammed the door shut, "from its, er, tail, if you'll pardon the expression, ladies."

The woman in black tutted, but she had put down her parasol and was busy unfolding a strange piece of sheet taken out from her bag. She was making a big show of spreading it behind the yellow lady. The carriage hadn't seemed to be dirty, but perhaps it was, with all the smoke and everything.

"There's always someone to cause trouble for other people," said the woman with the basket of strawberries, rolling her eyes. "Human nature, I suppose."

"But we can't let them make us afraid. If we don't go out and try to change things, then there can be no progress." The yellow lady sat up and wagged her finger like a vicar in church.

Bertie couldn't understand why anyone would want things to be different. He just wished life would stay as it was.

"Even so, miss, I should be careful," Old Ben muttered.

"Here, let's all have one of these." The woman opened up the strawberry basket again. "You all look as if you could do with something to cheer you up and there's nothing like a strawberry for that."

Old Ben took a handful.

"Thank you kindly, missus. Can't beat a good strawberry and these look lovely," he beamed, taking a couple from the pile he'd scooped up and putting them into Bertie's lap. "There you go, young 'un, get them down you. A couple of these won't hurt."

∪ ∪ ∪

The rest of the journey to Suffolk passed without incident and John, one of the grooms, was there to meet them at Newmarket. Bertie and Reg clambered into the back of the cart with their bags. The landscape was different here. The sky was bigger but there were no hills. Bertie peered over the big hedges and into the green paddocks. The sight of the grazing horses in the fields took his eye. Old Ben was up in front giving the driver a few pointers on handling.

"Watch this corner now, John, there's a funny slope here." Old Ben was interrupted by the crash of the wheel dropping down into a pothole.

"Not long now, boys." Old Ben turned round. "You won't have seen nothing like Egerton. The Guv'nor built it specially. You'll soon know it when you see it."

Bertie didn't understand. His head was boiling and he wanted to go home. The horse plodded along. Reg was on the opposite side of the cart, his arms stretched along the wooden rim, face turned up to the sun. The leaves hung heavy on the branches that reached across the lane, catching the light and casting strange patterns on his brother's skin.

"Are you scared, Reg?"

"Am I what?"

Bertie quickly checked that Old Ben and the driver couldn't hear him, but they were still in deep conversation.

"Scared, are you scared?"

"Why should I be scared?"

"Well, leaving home, being away from everyone. It will all be different."

"So?"

"What if everyone hates us? What if … ?"

"Look Bert, there's not a lot of point in what-iffing now, is there? We've not got a lot of choice. You've got to learn that things can't just stay the same, so stop moping and make the best of it."

Bertie crossed his arms and looked at his feet. No one seemed to understand. But a few minutes later there was a tap on his ankle. Reg had stretched his leg out across the cart.

"Oi you, come on now. You'll love it. Horses everywhere, no more school, just horses."

Bertie smiled. It was true, he would like being with the horses all the time and he had never been a great one for books.

"Reg?"

"What?"

"Glad you're here."

"Oh shut up, you big girl!" Reg flicked him with his boot a bit harder this time and looked away.

The large white six-bar gate was open and the cart turned left into a wide lane. Its surface was smooth and new, better than the vast roads running to London. On and on the lane went, disappearing into a line of trees. Old Ben chattered even more than ever, becoming louder the closer they got. His excitement made Bertie's breath quicken and even the pony seemed to feel it as she picked up her hooves and clipped along with renewed zeal.

"Here we are, boys. We're home." Old Ben gathered up his things.

Passing through the pillared archway with its well-ordered zig-zag pattern, the cart stopped in front of the carved-oak door.

"It looks like a castle," Bertie whispered to Reg, who was gazing at the towers either side of the entrance.

"Is this where Uncle Dick lives?" Bertie asked.

"No, it's where the horses live and you'll live." Old Ben stood behind them. "There are dormitories at the top. Then there's all the usual; the offices and storerooms, that sort of thing. You'll soon find your way about."

"If this is for us and the horses, then where is Uncle Dick's house?" Bertie persisted. "It must be a palace."

"Well, there's some as say that would suit the Guv'nor alright." Old Ben paused and shook his head. "But I wouldn't never, of course."

Bertie walked cautiously along the wall. Standing on tiptoe, he looked into one of the leaded windows. Big and hallowed, it felt like a church or somewhere that monks lived. Along the edge of the house was a grand yard; stables all around with a lawn in front and an exercise circuit on the far side. Bertie breathed in the familiar smells and smiled.

"Look at this, Reg," he beckoned his brother over. "I've never seen anything like it."

∪ ∪ ∪

A bell rang, echoing like the one in Bertie's old schoolyard. The sound of feet on the floorboards told him that the others were about. Old Ben was hurrying them along. Bertie hid under the covers for a moment.

"Come on, slugabed!" Reg gave him a shake.

Nearly toppling out of the strange narrow bed, Bertie uncovered his head. The bright whitewashed walls made him squint. He liked having his own spot in the dormitory between Reg and Old Ben. Old Ben had a larger area than everyone else, a whole corner near the door.

Everyone had their own cupboard for bits and pieces. Bertie and Reg had each been issued with two sets of clothes, an outdoor jacket, a cap and a new pair of boots.

"Now the Guv'nor is most particular about dress. You must always be clean and well turned out," said Old Ben.

The boots were kept in the cloakroom with all the outdoor clothes. Everyone had their own large peg that held their jacket and cap. Boots were lined up underneath. Bertie found the dubbin and some old rag. He gave his and Reg's boots two coats to make them last that bit longer and keep out the rain.

Old Ben ran everything with impressive precision. At breakfast, one boy put a cauldron on the table, another put down a large brown earthenware teapot. Old Ben himself ladled porridge in large dollops into the bowls that were passed around the table along with the teapot, jugs of milk and sugar. Every now and then, Old Ben would issue orders that made it clear that he must have eyes in the back of his head, and was quick to give Tiny Wal a slap when he started flicking bits from his spoon.

When it was finally time to go out into the yard, Bertie could hardly contain himself. He walked through the stables, past the lines of stalls. The horses were curious, straining their heads to take a look. He introduced himself to them.

Bertie had always liked tack rooms and this one was a source of endless joy: neat, ordered lines of bridles, bits, halters, saddles, brushes, buckets; all mud free and oozing polish. The odour of wood, leather and metal hung heavy. As the youngest new boy, he had to start with cleaning duties. Reg's experience meant that he went straight to exercising the horses. But Bertie was perfectly happy and, grabbing a broom and shovel, he made a start.

Uncle Dick, or the Guv'nor as Old Ben instructed them to call him, came to the stables in the afternoon. With him was Mr Smallwood, who managed the stables. Old Ben had pointed him out when they arrived. "A numbers man," he said tapping his temple. "Very clever but gives the Guv'nor a few headaches."

Mr Smallwood was very tall and straight. He wore tweed and a collar but was younger than the Guv'nor.

The lads all stood to attention as the Guv'nor approached. Bertie did the same.

"You settling in alright, Jones?" Uncle Dick called out in an unusually stern voice and his face wasn't smiling.

35

"Bertie is doing fine, and Reg too, thank you, Guv'nor," Old Ben bobbed up.

"That's one of Jack's boys," said the Guv'nor to Mr Smallwood.

"Alright now, boys, back to work." Old Ben clapped his hands. "And Bertie, remember to touch your cap to the Guv'nor when he speaks to you."

Bertie did as he was told.

"They'll be fine, Guv'nor. They're good boys," he heard Old Ben say.

υ υ υ

"I do like it here, Reg," Bertie followed his brother, who had asked him to come out for a walk after tea. "A nice table, piles of bread and jam."

"Yes, I saw you taking quite a few slices," said Reg.

"And everything is so clean and well set up. It's not home, of course, and it would be better to be there," Bertie added. "But if I can't be there, I'm glad I'm here."

Reg smiled at him. "It's alright, I understand, but you do have to watch out a bit."

"Why, what do you mean?"

"Well, the other lads, they will want to test you, to see what you're made of. It happened at Dad's stables all the time."

"Did it?"

"Of course it did. Don't you remember that chap from Belgium that Percy found tied to the cartwheel? He'd been left there all night. Well, that sort of thing."

"Oh, you mean the upside-down one without any clothes? Never saw him again after that."

"Exactly." Reg plonked himself down on a wall and got out his smokes.

The bread and jam felt heavy on Bertie's stomach and he wished he hadn't eaten that last slice.

"So, will we get tied to a cartwheel with no clothes on?"

"Well, maybe not that, but it may be something similar, so just keep an eye out."

"Will they do something to you, Reg?"

"Already done, Bertie, but I survived."

Bertie wanted to ask what had happened but checked himself. "Don't they like us?"

"It's not that. It's a hard world, and racing is harder still. There's a lot at stake, so if people can get rid of you, they will. Just survival of the fittest." Reg dug him in the ribs with his elbow. "Don't look so scared, Bertie, just remember that not everyone is as kind as you think they are."

Bertie couldn't sleep that night. He lay in bed imagining being kidnapped and dreading all sorts of indignities. At work the next day, he considered what to do in such circumstances and escape plans whirled around in his head, keeping his distance whenever anyone came too close. After two days, Bertie thought that he must be in the clear. Perhaps tackling one brother was enough.

One morning, when most of the horses were out being exercised, Little Wal approached him.

"Guv'nor needs Minty to have some exercise, just in the yard, and with a light weight on his back. Ben said you'd do."

"Are you sure?" Bertie was surprised as Minty was unbroken and marked out as difficult. "Didn't think I was allowed to ride yet."

Crooked Jim joined them. "They particularly asked for you," he said. "Better get a move on or there'll be hell to pay."

Bertie approached Minty's stall. The colt snorted but moved over for him. Bertie had already spoken to the colt a few times. He was a good-looking horse, especially now his dark-grey coat was starting to lighten.

"Well, Minty, the Guv'nor wants me to give you a turn round the yard. What do you say to that?"

Minty stamped his foot. Bertie took up a grooming brush.

"Let's just get you nice and calm, eh boy?"

Bertie placed his hand on the curve of Minty's back, the horse jumped and moved away. This didn't feel right.

"Come on, then." Little Wal stood in the doorway. "Not scared, are you?"

"No, but I don't think he's ready," said Bertie.

"You know better than the Guv'nor then, do you?"

"No, of course not." Bertie sighed and picked up a halter. "Now, it's alright, boy. I'm not going to hurt you. Nice and slowly now."

Minty looked at him, but didn't object as the rope went around his head. Bertie led him out.

"Up you get then." Crooked Jim gave one of his twisted smiles so that his face went in two directions. "We've all heard what a great little horseman you are."

"Ready, Minty?" Bertie took hold of the mane and lifted himself up so that he lay across the horse's back. He was glad now for all the practice his Dad had made him do on the wooden model they kept in one of the sheds. Minty stepped back but didn't throw him.

As he hung over the horse, Bertie could see the legs of other lads walking out of the stables to join Little Wal and Crooked Jim. Taking a deep breath, Bertie turned towards Minty's head and snaked himself up, levelling out his weight as best he could. Minty shuffled and swished his tail.

"I know you don't like this, Minty, and I'm so sorry," he whispered to the horse as he felt the animal's back dip and muscles tighten.

The other boys muttered. Bertie moved his legs out so that they were ready to move into position. He felt like a stranded starfish.

"Minty, I'm going to try and sit up now."

The colt jerked his head, blowing and whinnying. Bertie let him settle then began to ease his legs down and his body up, making sure to avoid any sudden pressure or movement.

A loud clap rang round the yard. Crooked Jim started shouting. Minty shrieked and kicked his hindquarters up. Bertie went flying, over and round. Wrists out and belly down, he landed heavily on the cobbles. Laughter was all around him, then the clatter of the horses back from the Downs made them run. His palms stung and his body felt crushed from the hard landing, but as his vision steadied, the old army boots of the Guv'nor stood before him.

Bertie struggled to stand. Warm blood filled his mouth; he tried to keep it in. Only Reg came forward to help him, passing him a handkerchief and holding him up.

"The horse?" Bertie heard the Guv'nor call out.

"I've got Minty, Guv'nor, he's fine, just a bit shaken," called Old Ben.

"Thank God for that," said the Guv'nor. "As for you, young man, what the hell did you think you were doing?"

Red-faced and barely stopping for air, the Guv'nor leaned over Bertie. He shouted so loudly that Bertie's ears throbbed with the sound. "What would I have said to your mother if that horse had killed you? Tell me!"

The Guv'nor stopped yelling and straightened his jacket. Then he turned back and started up again. "Really, you of all people, Bertie. I thought you had more sense. I thought you understood. What would your father say? I'll tell you, he'd send you packing with nothing but a good thrashing."

Bertie hung his head. It was only Reg's hold that kept him upright.

"Smallwood, can you sort this business out?" The Guv'nor bellowed, his words echoing round and round the yard. "Ben, you too. See if you can make some sense of it all." He strode away, cursing under his breath.

The questions went on for a very long time. Bertie just said that he couldn't remember and he'd been very stupid, but he didn't tell. He was given extra duties and a warning that any further misdemeanours would result in dismissal.

3
Back to Epsom, October 1892

Picking up a broom and shovel, Bertie got to work. His eyes were heavy after a restless sleep and his mind felt foggy, as if he was still in his nightmare and this was the dream. He heard the brisk military step of the Guv'nor in the yard. It was an odd time for him to be about as he was usually out on the gallops with the horses.

"Morning, Guv'nor. Are you looking for Ben, sir?"

"Morning, Bertie." His voice was much quieter than usual, almost gentle. "No, not Ben, I've come to see you."

"Me, sir?"

The Guv'nor stayed in the doorway.

"It all looks very clean and tidy in here. Good job, Bertie. You are doing well. Ben speaks very highly of you." He smiled, but there was something not quite right in his face. "Now put that broom down and come out here a minute."

Bertie did as he was told, placing the yard brush carefully in the corner against the wall. Reg was standing behind the Guv'nor.

"What's up?" asked Bertie, feeling his heart beat harder and faster as his mind tried to second-guess their words.

The Guv'nor motioned for Reg to go ahead. Bertie looked from one to the other.

Reg swallowed hard. "It's Dad, Bert, he passed away last night."

It took a moment or two for his brain to understand Reg's words. Bertie turned from them and bent himself double. "No, no, no," he said over and over again, as if a strong-enough denial would somehow make it right.

"A very sad loss, very sad," said the Guv'nor.

Reg touched Bertie gently on the arm. Bertie remembered where he was and stood up straight.

"The funeral is the day after tomorrow." The Guv'nor tugged at his cuffs, first one, then the other. He looked heavenwards, but Bertie could see the tears in his eyes.

They all stood there, very still.

"Right, boys." The Guv'nor rubbed his hands together, as if trying to find some warmth. "I'll send word to your mother. Mr Smallwood will sort out the arrangements. He'll tell you what to do and where to go. I'll be there with you."

The Guv'nor rushed away. They watched him go.

"I'll get on then, Reg, shall I?" Bertie spoke at last.

"Yes, that'd be best. There's a lot to do." Reg crouched down and looked into his brother's face. "Will you be alright?"

Bertie sniffed and nodded.

"Well, I'll see you later then," Reg said, pulling himself up and turning to go.

"I dreamt of our dad last night," Bertie called after him. "He was flying past on a big old steeplechaser, just like his old self."

ʊ ʊ ʊ

The funeral came round quickly and, as they travelled to Epsom, the Guv'nor became Uncle Dick again. At the old house, everything was familiar but different, smaller somehow. And it was no longer summer. Bertie always thought of home as a summerland, with sunbeams and birdsong, a place where bees danced round the borders like clockwork toys that never wound down, and where everything smelt warm. But now scratchy branches lurked in the lanes and slimy paths of mulching leaves reeked of damp and compost. It was crumbling and dirty, not at all how he remembered, and not at all like Egerton.

Bertie sat in the trap and watched as Uncle Dick got down, followed by Reg. Jess was at the door, dressed all in black. Uncle Dick put out his arms to her.

"Oh, Uncle Dick, it's so good that you are here. Thank you for coming." She gave him a peck on the cheek. "We were so sorry to hear about Aunt Sarah, I do hope she will feel better soon."

The Guv'nor's wife, or Aunt Sarah as they used to call her, hadn't been well enough to leave her room. Bertie had only seen her at Christmas time, when she had given them presents. He knew that his mother would be disappointed that she couldn't be there.

Reg hugged Jess. She hid her head in his shoulder. For a moment, Bertie wanted to run away, but he stayed stuck to the seat.

"Aren't you coming down then, Bertie?" said Jess, looking up at him.

For some reason, he jumped. He jumped as high as he could, flinging his arms out and landing close by her.

"Steady, Bertie," said Reg. "You'll knock poor Jess over if you carry on like that."

Bertie hung his head, feeling stupid.

Jess ushered them into the kitchen. Mother was in the chair by the range, with little William curled up on her lap like a cat. They were both asleep.

"Let her rest." Uncle Dick said quietly. "She'll be needing it. Where is … ?"

"In the parlour. Shall I … ?"

Uncle Dick knew what to do and guided them into the room at the front of the house. It was used only for best. The grate in the parlour was empty and the curtains were drawn. The room smelt of coal-tar soap and violet water. A single candle flickered on the mantelpiece. Black ribbons trimmed the edges of the mirror, turned reflection-side to the wall. In the middle of the room was the coffin, propped up between two dining chairs. Cushioned in white silk lay the waxen figure of their father, scrubbed, dressed and ready for heaven.

Uncle Dick stopped and bowed his head. Reg copied him, and Bertie followed. He stared at the body that had been his father. He'd seen dead things many times, but not a dead person.

"Dad must be in heaven; he's not here any more," Bertie thought to himself.

There was a rustling behind them. Bertie's mother walked in. "Jess should have called me. I'm sorry."

"Annie, my dear Annie." Uncle Dick walked over to her and held her tight. She started to cry. Bertie couldn't hear what else he said.

"I know, Dick, I know." She straightened herself up and patted his hand.

"And now, here are your boys, Annie." Uncle Dick pushed Reg and Bertie forward.

Bertie walked over to her as slowly as he could, feeling that he shouldn't run, given the presence of their father in his eternal sleep.

"Well, just look at you!" Mother hugged them, tears spilling down her cheeks. "It seems such a long time since you left. But how you've grown, and you smell different."

They stood there for a long time, it seemed. Reg stayed close and comforted her, but Bertie couldn't think of what to say, so he stared at his feet. Mother composed herself.

"Thank you, Dick, you've looked after them well. Jack would be proud, very proud."

Just then, Bertie sensed the presence of his father standing by him. He could smell his baccy and feel his warmth, but Bertie didn't dare look up in case it broke the spell, so he just smiled to himself.

"Well, Old Ben should take the credit for that," continued Uncle Dick. "He's like a mother hen with the lads. But he's still not past putting me in my place, and he was just the same to Jack. You know what he's like."

"But you wouldn't have him any other way, Dick," Mother wiped her eyes. "Now then, let's leave Jack in peace. Let's find you some tea."

They went back into the kitchen. Bertie sat down next to Bill, who was still sound asleep but found his way on to Bertie's knee.

"Our Bill has changed quite a bit since I last saw him" whispered Bertie as Jess brought him a cup of tea. "But then, everything seems to have."

Jess ruffled his hair, "Not you though Bertie, eh? You'll not change."

Uncle Dick was talking to his mother. "And you Annie, have you had a chance to think about the future?"

"Well, not really," she held her handkerchief to her face and lowered her voice. "With poor Jack being ill for so long, well, things have slipped here. We'll have to sell up and move to something a bit more suitable."

"Look, once the funeral is over, I'll get my man Smallwood to come and help oversee things for you for a day or two. I'll be glad to do what I can. You are not alone, Annie. Jack had a lot of friends and the other Epsom families will help. There will be plenty of takers for a good yard like this."

"Thank you, Dick. People have been very kind. I was thinking I might take on a small lodging house in the town. Jess will help. Our Ethel comes in when she can but she's a married woman now; she has her own house and duties to see to. Then there's all the little ones; I don't know what to do," she sighed. "Still, there's no point worrying about it now. We'll be alright, it's just a question of adjusting."

Bertie thought of his father lying in the next room and prayed. "Our Father who art in heaven, please look after our Dad, and make things easy for Mother, at least until Reg and I can help her."

4
Flora, November 1893

BERTIE BROKE HIS HORSE into a trot as he came down from the gallops. He'd been told to give this one some extra exercise but the mist was so heavy that the buildings in the distance were starting to disappear. The fine spray clung around his clothes and the air was so thick you almost had to swim through it. Bertie longed to dry off in front of the fire.

Coming along the lane going back to the stables, he heard a sneeze. There didn't seem to be a soul around. Bertie assumed he'd imagined it, but it had made the horse jump too, so there must have been a sound. He pulled up and looked about: nothing, but then someone sneezed again. It seem to come from the big oak tree, the one that was supposed to have been the gallows where the rebels swung in the time of King Henry, or so Old Ben had said. Perhaps it was one of them returning as a wandering spirit, but surely they wouldn't haunt with a cold? Anyway, the horse didn't seem particularly ruffled, and even though old Banjo was a bit on the stolid side, Bertie's trust in animal instinct made him feel a lot braver.

As they approached the tree, a small figure was curled up at the base of its trunk. Knees pulled up and head tucked in. Another sneeze shook the bundle.

"Are you alright?" asked Bertie.

"I'm not here," was the muffled reply.

"Yes, you are," Bertie said, not quite knowing what to do, but feeling that it was important to reassure the person, and himself, that they were in fact real.

"Not in my head I'm not."

"Well where are you then?"

"I'm back at the farm with the sheep in the orchard. The sun is shining and mother is letting us have tea under the apple trees."

"And what do you have for tea?" Bertie slipped off his horse and walked over. Peering through the mist, he could see it was a girl, a young lady, but her fine polished boots were muddy and water drops ran down her black hat and coat.

"Um. Well, there's strawberries and cream, fairy cakes and lemonade."

"Well, that sounds a lovely feast."

The bundle moved. A pale face appeared from the darkness.

"You're Bertie Jones, aren't you?" the voice became clearer and had a rather bossy tone. "I've seen you ride. Father says you've a special way with horses. And I've seen you in church, singing in the choir."

"Miss Flora?" Bertie looked closer. It was the Guv'nor's daughter. "Miss Flora, what are you doing out here? You'll catch your death." Bertie's voice trailed away as he realized what a stupid thing he'd said. "I'm so sorry, miss. I heard about your mother."

Flora looked up at him; the light caught her hair and it was golden.

"Your mother was a lovely lady, Miss Flora. Always very kind," Bertie added, trying to think what he would want to hear if it was him. "Tildy says that the souls of our dear ones are always with us, even if they are far away, even if they are in heaven."

That's a lovely thing to say. Who's Tildy?"

"Tildy is a gypsy lady. She always took care of us when we were running about the Downs. She's like an outdoors mother."

A blackbird gave an agitated chatter above them.

"Your dad died, didn't he, Bertie?" she asked, sounding much quieter now.

"Yes, last year about this time. Uncle Dick, er, the Guv'nor, your father that is; he took us back for the funeral." Bertie stumbled over the words. "It was strange going home after being away."

"I remember coming to your house in Epsom. It was one time when we were staying with Uncle Ned. We came round for tea. There were so many of you, Charles and I wished that we had lots of brothers and sisters too."

"Ha, we thought the other way round, because you said you had your very own room and in our house you never had anywhere to yourself."

"You had a big old dog that you were riding. And then you were doing somersaults; I think you must have been to the circus or something. The dog dashed away, then you fell into someone and your sister told you off."

"That was probably Jess. She's the bossy one, but a very good cook. She sends us food parcels. You'll have to try her fruit cake."

They both laughed. Bertie brought the horse nearer and crouched down beside her. She carried on talking and he liked the sound of her voice.

"Your house was always so jolly. Much nicer than here. I never feel cosy here. I liked it when we lived in the cottage. Mother did too. She missed Epsom. She'd tell me stories of all the escapades she and your mother would get up to when they were girls. She told me about a gypsy lady who could make spells and read fortunes. Perhaps that was Tildy?"

Bertie thought for a bit. "Perhaps it was."

"And your family, how are they now?"

"Well, I haven't been back home since Dad died, but I wouldn't know where to go in any case. Mother had to move and not everyone could stay with her. Jess and Bill, my littlest brother, are with her, but the other boys live in a church school. Ethel, she got married. Then there's Lily: do you remember her? Maybe you came before she was born. Anyway, she's my little sister, a year younger than Bill. She lives in Cambridge with my aunt, but even though she's close by, we don't really get to see her much."

"I'd like to see her one day, Bertie," said Flora.

"She'd like that. She gets lonely."

It was growing dark.

"I really think we should get you home, Miss Flora. It's getting harder to see. They'll be worried. You can ride back with me; it's a long way along the lane."

She stared at the horse chomping on the sparse tufts of grass.

"Oh, I'll be alright." She started to sound all clipped again as she stood up and brushed at her coat.

47

"But Banjo's a beauty, a lovely horse, a bit too nice really," Bertie stroked him. "See?"

She looked unsure.

"He won't hurt you, you know," Bertie said. "And I'll look after you, I promise."

"Do you mean that?"

"Of course. So don't worry. I'll always catch you if you fall."

"It's silly really, when you think I'm a horse trainer's daughter, but I'm a bit scared. Charles says it's pathetic. And I know it is but, well."

"Oh no, you're not silly," Bertie interrupted. "Horses can be tricky if you're not used to them. But look, I can jump on and then pull you up so you can ride in front of me; that's how we always carried the little ones."

Bertie brought the horse nearer and sprang up into the saddle.

"You really should work in a circus, Bertie," she laughed. "But I can't get up there."

"Yes, you can. I'll pull you up here."

"No, I'm bigger than you, so you'll never lift me up there."

"Don't be daft, you're only a little thing. I've lifted my sisters up like this and they can be quite a weight, believe me. Come on, give me your hand and we'll have you back home in no time."

Bertie held out his arm, and holding on to the horse with his legs, he leaned down and wrapped his arm around her waist.

"Now, when I lift you, put your foot on top of my boot," Bertie explained. "Don't be scared, I've got good hold of you, just don't be quite so stiff."

Bertie gently drew her up and placed her so that she sat side-saddle in front of him. She turned her head quickly, so that her hair flicked across his face, soft as silk it felt. The horse moved. Alarmed, Flora clutched at Bertie's neck and drew him close to her. Her nose bumped his.

"Ouch, sorry." She stopped. "All I can see are your eyes, Bertie, and they are so blue."

They walked along slowly, the three of them all quiet in a strange invisible world. The horse could smell his way home; he didn't need to be able to see.

Ahead a lamp swayed.

"Whoa!" It was the Guv'nor. "Who's there?"

"It's me, Guv'nor. It's Bertie. And I've got Miss Flora with me."

"Flora? So that's where you are."

The shape of the Guv'nor appeared out of the gloom. He snatched Flora from the horse.

"And what do you think you've been doing, young lady? Out in this, dallying," he spluttered and stomped off, dragging Flora behind him. Bertie could hear her trying to explain.

"Come on, Bertie, let's get you back." Mr Smallwood was next to him.

"Have I done something wrong?" Bertie asked. "He seemed so angry."

"No Bertie, it's not you. He was just worried about her. She was gone for hours."

ʊ ʊ ʊ

Bertie came in from the gallops. Old Ben had put out a mug of hot tea for him. The warmth seeped through the thick pottery, warming his cold chapped hands until the blood tingled. Master Charles was there, back for the Christmas holidays, he guessed, and begging at Old Ben.

"Can I help Bertie, please Ben?"

"Now, Master Charles, what does the Guv'nor say about that?"

"He says I might learn some sense."

"Does he now?" chuckled Old Ben. "Well, I dare say Bertie could do with a hand … What do you say, Bert?"

Bertie winked at Charles. "There's a lot of tack to clean this morning."

He always enjoyed it when Charles came back from boarding school. He would tell Bertie stories about the masters and the other boys. Charles reminded him of Percy, only better behaved, but Flora always laughed when he said this. "You don't see him at home, Bertie, always up to something, anything to try and not have to stay indoors with his studies. Father despairs of ever making a gentleman out of him."

Bertie thought about the church service last Christmas. Charles liked to feed the mice and had made them quite tame. He scattered

49

crumbled mince pies around the flagstones. From the choir stalls, Bertie could see the mice darting under the pews. They were particularly drawn to the long skirts of the ladies and liked to hide there. The ladies flapped and shuffled but were too embarrassed to say anything. There was always something afoot when Charles was around.

"Right, saddle soap, cloths, water." Bertie set the three piles on the little table and drew up a stool. He passed a strap to Charles and started on one himself. He liked the rhythm of working in the mixture, then polishing it up until the colour and suppleness of the leather returned.

Charles was making great progress and seemed very pleased with himself, as he was getting through twice as many as Bertie. Bertie didn't have the heart to tell him that they would all need doing again.

"If you put yours in a separate pile just there, Master Charles, I'll put them away later," said Bertie, interrupting Charles's story about a housemaster and a walking stick.

Charles nodded good-naturedly and carried on.

PART II
THE YEAR OF THE
DIAMOND

5
Egerton, April 1900

"DIAMOND JUBILEE IS DEFINITELY looking more settled now."
The Guv'nor gripped his field glasses, hardly able to take his
eyes off the colt as he watched Morny Cannon riding him around
the private gallop.

Bertie craned his neck to get a better view. He tapped out the
rhythm of hooves in his head.

"How's he been behaving in the stalls, Bertie?

"He's coming along, Guv'nor, that's for sure." Bertie chose his
words carefully.

"Really, he seems so much better now. Perhaps he has finally grown
out of those tantrums of his." The Guv'nor took another look. "Yes, I
think we've every chance in the 2000 Guineas, especially with Morny
up in the saddle. His Royal Highness will be very pleased."

"Well, Guv'nor, you've got Bertie to thank for that," Old Ben
spoke loudly, right in the Guv'nor's ear. "That horse will do anything
for him, and Bert's worked hard to get him that way."

"Of course, I'm very well aware of all Bertie's efforts, thank you
Ben." The Guv'nor turned away from Old Ben, but patted Bertie on
the back. "And you have done a jolly good job, young man, so you
have. Oh look, here they come."

Morny pulled the Diamond up and brought him off the gallop.
With a grand sweep, the jockey swung one leg over the horse's back
and dismounted with a graceful bounce. The Diamond cut him a
glance, but stood calm and still.

Allowing himself a rare smile, Morny led the Diamond towards
them. But Bertie knew something wasn't quite right. Something in

the tilt of the Diamond's head, the white of the eye, or a twitch of muscle: it was difficult to place exactly, but that horse was up to something.

Slipping under the fence, moving swiftly but steadily, Bertie approached just in time to see Morny disappear under the sinewy bulk of the horse's body as he was tossed and shaken by the unyielding clamp of the animal's jaw. The Diamond, with an evil glint in his eye, moved up on to his hind legs.

With his face set, Bertie walked straight up to the Diamond, unhurried, unhesitating and unmoved. Taking firm hold of the bridle, Bertie brought the horse down safely to one side of Morny, who was crouched on the ground waiting for the hooves to fall. The Diamond looked at Bertie and hung his head. The others arrived and rolled the cursing Morny out of range, guiding him back to the stable offices.

"Bertie, you alright there? Need a hand?" Old Ben was behind him.

"I've got him, Ben, he'll be fine now. I'll walk him round a bit to calm down, then bring him in."

"Good boy, Bertie. I'll go and help the Guv'nor with Morny." He ambled off cackling to himself. "Think there's a bad case of tumbling pride about to break out."

"See what you've done, Diamond," Bertie shook his head at the horse, who mirrored the gesture back at him.

"What was that all about? He wouldn't have hurt you, not Mr Cannon. You're lucky that he was willing to ride you at all after what you did to Mr Watts." Bertie tutted. "The finest jockeys in the land are willing to take you on and what do you do? Act up like a spoilt brat."

All the madness gone, the colt just blew noisily through his mouth and came closer, ears up, wanting to be petted.

"Don't you try getting round me." Bertie pulled him up firmly. "Come on, let's check you over and see if you've damaged yourself. You can't go round doing that sort of thing to people."

Bertie ran his hand along the horse's body, pausing at the joints, checking for any swellings, lumps or bumps. The Diamond shivered with delight at the attention.

"Well you seem alright for all that. Just as well as they'll probably sell you to the French now. And I'll get the sack for letting you have too much of your own way."

The Diamond tried to nibble the back of Bertie's shirt.

"Now stop that. It's too late to be acting all soft. What am I to do with you?" Bertie glanced over at the commotion going on at the other end of the yard. "In the end Diamond, I'll forgive you, I always do. But the others, I can't say the same for them."

Nuzzling his head forward into Bertie's neck, the Diamond sighed.

"Come on then, and let's get this saddle off you."

"Just look at him now. Like a different horse." Reg arrived carrying a horse blanket.

Bertie kept his head down, unpicking the leather straps sticky with sweat.

Reg paused. "You alright, little brother?"

Bertie shrugged. "I dunno what gets into him sometimes, Reg. It's a puzzler. I knew he had something planned though." He pulled off the saddle.

"Give us that here, Bert." Reg took the saddle from him and passed him the blanket.

Bertie plucked tiny strands of straw off the cloth.

"What are they saying, Reg?"

"Well, I don't think Morny Cannon will be up on him again, that's for sure, which puts the Guv'nor in a bit of a spot."

Pulling the blanket over the Diamond and adjusting it so that it was smooth and tidy, Bertie looked at Reg. "Alright, we're ready. Let's go and face them."

∪ ∪ ∪

Two days later Bertie and Reg were returning from exercising the horses on the heath. The Guv'nor was waiting for them and waved them over. They turned off from the others.

"He's got Lord Marcus with him and he's looking a bit upset," said Reg.

Bertie looked at the grand figure of the Prince of Wales's racing manager, with his bushy white moustache and wrinkled eyes. He'd always thought of Lord Marcus as a kindly gentleman, or perhaps a grand wizard like Merlin, although stouter than Merlin appeared in the picture books.

"I think he looks worried, rather than angry," said Bertie.

"Whatever it is, it must be something important by the way Old Ben is pretending to be busy just within earshot."

"Well, I just hope that the Diamond doesn't play up." Bertie patted the horse. "Do you hear me, Diamond?"

The Diamond snorted back.

Bertie let Reg go ahead on Fronti. Reg tipped his cap at Lord Marcus and then the Guv'nor. Bertie followed his lead.

"Good job, boys. Very nice indeed. We saw you up on the gallops." The Guv'nor spoke faster than usual. "Now then, how are these two behaving themselves?"

Bertie looked at Reg.

"Coming along well, Guv'nor, I'd say." Reg always found the right words. "The Diamond's always happier when Fronti's around."

Lord Marcus approached the Diamond and stroked his neck. "He really is quite an exquisite creature. Quite perfect. And you've got him in to magnificent form, Marsh."

Bertie felt Lord Marcus's gaze fall upon him.

"And you, young Jones, you've been keeping him in order, I hear."

"Trying to, my lord." Bertie drew a deep breath. "Always a bit of a handful though. But we find that … "

"Alright that's enough, thank you, Jones," Richard Marsh butted in and signalled for them to go.

Reg touched his cap again and Bertie followed suit. They set the horses walking towards to the stables.

"I said too much, didn't I, Reg?"

"Shh for a moment." Reg was straining his ears to the conversation behind them. The Guv'nor was talking.

"You see how quiet the Diamond is with him. The horse adores him. He's the only one who can do anything with him. Lord Marcus, I say it is worth the risk."

"What are they … ?" Bertie asked, but Reg shushed him again, signalling for him to go as slowly as the horses would let them.

Lord Marcus' voice carried over the yard. "Yes, young Jones has talent, but he is not an experienced jockey. What about the older brother?"

The Guv'nor replied but they couldn't catch what he said.

"But Marsh, really, the boy is not yet out of his teens and you are suggesting putting him up on the Prince's horse in a classic race! Isn't it too much to ask of him?"

"I tell you, Lord Marcus, I've seen him time and time again with that horse and Jones can do it. He's a first-class rider, like his father, but he needs the chance to prove it." This time the Guv'nor could be heard loud and clear. "We can't just let all that work go to waste and the Diamond will just act up again if we try anyone else. In any case, no jockey worth his salt will touch him after the incident with Cannon."

Everything went quiet. Bertie wound the reins around his hands. The Diamond's ears twitched.

"Well, to be honest, Marsh, the Prince is pressing for another winner. We need the people to cheer rather than jeer at him, and a royal victory would help morale no end." Lord Marcus stopped. "Alright, I'll put your proposal to HRH."

There was a crash and the sound of cursing as Old Ben sent the broom he was leaning on flying into a metal pail.

ʊ ʊ ʊ

Bertie was in the corner of the tack room sitting on his wooden stool, absorbed in dismantling a bridle. Lines of leather and pieces of smooth shiny metal were arranged all around him, with polish and cloths piled in a dark wicker basket. An early arrival of house martins dived through the eaves, searching out the familiar smell of their usual nesting quarters. Spiders spun their webs with renewed vigour as the early sunshine promised a fresh crop of hatching insects. He paused to feel the breeze as it blew through the saddles, ropes and brushes hanging on the walls, chasing away the winter dust from the shelves of implements and balms.

"Bertie?" Reg double-backed as he rushed by, throwing his arm round the doorpost to avoid flying past. "There you are. Come on, quick!"

"Everything alright?" asked Bertie.

Reg caught his breath and waved him over.

"Just come with me."

"I'll just tidy this lot away, look, and I'll be right there."

"No Bert. Now." Reg marched over and pulled him up by the arm. "You've no time for that now, just leave it. The Guv'nor's looking for you. Urgent, he said."

Reg practically frog-marched him into the yard and over to the Guv'nor. Standing next to him was Mr Smallwood, a large ledger in his hand. Old Ben was there, very obviously trying to peer at a piece of paper that the Guv'nor held in his hand. They looked up and smiled. Bertie turned around to see who was there. No one, just the stables with a few horses peeping out smelling the air.

"Now Bert, the Guv'nor's got some news for you," said Old Ben.

"Thank you, Ben." The Guv'nor stepped forward quickly, almost hiding Old Ben with his shadow, and cleared his throat. "Well, Bertie, I've just received this from Lord Marcus." He waved the piece of paper, thick bonded notepaper with a crest at the top and a watermark that glowed silver in the sun. "It says 'The Prince quite agrees for Bertie Jones to ride the Diamond'."

There was a long pause. Bertie stood there, not sure what to do.

"So, young man, what do you say to that?" The Guv'nor had barely spoken before Old Ben had stepped round him.

"Yes, Bertie, what do you say to that?" Old Ben repeated.

Bertie's eyes went from one face to another; his mouth dropped open and shut again. No sound came out. Reg gave him a nudge.

"Go on, say something."

"Me?" was all he could manage.

"Yes, Bertie, and that doesn't just mean exercising him, you will be his jockey," the Guv'nor explained. "Your first race will be the Guineas. Not long now, so there's a lot to be done."

"Lots to be done, Bert," Old Ben repeated.

"Me? In the Guineas?" Bertie said again. "On Diamond Jubilee?"

"No one can handle that horse like you can Bertie, we're all of one mind on this," said the Guv'nor, his voice vibrated so that his words echoed around the yard.

"All of one mind, Bertie," Old Ben butted in.

"The Prince, Lord Marcus and I, we are all of one mind," the Guv'nor carried on emphatically.

57

"And it's what the Diamond wanted," said Old Ben. "In fact I reckon that horse planned it all along. He planned it all, just to get Bertie up in the saddle."

The Guv'nor gave a sigh. "Well, I wouldn't put anything past that horse, but really … "

"And I'm sure young Bert is very grateful for the opportunity too," added Old Ben, "aren't you, Bert?"

"Alright, Ben. Now, is there anything else you'd care to add before I carry on?" asked the Guv'nor.

Old Ben thought seriously for a moment.

"No I don't think so, Master Dick, but thank you for asking, sir."

"Well then, to business." The Guv'nor turned to Bertie. "We'll draw up a new training plan tomorrow. The horse is already in very good shape, but we need to build up his stamina for the more demanding races. Reg will be riding Fronti, so you'll have him alongside. It'll help calm the Diamond to have his stable mate with him."

"And me too, Guv'nor," Bertie chimed in and glanced over at Reg, who winked at him.

"And of course we'll have to get you measured up for the royal silks."

Later that day, Bertie saw the Guv'nor walking across to the big house from the stable office. "Excuse me, Guv'nor!" he called, his voice sounding weedy and squeaky as he tried to call out. "Mr Marsh, sir!"

Bertie ran over, removing his cap and clutching it to his chest.

"Yes, Bertie?"

"Pardon me, sir, I just wanted to, er, say," Bertie felt his tongue fur up. The words in his head refused to come out. "I, er, … wanted to thank you for … "

"It's alright, lad, you've worked hard for this. It's not going to be easy for you, but I know that you won't let me down, Bertie."

Bertie watched him go on his way and prayed to God that he wouldn't.

υ υ υ

Reg was sitting on the broken boundary wall at the yard and looking out towards the woodland. A final burst from the sunset gave him a golden silhouette that glowed against the sapphire bluebells and the green haze of sprouting branches. The musty smoke from his roll-up mingled with the spring-sweet sharpness that reached them from the flowers. The trees creaked as the sap rose and the old branches grew heavy with the weight of contented wood pigeons.

"Reg? You alright there?" Bertie spoke quietly, not wanting to disturb his brother's peace.

"Yep. You?" Reg shuffled over and made some room.

Bertie heaved himself up on to the cold dew-covered stones and swivelled round to face the same direction as Reg. He tucked a flapping stinging nettle out of the way with his boot and let his legs hang free.

"Smoke?" Reg waved his baccy tin.

Bertie shook his head.

"Never liked the stuff, did you?" said Reg.

Bertie shook his head. "Find I can't get my breath."

"Takes my mind off the hunger," said Reg.

"Well, there is that," agreed Bertie.

They sat quietly.

"There's a little fox in there." Reg pointed into the dark woodland. "Sometimes you can see him in the shadows. He doesn't like coming out into the light much though. If you sit quiet, we might see him."

Bertie followed Reg's gaze and strained his eyes into the undergrowth.

"What do you think about me riding the Diamond?" Bertie asked at last.

"I think it's a tough one for you, Bert." Reg opened his tin. Drawing out a paper from the red Rizla packet, he flattened it carefully. "It's a difficult horse but you get the best from him. It's brave of the Guv'nor to put you up, no one knows you outside of the stable, but he wouldn't do it if he didn't think it was the right thing."

Reg dipped the forefinger and thumb of his right hand into the tightly woven rectangle of tobacco, carefully extracted a few strands of the brown weed and drizzled them along the centre of the outstretched paper. Bertie watched the cigarette form as Reg rolled it back and forth, little hairs of leaf hanging out of the edges.

"I don't want to let him down, Reg."

"You won't do that. Don't forget, you may still think of him as genial Uncle Dick but he's very canny, particularly when it comes to horses. He has to be, what with this place to run and all his fine patrons to keep happy." Reg paused to run the cigarette paper along the tip of his tongue. "You'll be alright. And anyway I'll be out there with you."

Dusk was settling in quickly now and the air cooled fast.

Reg struck a match and lit his ciggie. Bert turned to him.

"And Reg, you don't mind me riding in the Guineas, do you?"

"You what? Of course not; I'm really pleased for you. The Diamond's way out of my league. I'm not a bad rider, but you, Bert, you've always had a special way. A God-given gift."

They fell silent again, both looking out on to the wood.

"Daft idiot you are." Reg made a grab for Bertie's cap. Bertie neatly ducked, almost toppling off the wall. Reg put his arm out to steady him.

ᴗ ᴗ ᴗ

The Diamond was frothy with sweat after his work on the gallops, his coat glittering in the sunshine like a beautiful golden statue brought to life. The colt snorted and blew, turning his neck round to try and reach Bertie.

"Yes, Diamond, you did well." Bertie tickled his ears. "Good boy."

The Diamond did a little dance, tip tapping, and looked back to see where Fronti and Reg were.

"They're just coming, but we need to get you all nice and dry as quick as we can. Come on, boy."

Bertie sat back as the Diamond sauntered back to the stables. Old Ben was waiting, twitchy with excitement.

"He's been watching you out there with the Diamond," he whispered, coming forward and taking hold of the bridle.

The Diamond tensed, his dark brows furrowing.

"Come on, Diamond, it's just Old Ben, you know him."

The Diamond swayed his head but did as he was told.

"I tell you, he's been watching you out there on the gallops with the Diamond," Old Ben hissed.

"Who has?"

"The Prince. He's here with Lord Marcus. They're waiting for you."

"I ought to get Diamond brushed down first and put a bit more cover on him," said Bertie, reckoning that by the time he had done all that, Reg would be back and could go with him.

"You'll have to pass them, Bertie, so you'll need to stop on the way. The Guv'nor won't let you hang around too long if the horse needs seeing to."

Bertie shivered. The warm sweat trickling down his back turned cold and his skin prickled with goosebumps. He'd seen the Prince many times talking to others, including his father, but had never been involved other than to hold a halter.

"You'll stay with me, Ben, in case I need some help?" He slipped out of the saddle.

"I'll be there Bertie." Old Ben stood up as straight as a soldier, or at least much as his rheumatism allowed.

There was quite a group waiting as they turned into the yard. The Guv'nor and Mr Smallwood were listening to the Prince of Wales, who stood immaculate in the brown suit and bowler hat that he always wore when visiting the stables. Lord Marcus was next to the Prince. The Duke of York stood slightly away from them. Various other attendants gathered, straining to hear the Prince's words.

"Ah, Jones, here you are," called the Guv'nor. "Now, let's see the Diamond."

Bertie walked the horse round, keeping a tight hold on the reins and making sure he was carefully positioned between the animal and the royal party, far enough out for them to be able to see but close enough to react in the event of any problems. He willed the Diamond to behave.

"Perfect. He looks even more perfect, if that is possible." The Prince stood back, clapping his hand together. "Do remember that time, Marsh, when you won that fiver from Lord Chaplin?"

"Indeed, sir."

"He wagered that there was no such thing as a horse that could not be faulted." The Prince addressed the others like a performer on a stage, even giving Bertie a wink. "But he had to throw in his bet after seeing our Diamond here."

Everyone laughed heartily. Bertie wanted to comment, but kept his mouth shut. Only speak when spoken to, he reminded himself.

"You're doing fine work here, Marsh, if we can just keep the Diamond's temper steady," said the Prince, turning towards his horse but keeping a safe distance.

"Well, the colt certainly seems to be going well with you, young Jones. A good show on the gallops," said Lord Marcus.

"Thank you, sir." Bertie blushed like a girl. "He is coming along, even on the longer distances. There is no finer horse out there, or so I reckon."

Bertie's voice tailed away. He probably sounded a right idiot, but he wanted them to know how well the Diamond was doing.

"Hear, hear," they replied to his surprise, as Bertie wasn't sure that they had even heard him. Even the Guv'nor looked on approvingly.

The Prince came nearer. "I remember your father well, Jones. He did a fine job down in Epsom with my steeplechasers, very good in the saddle too. Glad to see you carrying on the family tradition."

"Thank you, Your Highness, sir," replied Bertie. "My brother … " He wanted to explain about Reg, but they were no longer listening.

The Prince slapped the Guv'nor on the back.

"You and Jack Jones, eh Marsh? Quite a handful, I recall. What do you say Lord Marcus?"

"Indeed so, sir. There was that time at Aintree, do you remember? With the ginger whiskers and bottles of stout." Lord Marcus tugged at his thick white moustache. "When was it? Seventy-two?"

Richard Marsh coughed "Em. Well, off you go, Jones, best settle the Diamond down after his exertions."

Bertie touched his cap and led the horse away.

"Well done, Jones," the Prince called after him. "See you at the Guineas."

ひ ひ ひ

Diamond leaned out of the stall, his upper lip curled as his teeth nibbled to get a grip at the bolt as he saw Bertie approach.

"Alright, Diamond, give me a chance," he laughed and started undoing all the locks. "If you weren't such a escape artist, it wouldn't take so long to get in, would it?"

Bertie walked around the box, plumping up the hay and checking the water. The Diamond followed him round, inspecting everything too.

"Anyway, you knew I'd come and see you. Settle you down, what with us both a bit nervous about tomorrow. Eh, boy?"

The horse grunted in agreement.

Bertie took the nice soft-bristled brush from his pocket and swept it slowly along Diamond's neck and body.

"Now, Diamond, we need to have a serious talk about tomorrow. No one else'll ride you now, only me. And a lot of people are relying on us, you see. So you've got to behave. Understand?"

The Diamond nodded his head.

ʊ ʊ ʊ

"Ready for the big day tomorrow, Bertie?" asked the Guv'nor.

"Yes, thank you, sir. The Diamond seems alright and at least we're only up the road, so we can walk him there," Bertie replied.

"We thought that last year though, didn't we?" Old Ben joined them. "Do you remember at the July course? Even shorter walk to there, but that didn't help."

"But this is different, Ben." The Guv'nor gave him a hard stare, but that didn't stop Old Ben.

"We thought then he'd be alright. The Diamond looked as smart as can be and was the favourite in no time. Then he unseated poor old John Watts going down to the line." Old Ben laughed. "Almost at the starting post they were, tossed him off and went tearing off in the direction of Egerton."

Old Ben poked Bertie in the ribs. "You caught him, Bert, didn't you? Trying to get home, he was. Never cared for the crowds did the Diamond, nor for his jockeys, excepting you Bert, of course."

Bertie gave a nervous cough.

"But give him his due," Old Ben carried on. "Watts got back on. But the Diamond had the devil in him and played merry hell. Came in last, 'though that he came in at all was a miracle. Shouldn't laugh but it was very queer seeing him dance along that turf. 'Course John Watts didn't think it was funny but then he never had much of a sense of humour, did he, Guv'nor?"

"Well, I think in the circumstances … Oh really, Ben, I really don't think this is helping." The Guv'nor shook his head and walked over to the stables.

"It's alright," Old Ben whispered to Bertie. "He's just a bit nervous."

6

2000 Guineas, Newmarket, 1900

"YOU SURE YOU'VE GOT everything, young Bert?" asked Old Ben again as they stood outside the door to the jockeys' room.

"He's checked a dozen times at least," said Reg.

"And you checked for me too, didn't you?" Bertie inspected his bag again and went through the list in his head.

"Yes, Bert, so nothing to fret about." Reg came closer. "I'm sorry I'm not racing with you today, the Guv'nor says the ground is too hard for Fronti. But we'll be there at the parade and ride down with you to the start. It's all been arranged."

"The Diamond and me, we'll like that," said Bertie, keeping his head bent over his bag.

"And be careful who you talk to, there's all sorts who'll take advantage of a young jockey starting out," Old Ben waved a finger at him. "One slip, that's all it takes and you're in their power for the rest of your life."

"I know, I know and I will," promised Bertie.

"Many a fine career has been ruined … " started Old Ben.

"Careful now," Reg interrupted, "or poor Bertie will get so worried, he'll bolt."

"Of course I won't bolt," although as he said it, the idea was suddenly appealing.

There were people everywhere in the enclosure, all dressed up to the nines, even in this heat. Some walked with a purpose, brisk, business-like. Others sauntered. Smart, languid couples arm in arm, laughing groups waving their racecards. Occasionally they would look over.

Two racing types, with their binoculars and pink 'uns tucked under their arms, paused nearby.

"Diamond Jubilee looks in cracking form," said one.

"Well, the smart money's not on him, too unpredictable. None of the decent jockeys will touch him, they've had to rope in some little stable lad."

They snorted to one another and ambled off.

Bertie felt a bit sick. What was he doing? He tried to turn his eyes back to the others but couldn't face them. Old Ben was still offering words of advice. Reg fidgeted nervously.

"No need to worry about Bertie, he'll be fine." The Guv'nor burst in. "You've been around racing long enough to know what's what, eh Bertie?"

Bertie tugged his cap "Yes, Guv'nor," he answered.

"And how are you bearing up, young man?" The Guv'nor beamed, tapping his stick on the ground and adjusting his binocular strap to a more comfortable position across his front.

"Eh, alright, sir, I think?" replied Bertie, squinting as the sun shone full in his face.

"Come now, Bertie. No one can ride that horse better than you. Just like your father, isn't he, Ben?"

"Beg pardon, sir, what was that?"

"Bertie's just like his father, like Jack. Remember?" he repeated a bit louder and more slowly.

"Oh yes, Guv'nor, he is. It's like going back thirty years," Old Ben joined in enthusiastically. "I could tell some stories about those days, eh, Master Dick?"

Richard Marsh put a hand on Old Ben's arm. "I think Bertie should prepare himself and we should go to see about our other young man. Don't you?"

"Oh, the Diamond'll be alright. He's got Fronti there." Old Ben was about to start off on one of his tales, but the Guv'nor gave him one of his looks and this time Old Ben jumped to attention. "Thinking about it, you're right, sir. We don't want him getting restless, do we?"

"That's right. And Bertie, you'll be fine. Just nerves – a good sign in a jockey, just like in a horse."

Old Ben did a little thumbs up to Bertie behind the Guv'nor's back. "A good sign in a jockey, that's what he said, Bertie, see."

Bertie walked into the jockeys' room. It felt like the first day at school, with the tall whitewashed walls pitted with large iron coat-hooks and long wooden benches. His footsteps on the stone floor sounded unnaturally loud. Muffled voices came from the back of the room, but he couldn't see anyone.

"Can I help you, Bertie?"

Bertie jumped, caught unawares as someone came up behind him. It was George from the cricket team. He played a good game of football too, Bertie remembered. "Didn't expect to see you here?"

"I'm one of the valets." George flushed pink from the top of scalp that showed through his thin blond hair right down to where his neck disappeared under the floppiness of his collar.

"Sorry, George, you gave me a start. I didn't recognize you for a minute, all dressed up in your work clothes."

"I heard about your big ride. What a bit of luck."

"Well, we'll see. It's very quiet round here, thought it would be full, it being Guineas day."

"It's between races, and you're a bit early. It'll start filling up in a minute. We have to keep an eye on the comings and goings though, especially those Americans; you have to watch them, if you know what I mean."

"Well, I've heard things, but I don't know. They seem alright to me, a bit loud." Bertie shrugged. "Maybe people just don't like it because they keep winning."

George got even redder. "No, Bert, really, there's some odd things going on. Better not be seen chatting though or I'll be in trouble with the master. We're not supposed to fraternize. When you're all done, just go through to the weighing room, but call me if you need anything, that's my job."

"Thanks, George," he said, unsure about what he could possibly need. "And see you at practice on Sunday."

Bertie went over to an empty bench. He turned around to say something else but George had gone – perhaps it was too much fraternizing – so he put down his bag and sat next to it. Coats and shirts hung on the pegs opposite, shoes lined up underneath. He wondered about their owners. The sensible brogues were probably Morny Cannon's, the sleek black boots looked a bit foreign so they could be Otto's from one of his continental trips, the fancy spats were a bit flash so maybe they belonged to one of the shady Americans that everyone seemed to be talking about. Bits of material poked out of one of the closed lacquer-wood lockers that lined one wall, Bertie resisted an urge to tuck them in.

Behind the frosted glass doors across the way, there was a tiled bathing area, hospital clean. Clammy white wisps of vapour seeped from the steam rooms and condensed on the shiny surfaces. The tang of stale water was overwhelmed by the strong scent of carbolic. The smell took him back to bath night in the scullery at home a long time ago. No running water and flushing toilets there, just a big tin bath in the middle of the room, a hot copper in the corner. The towels were folded on the rail, placed by the fire to keep warm. Bathing was in strict order of size: smallest first. "Hurry up, I'm freezing!" they'd call as they waited their turn. Quickly diving in, they'd rub in a bit of soap and rinse, ducking down in the water. The bitter scum filled their ears and nose made them splutter and shriek. The older boys had to see to the younger ones, rubbing down one, then the next. Mother sometimes did a spot check and heaven help you if she found a tidemark on your neck or a speck of dirt under your fingernails.

If you were lucky you'd get one of the towels nearest the heat, all baked and fat. But it always ended up a bit of a free-for-all, with Percy tipping jugs of cold water over the little ones who'd splash with the shock of it, soapy liquid slopping over the side and slithering over the stone slabs. Bertie and Reg would have to make sure it was all sorted out before Dad came. Dad was always last for some reason. They'd all have to clear off once he came in, as he liked his bath in peace. Bertie couldn't understand why he never went first, but he didn't.

The lads who lodged had their own bath night. They would slip in and out as fast as they could, before any of Percy's pranks could humiliate them in front of their peers or, even worse, the women of the house.

Laughter from outside broke into his thoughts. Bertie picked up his bag. Piece by piece he removed each article, laying everything out neatly. He smoothed out the purple body of the shirt, feeling the swirls of the braid with his fingers and pulling the bright scarlet sleeves straight. He took the black velvet riding cap from its case and brushed it, adjusting the gold fringe carefully so that the button stood clear in the middle. His breeches and silk scarf were bright white, new and crisp. Only his riding boots were familiar; he'd been breaking them in over the last couple of weeks to make sure that they were soft enough to mould the tiniest movement from his legs on to the horse's body. Looking at it all there in front of him, Bertie shook his head. Crikey, he thought, I'll wake up in a minute.

Bertie sat back down on the bench. Pushing his arms out in front and linking his fingers, he stretched as far as he could reach. Someone who was vaguely familiar walked past wrapped in towels, skin all red from the sauna. Bertie smiled, but didn't get a response. He cleared an imaginary lump in his throat and sat still again for a while. The clock hadn't moved much more than a minute or two, so he went through all his things one more time and rearranged them just to be sure.

It was cool in the room, but he decided to take a shower anyway. He picked up a towel from the open cupboard; the material was thin and harsh. Walking towards the tiled area, he passed the lavatory cubicles. Someone was heaving away a couple of last desperate pounds. At least that was one thing he didn't have to worry about.

Twenty minutes later, Bertie presented himself at the weighing room.

"My word, you look well scrubbed, young man. Nice to see such a healthy-looking jockey," said the official, all dressed up in his top hat and tails. "It's young Jones, isn't it? Big day, eh? Well, you're a bit early so you'll need to wait there. I'll call you over as soon as I can."

Bertie stood in the corner and watched people filling in forms, chalking on boards, adjusting scales: it was more like a bank than a racecourse. He felt like a spare part, a fish out of water, not at all like a proper jockey. The chatter of the crowd filtered in. More noise came from the room behind him as it filled up with the other riders, calling out loudly, teasing, arguing, swearing.

"Americans," said one of the black-coated clerks to another and they both raised their eyes.

After finally climbing on the scales, Bertie hurried out of the weighing room. Morny Cannon came along with another couple of jockeys. He should be riding the Diamond today by rights, thought Bertie, feeling his blood sink down to his boots. Morny glanced in his direction, but showed no sign of knowing him.

Bertie wandered outside. It was even busier. People shuffled along the paths, barely able to pass one another. The bright sun made him feel light-headed. Taking a deep breath, Bertie launched himself out along the path to the parade ring. Many in the crowd paused and went quiet as he walked past. He could make out the odd words as they muttered: "stable lad", "royal colours", "mad horse".

"Good luck, young 'un!" someone called out.

Bertie went to smile.

"He'll bloody well need it," called another.

After that he kept his head down. The walk to the paddock seemed endless, and, all the time, pictures of what the Diamond might be up to went through his head. Please behave today, he thought.

"Bertie!" Mr Smallwood appeared in front and waved to him.

Never had the sight of Mr Smallwood been so welcome. Bertie almost threw his arms around him but managed to content himself with a two-handed hearty handshake.

"You alright there, Bertie?" Mr Smallwood checked him over, as if he were one of the horses.

"Yes, sir, I'm fine, but very pleased to see you, I must say," replied Bertie quietly.

Mr Smallwood smiled down at him. "Shall we go down to the paddock?"

"How is Mrs Smallwood, sir? And little Stanley and baby Doris?" he asked in as normal a voice as possible.

"They're fine, thank you, Bertie. They asked to be sure to send their regards. The children have been busy playing out the race. You'll be pleased to hear that you and the Diamond always win."

They laughed.

"You must come for tea again soon, you and Reg."

Thank you sir, we'd like that, I'm sure. You and Mrs Smallwood have always been so kind to us." Bertie had to stop himself gushing on.

"Pleasure, always a pleasure, my boy." Mr Smallwood patted him on the shoulder. "Now to business. Lord Marcus is down in the paddock and His Royal Highness has sent his equerry, Sir Dighton Probyn, to report back to him."

"And the Diamond?" asked Bertie.

"Well, so far he's not put a foot wrong. Mr Marsh is leading him round just now."

"Oh, that's a relief. I'll go straight and see to him." Bertie cheered up at the thought of getting on with things.

"Better come and pay your respects to Lord Marcus and Sir Dighton first, Bertie. That's the done thing," said Mr Smallwood, hauling him back and steering him gently inside the ring. Lord Marcus saw him coming and tapped Sir Dighton on the arm.

"Here's our boy," he called. "Can't wait to get going, eh Jones, I bet."

Bertie touched his cap. "Yes, sir."

"Good, good. We are all very much looking forward to this, aren't we, Sir Dighton?"

"Indeed we are. And I must tell you that their Royal Highnesses asked me to convey their good wishes," the equerry added.

"Diamond Jubilee is in fine form today. I even hear that the odds are shortening, he looks so splendid and well behaved." There was mischief in Lord Marcus's eyes and his mouth twitched, sending the hairs of his white moustache on a march up and down his cheek. "Rather different to last year when our Diamond chased you out of the Paddock, what eh Probyn, old chap?"

Sir Dighton stood ramrod straight and raised an eyebrow. "I'm pleased it caused you such amusement, Beresford."

Lord Marcus laughed so much that it was a miracle that his hat remained in place, but then everything about his lordship was always correct in that respect.

Bertie caught sight of the Diamond; his body was taut, his step rhythmic and calm. As if reading his thoughts, the Diamond stopped and swung his head round.

"Think you'd better go, young man." Lord Marcus motioned towards the horse. "Our Diamond is starting to pine for you."

Sure enough, the Diamond was refusing to move on. He just stood there, tapping a hoof on the turf. The gasps of admiration from the race-goers were not lost on the Diamond. The old devil was enjoying it for once. He stood proud, bowing this way and that to his grateful public.

"You're going to be impossible after all this fuss, aren't you, boy?" teased Bertie.

The Diamond cooed back at him and tossed his mane.

"Too clever by half," muttered the Guv'nor and turned to Bertie. "Now then, young Jones. You'll lead out on to the field as you are riding His Royal Highness's horse. Reg and Fronti will accompany you to the start. The Diamond is in a good temper, but any sign of a change just move him down to the line as quickly as possible. Another thing … " The Guv'nor glanced around and lowered his voice. "Give him as much space as you can. The Americans will try and box you in. Remember they don't ride by our rules. And that ridiculous monkey crouch, with their knees stuck up in their neck, means that they swing this way and that, so keep as clear as you can."

"Yes, Guv'nor."

"I've nothing else to advise, Bertie." He looked him straight in the eye. "I know you can do this."

"Thank you," Bertie paused, for a moment he wanted to call him Uncle Dick like in the old days. "Thank you, Guv'nor."

The bell rang. Bertie's heart started to beat faster.

"Leg up?" Old Ben increased his pace to keep up with the Diamond, then bent over and held out his cupped hands. Bertie sprang up, taking comfort in the brief, but unnecessary support, as he rose up into the saddle.

"Ready, Bert?" Reg asked, coming alongside.

At the start of the course they broke into a canter, leading the other horses and riders out on to the field and down to the starting line. People lined the course several deep all the way along. Bertie could hear them cheering for the Prince, and forgot for a moment that this was directed at him. The Diamond was relaxed and happy, almost skittish, glancing at Fronti and back up at him.

They were soon at the start.

"Alright then, Bert? I'll be leaving you now." Reg turned Fronti around. "See you at the other end, little brother!"

Bertie and the Diamond watched them ride away.

"Just you and me now, boy." Bertie rubbed the horse's neck with the flat of his hand. The Diamond walked demurely into position. Bertie focused on the course ahead, blocking out the riders around him as they chided each other using words that he could barely understand. The sun was high, the turf dry and unforgiving beneath them, there was a mere flicker of a breeze. Bertie adjusted his seat and the bridle until it was right for the Diamond and for himself. They were ready and when the flag went down, they flew forward.

Bertie didn't have to worry about keeping clear of anyone: the Diamond knew what he had to do and shot ahead without a second's hesitation. It was as if they were on a joyride over the gallops and they ran simply for the pleasure. Once or twice, the Diamond peeked back at him, almost laughing. In their own world, they were only aware of the course stretching ahead. Everything around them blurred as they swooped along. Bertie was sure there were no other horses nearby, but he didn't dare take his eyes away from the front to check. He could hear the drumming of the hooves behind him, so he knew they should be still racing. When the winning post came into view, Bertie allowed himself to sneak a look behind. It was like the hounds of hell were after them, a whole pack bearing on their heels, but he knew they wouldn't catch them now, there must have been four good lengths between them and the next horse.

It was the wave of noise from the crowds rather than the post that told him that the race was over. People ran on to the course. The stewards rushed out too, but they joined the crowds rather than held them back. Bertie let the Diamond canter on for a bit. He needed the time himself. Now it was over, everything inside him started to shake. He brought in the reins, and the Diamond huffed and puffed until Bertie comforted him.

Richard Marsh was running towards them, his arms outstretched.

"Wonderful job. Wonderful," the Guv'nor patted the Diamond, who was unusually patient, and shook Bertie's hand, then did it all again, before proudly leading them through. Well-wishers packed themselves in and gathered round, cheering and calling, jostling for a better view. The crowd went quiet and parted as the royal party, led by the Prince of Wales, the Duke of York and Lord Marcus,

73

approached. A large official-looking group trailed after them, all eyes on the beaming Prince.

"Easy, boy," soothed Bertie, as much to himself as to the Diamond.

"Well done, Marsh, magnificent show!" The Prince slapped him on the shoulder. "And you, young Jones, a fine ride, what? One of the best races I've seen in a long time."

Everyone clapped. Bertie bowed his head and shook the royal hand, being careful not to squeeze too hard as he'd heard that it wasn't good form. Cheering broke out again and a photographer brought out his camera. The Prince kept up a long series of questions to Bertie throughout.

"Expect you'd like to get down, young man." said Lord Marcus. "We don't want you or the Diamond catching cold."

The Prince waved his hand. "I think, Lord Marcus, you are trying to tell us in your charming manner that we should let Jones get about the business of weighing in. As always, you are quite right."

At the signal from the Guv'nor, Bertie slung a leg across the horse's back and slid off the Diamond.

"Phew!" he exclaimed, forgetting himself for a moment at the relief of being back on the ground. The royal party laughed.

Reg and Old Ben were waiting in the background. Bertie caught their eyes and grinned as they both put their thumbs up.

"I'll come and give you a hand once I've seen to this lot," Bertie mouthed to them.

"Think you've done more than enough for one day, young man," said Lord Marcus seeing the exchange.

"I reckon he's talking sense, Bertie," Old Ben spoke in a whisper that rang out loud and clear.

The Prince went off with his party. The heat from the warm bodies made the enclosure feel like a glasshouse. Bertie wished all the people would disappear. He gazed at the scene and tried to take it all in. A few yards to the right, fighting her way towards him, was Flora. She looked as neat as a daisy, tucking her hair back under her hat.

"I've never seen you race before. It was so exciting, my heart is still pounding." She patted her chest. "You scared me."

"Nothing to be scared of, Flora."

She stood so close that he could smell the freshness of her skin.

"I was worried. You were going so fast."

Bertie flapped the bridle, almost catching Old Ben with it. The Diamond started to sneeze.

"You better leave him, Miss Flora. He's getting himself all tangled up and the horse is getting worried." Old Ben stood between them.

Flora crossed her arms. "Well, that wouldn't do now, would it?"

"And you'll get muck on your frock," muttered Bertie.

"But he ran a good race though, eh, miss?" Old Ben turned to Flora and went on to describe in detail the more technical aspects of the course. Bertie laughed: that would teach her.

Two women paused in front of them. One nudged the other.

"How on earth do the jockeys manage to ride like that without falling off?"

The words blared out above the general drone.

"The movement from the waist down, dear girl, they have tremendously powerful thighs, these riders," her companion explained in an equally loud voice.

"Oh, really!" the first lady quivered.

Bertie felt people stop to look him up and down.

"That didn't sound very proper," said Old Ben.

The Guv'nor had arrived. "Really, ladies! I think you had better move along," he frowned.

Bertie turned back to his horse, all fingers and thumbs as he removed the saddle.

Flora came close again.

"Perhaps you can explain it all to me when we get home," she whispered in his ear.

Bertie felt very strange. All light-headed, as if he was full of laughing gas, he wanted to turn somersaults around the ring, to jump back on the Diamond and to ride off with Flora into the great unknown.

The Guv'nor observed them with a strange expression.

"Thank you, Miss Flora," Bertie coughed and dived into the quiet of the weighing room.

ᴜ ᴜ ᴜ

"Look at you in the paper, Bertie." Lily held up the picture for them all to see. "It says here that 'everyone was overjoyed and full of celebration at the victory of the Prince of Wales' horse in the 2000 Guineas. The only person who seemed to retain an air of calm was the jockey himself, the young Bertie Jones.' It goes on with lots about you, and mentions Dad. What about that?"

"If only they knew, eh, Reg?" laughed Bertie.

"I brought you something." Lily passed him a brown paper parcel. "Well, lots of little things."

Bertie looked at her suspiciously.

"Oh don't be like that, I thought it was important to celebrate your first race."

Bertie opened the package. Inside was a large black-sheeted scrapbook, with a swirling marble-patterned cover. There was also a tub of gum, which had been opened and was very sticky around the edge.

"Where did you get this from, Lil?" asked Reg.

"Well, Aunt Mary brought it for me years ago one Christmas and I never use it, but Jess told me that Bertie used to have one, with all the cards of the jockeys and horses in. So I thought he could have one for his racing history. A sort of heirloom." She gave a satisfied smile. "Oh, and you can go in there too, Reg."

"Very kind of you, Lil, I'm sure." Reg clipped his brother's ear. "Well, Mr Calm Cool Jockey, time for cricket. Let's see how calm and cool you are when I bowl you out for a duck."

7
Derby Day, Epsom, 1900

BERTIE AND REG FOLLOWED a few paces behind Morny Cannon as he strode out of the weighing room.

"Always something special about the Derby, don't you think, boys?" Morny called to them over his shoulder.

"It does seem busier than usual, sir." Reg walked faster and caught Morny up.

Bertie followed suit, struck dumb that Morny had even noticed that they were there, let alone that he was talking to them.

"The sun's shining, two royal horses and two brothers riding. That'll help make a good day," continued Morny, taking no notice at all of the big cheer that broke out from the crowd. "It'll be even busier next year with the new railway coming to Tattenham Corner."

Reg nodded. So did Bertie.

"Well, boys, there seems to be fewer of us English riders every year." Morny was in full flow. "All these Americans."

The muttering in the crowd got louder.

"It's Diamond Jones," someone called and the cheering started again. Reg nudged him. "They mean you."

"Welcome home, Bertie!" The phrase echoed from all sides, starting and stopping at different times as if they were all singing in one big round.

But there was another voice that made Bertie stop. It wasn't loud and may even have been in his head but when he turned round, there was Tildy swathed in faded black. He saw the smartly dressed people around her grumbling as she pushed forward, but they soon moved when he rushed over to pick her up and swing her round.

"Put me down, Bertie, or you'll do yourself a mischief before your big race."

"Tildy, you haven't changed a bit."

Reg joined them and took her hands, planting a big kiss on her cheek.

"My little Bertie. My handsome Reg. I brought some lucky heather for you, my darlings. Tildy's darlings."

She passed them each a little sprig of white flowers. Bertie laughed and tapped his empty pockets. "I don't have any money on me just now, but … "

"Oh Bertie, don't tease old Tildy. You know I don't want your money; there's enough daft ones here to see to that," she said, gesturing at the passers-by. Then her expression changed and she grabbed his hand. "But I am here to give you luck, boy, and a charm to make you go careful. Now Bertie, listen to me, watch out at the Corner, you hear, that's not a good place for you."

Bertie watched Reg tuck his heather into the pouch of his shirt and did the same.

"There you are, Tildy. We're all safe now," Bertie patted the spot where he had put it.

Mr Smallwood arrived, waving his watch. "There you are, boys. Now, the plans have changed as the Prince wants the Diamond in the parade. Of course, this is a worry."

"So many people and so much noise, he won't like it." Bertie's throat felt dry.

"I know, I know. We're bringing him on as late as possible, but you need to be there so that we can get him on to the course quickly if he starts to get jittery. So pay your respects to Lord Marcus as quickly as you can."

Bertie looked back for Tildy, but she was lost in the crowd. Reg steered him towards the small party representing the Prince. All dressed in their finery, pink from the heat of the afternoon and the enjoyment of the day, it was like walking into a grand painting. The men sweated in their tall hats and long tails. The ladies in their tight-fitting frothy dresses smiled under the lace shadows of their hats.

"Ah, the young Joneses." Lord Marcus came to meet them. "I think Marsh is keen to get the Diamond out of the public gaze as quickly as possible. And quite right too, you never can predict what that horse will do next. But I don't suppose I need to tell you that, Jones Minor."

Everyone laughed and strolled around and around them. Bertie was unsure where to stand, thinking it was rude to have his back to anyone, but it was quite hard to avoid it in the circumstances. So he kept turning, getting quite dizzy and thinking he should be with the Diamond.

One of the ladies sidled up to Reg. Her silk dress creaked and, as she came close, Bertie was sure he could smell alcohol beneath the layers of perfume.

"Should I put a bet down on you, Mr Jones?" she breathed, inclining her parasol over Reg until it clipped Bertie in the eye.

"Leave the poor boy alone, Daisy." Lord Marcus swatted her away. "He's got far more important things to think about than you making sheep's eyes at him."

Bertie didn't know where to look but Reg was as unruffled as ever. The lady shrugged and turned her attention to a tall man with a monocle and neat beard. Tipping his cap, Bertie walked away.

"He is a good man, that Lord Marcus is," said Bertie. "But I don't know what that lady was up to. A bit forward, it seemed to me. I'm surprised at how they carry on."

Reg was about to say something but Mr Smallwood interrupted.

"It is really not our place to think or judge our betters one way or the other, Bertie my boy. You'll see many things and, mostly, you just have to turn a blind eye. Keep your mind on the race and you'll not go far wrong."

As the bell rang, the Guv'nor took Bertie to one side. "This is the big one. The one we want to win, but remember every other trainer and rider out there wants that too, so be careful."

Bertie could feel his heart beating at twice its normal speed.

"Reg will pace you as much as he can. You'll know when to go," said the Guv'nor and he stood to one side.

Old Ben helped him up and, with one last look back, Bertie and the Diamond followed Reg and Fronti out and off to the canter. Bertie knew every last line of the Epsom course. Since he was knee high, he'd walked it, talked it, practised on it, dreamt about it. Now he was really going to race on it. From here, the Downs resembled a busy anthill. Open-topped charabancs, full of waving shapes, lined the course. He thought of his mother, his brothers and sisters; another couple of hours and they'd all be together. A man walked past: there was something in his step that reminded him of his father. Now what would Dad say if he could see him and Reg cantering down together in the royal colours?

The horses lined up. The Diamond twitched and fidgeted despite Fronti being close by. He was anxious to go. At last the flag came down. The race got off to a steady start; no one made a break. By the first quarter-mile Fronti had started to fall back, but the Diamond was in his stride by now and maintained a good pace.

As they got to the bend, the horses bunched up tight. They were packed so close that Bertie felt the breath of the jockeys and the heat from the horses. He kept the Diamond tucked in between Otto on Chevening and Sam on Forfarshire. They squeezed round Tattenham Corner. A mad battle-cry shriek started up from behind. Arms flapping and waving his whip, a jockey drove his horse through the field, swerving from one side to the other. Forfarshire was knocked badly and went out of sight. Bertie glanced over at the gritted face of the man riding next to him. Screaming obscenities, it was the American, Sloan, on the Yankee horse Disguise. The Diamond jumped as the irons from the other horse skidded across his flank and the flaying stick bit into his skin. The whip caught Bertie too, slicing through his breeches and drawing blood. The downward sweep of the Corner was no place for messing around.

Tildy's words came into Bertie's mind. He pulled the Diamond back, letting him ease for a moment, finding space for them to collect themselves. The Diamond started to sink but then together the two of them took an almighty breath, and shot forward through a line that had opened up from nowhere. They passed Disguise and Sloan. The finish was in sight. The crowd shouted and called.

"Diamond, I think we're going to do it," Bertie stammered as he realized where they were.

Then, in the corner of his eye, Bertie glimpsed another horse steaming along, gaining fast. It was the Duke of Portland's colours, so that meant Morny. Bertie wanted just to stop there and then.

I can't do this, I can't push poor Diamond any more; if I do he'll almost certainly give up, that's his nature. So Bertie loosened off the reins. The Diamond knew and slowed for a second, then heaved forward with a second wind. The Diamond had decided. With his head down and his eyes fixed ahead, the Diamond called to Bertie. Bertie leaned in further. The Diamond rallied and sprinted forward. The other horse and rider were on their tail. But the Diamond kept going. They kept going right past the post, continuing on for quite a few seconds before Bertie brought them up. The roar that greeted them must have been heard halfway across the country. The stewards could not contain the rush of the crowd that spilled on to the course.

Bertie felt as he was floating. The sounds all around travelled through him. Looking out into the distance, Bertie could feel Tildy watching.

"See Tildy, no need to worry."

"What was that, Bert?" shouted up Old Ben.

Bertie shook his head. "Nothing, just saying, in a bit of a hurry, you know, to see Mother tonight."

"Well, you'll have to hang on for a bit, it wouldn't be right to do otherwise."

Bertie glanced over to the Downs, but this time there was no one there.

The Prince met them before they reached the paddock, accompanied by Lord Marcus and a whole party of grand-looking people.

"So many people congratulating us, it was hard to reach you," beamed the Prince, taking the bridle. "Well, Marsh, as I said to Lord Marcus, you can relax now that your gamble has paid off. Bravo little Bertie and bravo Diamond!"

The Guv'nor and Lord Marcus exchanged looks.

"Well sir, at least now you can't send us to the Tower and cut off our heads," said Lord Marcus.

The Prince laughed so much that his body shook, sending quivers along the horse that Bertie could feel through his boots. The Diamond grumbled.

A brass band was playing the National Anthem not far away, and the crowd picked it up and sang along. They continued to sing it over and over again. Photographers set up their black boxes on wooden stilts, setting off blinding flashes that made everyone, even the smiling Prince flinch. Wave after wave of people came up to pay their respects them. The Diamond played his part very well. Bertie just sat there and let it all happen around him; even with all the commotion he felt a separateness from it all. He smiled and shook the many hands held up to him, but it didn't feel at all real. When the Guv'nor told him that he could dismount and get weighed in, he was pleased to have his feet back on the ground. Bertie patted the horse and went to walk away, but the Diamond stretched his neck out after him and let out a cry of distress.

"You'll be alright, Diamond," he turned and let the horse nuzzle him. "I've got to go now but I'll see you in the stable. Ben will look after you."

The Diamond started to rock from foot to foot.

"It's alright, Bertie, I've got him. You go." Old Ben took the weight of the animal. Bertie carried on but he could hear the loud whinnying behind him.

It was hot and crowded inside the weighing room. There was loud applause as Bertie came in and by the time he was off the scales, Reg was there to congratulate him.

"I'll get cleaned up and we can go off to mother's," Bertie said.

"You Jones boys sure know how to celebrate." Tod Sloan paused in front of him, in his silks and ready to race again. He spoke so loudly that his voice drowned out the noise outside.

Bertie saw the unpleasantness in the other man's face. Tod stood a little too close. He held his whip in his hand and tapped it impatiently against his leg. Bertie stayed where he was, looking around him for some inspiration on what to do next. Slow footsteps approached, another of the Americans came alongside.

"Hey, Reiff, d'you fancy a nice cup of tea round at Mater's?" asked Sloan in a mock English accent, distorting his mouth into slow ugly movements and unnatural sounds.

"Don't mind if I don't, old boy," replied the other American in a similar tone.

"And you, Bertie boy, you should get back to the stables. Mucking out, that's what you stable lads do, isn't it?" Sloan sneered. "Even sleep with the horses, that's what I heard."

Bertie was hot and tired. The cut on his thigh was sore and he just wanted to be left alone. "I'm not ashamed to care for a horse but I would be ashamed to use a whip without very good cause."

The room became very quiet.

Reg swore under his breath and moved in front of Bertie. From the back of the room, Morny stormed over.

"Just ignore them, boys." Morny towered over Sloan. "We've all had quite enough of you and your ways. And don't go thinking that things haven't been noticed."

The other jockeys all came closer, most in various stages of undress. Like Bertie, they all looked at Morny in amazement. The stewards and the other staff had appeared too.

"Mr Cannon, sir." The stewards tried to pacify him.

Morny turned his eyes on Bertie. Bertie felt everyone else shift their gaze too and he felt more nervous than he had all day.

"Don't let them upset you, young man." Morny waved his fists in the air. "That's what they are after. After all, *you* ran a fine, honest race and still managed to win."

Sloan swept off, followed by Reiff.

"Good riddance," called Morny.

A jockey came over that Bertie hadn't seen before. He was dressed ready for the next race and wore a grin as wide as his face, just like the Cheshire cat. You couldn't help but feel cheerful.

"Hi, I'm Danny. I'm new over here," he said.

Bertie's smile faded when he heard the American accent. He'd about had it with Yanks for one day.

"Oh, please don't look so anxious, Mr Jones." Danny had a look of real distress in his eyes, but the grin stayed just as it was. "We're not all like Sloan. He is quite unique, but somewhat unconventional."

"Ummph, that's one word for it," Reg muttered.

"No hard feelings?" Danny put out his hand.

Bertie shook it and had to grin as Danny nearly wrenched his arm off with his enthusiasm.

The friendly American left for the weighing room. He seemed to dance rather than walk. "Now I'm seeing things," Bertie said, shaking his head.

"Don't you worry sir, that's Mr Maher. Dancing Danny, they call him. Says it keeps him trim. But he's a good sort generally, unlike most of them that have come over," said the valet, handing him some towels. "Mark my words, it'll all come to a head now though. When a gentleman like Mr Cannon starts getting upset, something has to happen. He's been talking to the stewards about Mr Sloan's riding tactics."

Bertie steadied himself against the bench as he thought about Sloan's violence. There was never a need for that, however much you wanted to win.

"Sorry, sir, just me getting on my soapbox," the valet continued. "But we have to set an example to the punters, otherwise God only knows what. People will be running out and trying to take over the races themselves. And what would that be like? You answer me that."

"You're right, but let's forget about all that now. We can't let this ruin the day," Reg interrupted. "Hurry up, Bertie, then we can have some of that tea those Yanks were so keen on."

∪ ∪ ∪

Bertie was wearing the new clothes that the Guv'nor had sent him to buy at the outfitters in Newmarket. He had butterflies in his stomach. It was so long since he had seen Mother. He and Reg had not been back since Dad's funeral and they hadn't yet visited the new house.

Walking out of the jockeys' room, Bertie chattered on to Reg. "We'll call into the stables and check on the Diamond, and then perhaps we can cut through the hill and back past Dad's stables. What d'you think?"

Reg stopped in his tracks. Bertie looked up. The sun was in his eyes. A host of shining ghostly shapes were all around, moving like the patterns in a kaleidoscope. For a moment there was silence, then they called his name from all sides and so loudly he thought he would be swallowed up by the sound. Bertie swivelled left, then right. There was nowhere to go. He gasped and ran back inside, slamming the door after him. Pressing his back against the wall, he stood rigid, his eyes fixed ahead, panting. Reg rushed in.

"What's the matter?" Reg tried to prise him from the wall.

Bertie pulled himself back.

"Come on, Bertie, you've been through this already once today already, it's just the same."

"No, it isn't the same at all. I had my silks on then and I was up, now I'm just I'm me."

"Don't be daft, Bert. You can't stay in here." Reg paused. "You want to see Mother, don't you?"

"Of course I do."

"Well, unless you can make yourself invisible and fly, you're going to have to get yourself out at some point."

"It wasn't like this at Newmarket," said Bertie.

"Newmarket may be racing's headquarters, but Epsom is its heart. It's different," said Reg. "It's a big day today and people come from all over. The Derby is special. You know that, Bertie, you remember when we used to come and watch. Come on, don't be such a baby."

Bertie was quiet. That was what Dad would have said, although he'd probably have told him not to be so bloody stupid, and if people had bothered to turn up for him the least he could do was to give them a smile. Bertie remembered standing for hours to get a glimpse of the winning jockey. But never did Bertie ever imagine that so many people would be waiting to see him.

"Try again, shall we, Bert?" Reg put his hand on Bertie's shoulder.

"Alright, but don't leave me, Reg."

"Of course I won't. You are a daft one."

They walked outside. The crowd was still there and seemed bigger if anything.

"There he is, Diamond Jones!" someone called.

A big cheer went up and the people gathered round.

"It's our Bertie!" a man shouted.

Bertie glanced over expectantly but it was a complete stranger.

"Thought we'd lost you there, Mr Jones." A large boy stood in front of him holding out a greasy crumpled racecard in his hand.

"Oh, yes, I just forgot something." Bertie took the stumpy pencil and signed the card. "Sorry, have you had to wait long?"

"That's alright, sir, it was worth it," the boy replied.

Bertie was surprised to be called sir by someone not much younger than himself and pointed towards Reg. "My brother rode in the Prince's colours today; he'll sign too if you ask him, won't you, Reg?"

Reg took the pencil and added his name, smiling good-naturedly.

"It's you they want to see. I am happy for you, Bert, so stop worrying," Reg said quietly in his ear.

Bits of paper were waved at Bertie. The jumble of hands and fingers came towards him, bruised black, gnarled red, nicotine yellow, baby-plump pink, lady white. People closed in around him, some silent, some wanted to talk.

"I remember your dad. You're just like him."

"Thank you," said Bertie.

"Would you sign my card too, Mr Jones?"

"Yes, of course."

"Congratulations, Bertie."

"Very kind of you."

"Your mum lives just round the corner from me."

"We're nearly neighbours then."

"How is Diamond feeling?"

"He was alright when I left him, but I'm going to check on him now."

"Mr Jones, could you sign this one and make it out to Percy, my handsome clever younger brother?"

Bertie started to write and it was only when Reg gave him a nudge that he looked up and did a double-take.

"And here's Jack." Percy pointed at the dark-haired chap standing next to him.

"Little Jack? Well, not so little Jack."

Then, Percy pushed a smaller lad forward.

"This one can't be our Bill, can it?" said Bertie. "Look at you!"

Bill fidgeted, before flinging his arms round his brother's waist and burying his head in his chest.

"We saw you win," he whispered. "We had a bet too. Percy put one on for me. I won some money."

"Did you now? Well, that's more than me and Reg did," laughed Bertie. "We're not allowed."

People drew back. Bertie realized that they were watching. He didn't know what to do, so he pleaded to Reg.

"Alright, you lot stay there," said Reg and turned to the crowd. He flushed bright red but called out. "You see, they're our brothers. We haven't seen each other for years."

"Ahh," sighed the crowd all together, with smiles on their faces. One woman started to cry.

"You go and see your family, lads, and God bless you!" they called.

The crowd gave a cheer, and parted for them.

∪ ∪ ∪

The next day, they were all ready to go down to the station and load the horses on to the train home. Mr Smallwood came over.

"A very favourable review of the Derby and of you, Bertie. The Guv'nor is very pleased. And look at this." He passed the paper over to Reg.

"The Stewards, having observed the confusion that occurred near Tattenham Corner, subsequently made enquiries of the jockeys riding, and severely reprimanded Sloan for his breach of Rule 140, forbidding crossing." Reg read it out. "No wonder he was in such a state."

"Well, he came through the Corner like a steam train, barging anything and everything out of his way. Me and the Diamond, we were lucky really," Bertie shuddered.

They all shook their heads.

"No good ever comes of foul riding," pronounced Old Ben. "About time something as done about it in my view, it sullies the name of English racing."

"Sloan fancies his chances as first royal jockey now that John Watts is retiring," said Mr Smallwood.

"Poor old John, I think our Diamond was the last straw," chuckled Old Ben. "But surely we can't have an American royal jockey?"

"He's a good horseman, but I can't say I took to him," said Bertie. "A bit too fond of the whip, which wouldn't go down well with the Guv'nor, but he's won a lot of races. I would have thought that Mr Cannon would be a better choice."

"Oh, well, it will all get sorted out at the end of the season," shrugged Mr Smallwood.

◡ ◡ ◡

They walked the horses down the lane towards the station. At one of the gates, Tildy appeared. She was almost hidden by the cow parsley that framed the fields with its lace flower heads. Bertie waved and walked over with the Diamond dragging his heels.

"I knew you'd come," Bertie grinned. "Here, I've been carrying this round for you."

He untied his bag and dug down into it.

"Here you are." He presented her with a little box neatly wrapped in brown paper and tied with a bow.

"Open it later, I'd better run," he said, turning to join the others.

But Tildy had already opened the package.

The Diamond swung round and snorted in her direction.

"Don't you do that," said Bertie.

Tildy stared at the horse full in the eyes and muttered some words in Romany. The animal skulked back. "Poor demented creature," she said in English to the horse.

Bertie tightened his hold on the Diamond. "If you behaved better, you wouldn't get told off now, would you?"

As Bertie looked back, Tildy waved the new shawl.

"See you next year, Bertie." Her words caught on the breeze and echoed around him. Next year, next year.

8

Newmarket, July 1900

"I THOUGHT WINNING THE DERBY was an experience that could not be surpassed, but it pales against my happiness today." The Guv'nor beamed at his bride.

The new Mrs Marsh blushed as loud cheers broke out.

"Please, my dear family and friends," he continued. "Enjoy this evening with us."

Lanterns were lit in the garden as the light faded. The orchestra in the corner of the terrace played a waltz.

Flora walked over to Bertie. "Dance with me."

He shook his head. "No, Miss Flora, you know I'm a terrible dancer."

"Please, Bertie."

"Will I do?" Danny appeared and waltzed her round a couple of times. "Tell me pretty maiden are there any more at home like you?" he sang and she giggled.

"Now, I have a treat for you all." Danny took a sheet of music from inside his jacket and put it in front of the pianist.

The pianist shook his head, but Danny was not one to give up. He asked the conductor, who scratched his chin. The violinist joined in, tapping away with his stick. He and the pianist prodded at notes until they seemed satisfied.

"Ladies and gentlemen," Danny went to the centre of the room, clapping his hands like a fairground hawker. He winked at Bertie. "In honour of this auspicious occasion, a friend of mine from back home sent over something special for your entertainment. So I'd like to introduce you to ragtime. And this is the Maple Leaf Rag."

The pianist plonked out the notes. Danny grabbed hold of Flora and did some strange strutting. Some of the other guests tried to follow, but got into a terrible tangle. Bertie laughed at their antics.

"You find it so funny, let's see you try." Flora pulled herself away from Danny and dragged Bertie over.

To his surprise, Bertie quite liked the strange beat of the music and was soon parading around the terrace with Flora at such a speed that she could hardly keep up.

"You've got natural rhythm, Bertie boy." Danny slapped him on the back. "You just need to loosen up a little."

"Oh Dick, let's try," said the new Mrs Marsh.

The Guv'nor coughed. "Certainly not, Grace."

"Shall I assist, Guv'nor?" Danny volunteered.

Grace smiled and held out her hands.

"No, no." The Guv'nor looked furious and waved at the orchestra. "That's quite enough of that now, let's have a nice waltz. What about 'Always'?"

The conductor tapped his baton on his music stand and led the musicians into a more sedate melody.

"See Bertie, that's what happens when you marry a man old enough to be your father. You end up waltzing when you want to be maple leaf ragging. But I've no sympathy." Flora put his arm around her waist. "But now I've got you on your feet, we can at least enjoy ourselves."

"I think you're a bit giddy, Miss Flora. Perhaps you should sit down."

"On the contrary, Bertie," she replied, her voice becoming very shrill. "I think I should dance all night, with you."

"No, Flora. You mustn't." He took a step back.

The music stopped suddenly. Flora stamped her foot and ran off. The other guests turned towards him in astonishment.

"What's going on, Bertie?" asked the Guv'nor. "Is she ill?"

"I don't know, sir, she went off in a bit of a hurry. Shall I go and see if she is alright?"

"No, I should leave her. She'll be fine."

"Well, I ought to check on the Diamond, so I'll be turning in myself. Good night Guv'nor, and Mrs Marsh. Congratulations again to you both."

Bertie waved at the others and walked off towards the stables. He got halfway across, just reaching the trees, when he heard something move. Bertie instinctively ducked out of the way.

"Oh Bertie, don't run away from me." It was Flora.

"What are you doing out here by yourself? You can't go running off on your own like that."

She flung her arms around him. He felt the rise and fall of her breath, the warmth of her skin through the thin lace of her dress.

"Do you remember, when you rescued me in the fog? You said you'd look after me."

"Of course I do, and of course I will."

Flora puckered her mouth and closed her eyes.

"Now stop this right now, Flora. Really, what would your father say?" Bertie tried to disentangle himself.

"You are very strong, Bertie. You could throw me off you in an instant and you haven't completely, so perhaps you do like me a little," she giggled.

"I'm trying not to hurt you. And you have had too much to drink. I don't want you to fall," he tried to explain.

"Don't you want to kiss me, Bertie?"

"That's not the point, you know it isn't. The vicar's just over there, and everything."

"Then you do want to kiss me! No one can see, Bertie."

"It doesn't matter who can or can't see. It's not proper. For heaven's sake, think of your reputation, you'd ruin yourself!"

"No I wouldn't, because you'd have to marry me," she insisted.

Bertie stopped struggling for a moment and stroked her face.

"You can do a lot better than me, Flora. Your father has great hopes for you. Now you go back. I'll watch you and make sure you're safe."

"Just one kiss, Bertie, and I promise I'll go back. Just one little kiss."

Bertie squirmed. "I don't think it would be a good idea, Flora, really."

"I promise to go back quietly, like a little mouse," Flora moved closer. "Eek, eek."

He didn't push her away but stood tense.

"Just one little kiss, my Bertie," she whispered.

9

St Leger, Doncaster, September 1900

"How's the diamond? any better?" Bertie weighed out as quickly as he could and ran out to join Mr Smallwood.

"No, worse if anything." Mr Smallwood shook his head. "He's refusing to come down off his hind legs. He won't let the Guv'nor near him, so heaven knows how we'll saddle him."

Bertie sighed. It had been a long journey north and the Diamond had kept him up most of the night with his antics.

"Today of all days. I'm sure he knows."

"Well, Mr Marsh says we'll have to go straight to the start, we can't take the chance of parading him," Mr Smallwood added.

They walked over to the stables and could hear the Diamond screeching well before they got there. The horse had worked himself up into a dreadful temper. He was all lathered up and tottering round on his two back legs, striking out with his front hooves like a thing possessed. The Guv'nor was not in a much better state. Two grooms held on to the Diamond's bridle and halter, both strong and experienced men, but they struggled to keep control.

Bertie passed the saddle to Old Ben and went towards the Diamond. The horse saw him but just rose higher on his legs, kicking out more furiously.

"Diamond!" Bertie sighed. "Do you know how important this race is? We can't throw it all away now."

The horse dropped down, huffing and puffing, but stood still. He wouldn't look at Bertie, turning his head away and flicking his tail. The Guv'nor took full advantage of this distraction and flung the saddle over his back, fastening the girth as the horse rose up and narrowly missing the left hoof as it hit out at him. They let the animal thrash about.

"He'll be exhausted before we even get to the start at this rate," remarked Old Ben.

"It's fine," Bertie assured him. "He's just got himself a bit worked up."

The Guv'nor didn't look convinced. Fronti was brought out and stood quietly to one side. The Diamond was pleased to see him and became still.

Taking a breath, Bertie jumped up cat-like from the ground straight on to the Diamond's back. The horse let out a shriek and leapt up on his hind legs again, twisting and turning like a mad snake. Bertie caught the reins. The stirrup irons slid back as the angle steepened, and Bertie slipped his feet through the metal and felt their support. Once he was in place nothing would get him off. The Guv'nor stood back, relieved.

"I'm sorry Diamond, you can't have it all your own way." Bertie spoke through gritted teeth. "Sometimes you just have to behave and do your job."

The Diamond didn't listen and didn't give up. He walked upright most of the way from the paddock to the starting line on his hind legs. Feeling like an under-rehearsed circus act rather than a royal jockey, Bertie patiently held his position while the Diamond continued his angry trot. Reg stayed as close as he safely could, but even the calming presence of Fronti didn't help any more.

The other horses and riders were all ready. Bertie's body shook, partly from the exertion of holding himself up and partly from the worry of what the horse would do next. The Diamond swaggered up to the start, finally dropping down on to all fours.

Straight away the starter sent them off. The Diamond's bad temper worked in his favour as he flew out in a terrible fury, ripping along the turf after Fronti, who was first away. They were well out ahead, but Bertie sensed the Diamond flagging. Morny was on his heels.

"Come on Diamond, don't give up now."

But the Diamond was tired, his stride slackened. Bertie shifted his weight. All he could do was urge the horse on; the Diamond had to find the will to win. By now Bertie was leaning in so much that he was almost at the Diamond's head. He knew the horse could see him.

"Diamond, please, just a bit more?" Bertie pleaded. "Just for me."

The horse's ears went up. The Diamond stretched out his neck. The finishing line was just ahead, but Morny was very close. Bertie flung himself forward and the Diamond went with him. They passed the post in first place. They'd done it. After all the fuss beforehand, Bertie couldn't believe they had really won.

When their number went up, he jumped up on the saddle and waved his arms above his head, triumphant. The crowd cheered even louder at this. The Diamond looked back at him and laughed, then, not to be outdone, trotted round with his head held high. The Guv'nor was in tears, weeping into Old Ben's jacket. None of them ever imagined that the Triple Crown would be theirs.

10

Egerton, September 1900

BERTIE WAS GETTING THE Diamond settled for the night. He tidied the bedding, checked the water and topped up the net with hay. Reg had already seen to Fronti and gone off to the dormitory. Judging by the snoring coming from the other stall, Fronti was flat out. That horse never had any trouble getting to sleep.

"Just one last brush down, Diamond, and then we can both get some rest."

The Diamond gave a short snort and stepped away. Bertie looked up.

"What's up, boy?"

The horse swung his neck towards the side of the stall. In the flickering lamplight, Bertie saw the top of a flowery straw hat float past.

"Flora?"

The hat disappeared. She popped her head around the side of the dark wood panel.

"And who else would you be expecting?"

"I wasn't expecting anyone, and especially not you." Bertie kept his face turned away from her. "Flora, you shouldn't be here. The Diamond can get dangerous and it's not proper."

The Diamond lurched from side to side, shaking his head and sneezing.

"Easy, there's a good boy," Bertie caught the halter and stroked the horse's nose.

"I don't care what's proper. I had to come out here, otherwise I would never get to see you." Flora picked up a piece of hay and wrapped it round her finger like a ring. "Anyway, I hear you've got lots of admirers now. The ladies like to follow you around the racecourse, so I understand."

"What? Oh, for goodness sake, Flora. Who told you that? It's silly talk. You know … " Bertie stopped himself. He took up the soft brush and started running it over the Diamond's coat.

"But I don't like to think I've got competition now, do I?" Flora edged nearer.

"Now you're really talking daft," he replied, brushing the Diamond with more effort than was needed.

The Diamond started to protest. He didn't like his routine disrupted.

"I'll take that as a no then, shall I, Bertie?" she peered over his shoulder.

"No? Yes? I don't know what you are asking me." He wiped his forehead and moved her away from the horse. "Look, let me take you home before anyone sees you."

The click of a latch made them stop. The Diamond flicked his ears forward and even Fronti went quiet. They listened, but there was nothing, not even the far-away call of a hunting owl. Bertie was about to say that they must have imagined it, when there was a scrape of metal. He put his fingers to his lips and signalled for Flora to hide in the hay bales in the far corner. Stretching his neck out, the Diamond gave a high-pitched call. Bertie put his hand out to reassure the horse then walked towards the stable door. Fronti shuffled up.

In the gloom, Bertie could see that the door was ajar. He turned back to check that Flora was hidden. At that moment, someone grabbed his arms, pulling them up so tight behind his back that his shoulders burned. Bertie struggled but too late, the grip held him firm. Two other men entered. They looked like spectres with their long coats, high collars and pulled-down hats. One was jockey height.

"Let's see to the horse, then we'll look at Bertie boy here." The American accent had a sneer in its tone that was unmistakably the voice of the jockey Tod Sloan.

As Sloan and the other man went towards the Diamond, Bertie took in the situation and tried to calm his thoughts. There wasn't much time. He offered a quick prayer for guidance, all the time working through the options in his head. Whatever these men were after, it was nothing good. He had to get rid of them, and he needed the Diamond to play his part.

Bertie relaxed his body and stilled himself, concentrating all his attention on the Diamond. He wasn't at all sure he could do this, but he kept his eyes lowered in case Sloan could read his thoughts. Being with the Diamond, becoming the Diamond, Bertie focused his mind on the horse until he shared the anxious heartbeat and the quickened breath. With all his might, Bertie tried to send his words to the horse: "Wait, Diamond, wait and follow."

The Diamond stood straight and alert. Ignoring Bertie, he watched the intruders with steady eyes.

"Thought he was supposed to be mad, this horse," said the other man, also a Yank. "Seems pretty calm to me."

"He's a clever horse. He's weighing us up. Aren't you, boy?" said Sloan, unravelling a piece of cloth and holding up a large syringe. "Anyhow, if he is standing still, it will be easier to get the needle in."

The Diamond took a step back and moved his mouth as if he was chewing.

"See," said Sloan. "He knows who's boss. Now, get hold of him nice and gentle."

It was time. Bertie exhaled, relaxing all his muscles, so that he slumped, becoming limp and lifeless.

"What're you doing?" said the man pulling his arms further back until Bertie felt that they would tear from their sockets. "Fainting? Can't you take it, little man?"

"Told you he was a mother's boy," Sloan turned and laughed.

Bertie said nothing but kept breathing out, until his lungs were empty and hollow. Then he sprang up, forcing the air down deep into his belly.

"Now!" he shouted.

The Diamond shrieked and flew his hoof into the face of the man who was reaching for his rope. At the same time, Bertie kicked his right boot back, as hard as he could, into the knee of his captor. The man buckled and loosened his grip. Bertie felt slightly sick, but flipped himself up. He somersaulted and landed on Sloan. Sloan fell to the ground and dropped the syringe. Splintered glass crunched underfoot as Bertie righted himself.

But Sloan was an athlete. He bounced right up from the fall and ran at Bertie, his head lowered like a battering ram. Bertie waited until the last moment, then jumped to one side, almost colliding into the Diamond. Sloan carried on into the brick wall.

Flora rose up from behind the bales. She was waving a shovel. Her face was pale and grim, but there was such fire in her eyes and with the sprigs of hay sticking out from her hair, she looked like a demonic corn dolly. She raised the shovel, aiming at Sloan's head. Sloan curled himself up, ready to receive the blow.

"No, Flora, no!" Bertie ran to her and grabbed the shovel. His ears rang from the cries of the Diamond. "You'll kill him. You mustn't."

Bertie dragged Flora away. "Stay back there, until I tell you," he said.

"No, Bertie, I'll go to get help." She slipped from his hold and ran out into the night.

Sloan pulled himself to his feet. Bertie stood in front of the Diamond, wishing he'd held on to the spade. The alarm bell clanged across the yard.

Sloan swore and lumbered out of the stables. The other intruders staggered after him, one bleeding heavily from his nose and the other limping. Bertie followed. They made for a motorcar parked along the lane. The engine chugged and a figure of a man moved alongside. Silhouetted against the moonlight, he seemed to be dancing. Bertie watched as they bundled into the vehicle and raced off into the darkness.

Old Ben and Reg shouted to him. Others followed, carrying buckets and blankets. Bertie tried to find Flora, but she had gone. Inside, the Diamond tugged at his rope and pawed the ground, calling for him. Even Fronti was kicking at his stall. Bertie looked around at the mess and wondered how he could possibly explain what had gone on.

In the nights that followed, Bertie found it impossible to sleep. The slightest noise would wake him. He sat on the steps of the stable looking up at the stars. Behind him, the Diamond sighed and muttered. At the sound of approaching footsteps, Bertie jumped and held his breath. He noticed that the Diamond too had fallen silent.

"Thought you might like a mug of tea, Bert." It was Reg. "Still worried about the other night?"

Bertie took the mug and sat back on the steps. "It's just I feel such a fool."

"Why? You got rid of them without anything bad happening to the Diamond or to you, or anyone else for that matter. Sounds to me that you should feel anything but that."

"But, Reg, you don't understand. It was awful, and the worst of it was how it made me act. I didn't think that I could do such harm to someone, but I had to stop them."

"Sometimes, Bertie, we have to do these things. And these were bad people."

"Oh, I don't know." Bertie drew his hand across his chin. "I don't understand."

"Have you heard of the Yankee Alchemists?"

Bertie shook his head.

"Did you know that the syringe contained cocaine?"

Bertie shook his head again.

"Mr Smallwood had it analysed. He thinks that they were trying to set you up. They would give the Diamond the drug, and you too probably, then call in the Jockey Club. It would all point at you, and most likely all the Diamond's wins would be struck off. So you see, you had no choice."

"But, I should have heard them creeping around. I wasn't concentrating, you see." Bertie felt hot tears roll down his cheek. He buried his head in his arms. "I wasn't doing my job."

"Why, because a certain young lady was there?"

"But, how do you know? I didn't ... I mean she just turned up." Bertie felt his throat tighten. "Does anyone else ... ?"

"Calm down, Bertie. I saw the hat in the hay and hid it. I don't think anyone else knows. She must have rung the alarm. I saw someone in a white dress running from the tower, so she was brave."

The scenes came back into Bertie's head.

"They ran off then ... There is something else too. I haven't said, but I think I may have recognized one or two of them."

"Well, to be honest, Bertie, I suggest you keep quiet. No harm done, so there's no point in stirring up more trouble for yourself."

"I don't like all this, Reg. I just want to ride my horses and do a good job."

"Bertie, you have to learn, it's a tough world and sometimes people don't play by the rules." Reg passed him a handkerchief.

"It doesn't make it right though."

"No, of course not." Reg ruffled Bertie's hair. "Be careful though, little brother, don't let yourself get distracted. Racing and women don't really mix and you have a fine career ahead of you."

11

Jockey Club Stakes, Newmarket, September 1900

THE RAIN HADN'T LET up for twenty-four hours. Bertie ran from the weighing room to the paddock, splashing past bedraggled punters huddled under umbrellas. As soon as he saw the Diamond with the Guv'nor, it was clear that something was wrong.

"The devil lulled me into thinking he'd be alright. Not a murmur when I put his saddle on, now look at him." The Guv'nor scratched his head.

Bertie took the halter and tried as hard as he could to persuade the Diamond to walk on, but he did no better than the others. The Diamond dug his hooves into the marshy grass, stuck out his hindquarters and shook his head.

"I think he's just had enough, Guv'nor. It's all got a bit too much for him lately. Poor old boy."

"It's true, he's worn out, look at him," said Old Ben. "And you don't look so good yourself, Bertie."

"It's been a long season," agreed the Guv'nor.

"He's not sleeping, neither," added Old Ben.

"The Diamond?" asked the Guv'nor, surprised. "I hadn't noticed that."

"No, he's alright. It's Bertie, I mean."

Bertie rolled his eyes. "Me? No, I'm fine, honest, Guv'nor."

"You ask Reg then, if you don't believe me." Old Ben wagged his finger at the Guv'nor. "Young Bertie needs a rest."

"Alright, Ben, I have got eyes, you know," the Guv'nor snapped. "But for now we have to stick to the job in hand."

One of the lads from the course joined them.

"Excuse me, Mr Marsh, sir. They're calling for Diamond Jubilee to come down to the start." He tugged his cap at the Guv'nor and moved towards the Diamond. "He really is the most beautiful horse I've ever seen."

"Handsome is as handsome does," said Old Ben and put out his arm to shield the boy. "I wouldn't get too close, especially when he's like this."

Reg arrived with Fronti. The Diamond put his nose out to Fronti and straightaway became less tense.

"Right, up you go, Bertie," said the Guv'nor.

Old Ben held his hands out for him, as he liked to do, and Bertie jumped up. The Diamond pretended not to notice. With a signal from the Guv'nor, Reg moved Fronti forward a step at a time. The Diamond took a sideways glance, but other than a slight readjustment of his legs, stayed still.

"Keep going, Reg, nice and slowly," said the Guv'nor. "Ben and I will stand back, or he'll stay put out of awkwardness."

Bertie kept a neutral position, holding the Diamond back if anything. It had the desired effect as the Diamond moved off in pursuit of Fronti, calling to say he was coming. Once they were on to the course, Reg increased their pace to a canter. The Diamond followed, glowering at the crowd, but he lined up without further trouble. Reg and Fronti slipped away. The starter set them off without delay.

The Diamond snorted as they leapt forward. Sam Loates took an early lead. As they went along, Bertie let the reins loosen. A shudder of the old excitement went through the body of the Diamond. The horse's ears perked up and he fired to the front. It was like they were back at the start of the season, full of energy, full of life. For most of a mile they kept up the pace, but the ups and downs as they reached the Bushes were too much. At the last few furlongs, the Diamond had no reserve left and nor did Bertie. Morny passed them at the post.

"You did your best, old pal." Bertie patted the Diamond, but they both knew it was the end.

∪ ∪ ∪

Back at the yard, Bertie was helping the young lad with the Diamond.

"All hell's broken loose," Old Ben called out, as he limped into the yard with a rarely seen haste, full to bursting with news.

The commotion startled the Diamond. The lad jumped back nervously. Bertie took over brushing down the horse.

Some of the others heard and came over to join them.

"Where's the fire then?" Mr Smallwood came out of the yard office.

"More than a fire, sir. A big to-do. I ran into one of them from the Jockey Club. Heard it all, he did." Old Ben waved his arms as he tried to catch his breath. "Hang on a minute, I'll have to sit down, I ran back as soon as I could to tell you all."

Old Ben settled himself on a ledge. They gathered around and waited. He started to reach for his pocket.

"Come on Ben, spit it out. We've all got work to do," Mr Smallwood called out good-naturedly.

Old Ben took no notice and filled his pipe. "Well, it seems that Sloan, you know, the American, had thought his mount was in with a good chance at the Cambridgeshire. But to make sure, he wanted to take a gander at Phillie's yard, as Phillie's horse, Berrill, was said to be his main threat. So Sloan's blokes went round to his yard and offered to exercise Phillie's horses. People thought this was a bit strange at the time. Anyway, Phillie had kept Berrill out of the gallops for a while as he'd strained a ligament in his last race. The Americans kept on, which made Phillie suspicious, so rather than find an American jockey as the owner had asked, he had someone who he knew was an honest fellow come over from his home town in Ireland. The jockey, John Thompson, arrived and this afternoon rode Berrill in the Cambridgeshire. Berrill looked in pretty bad form, as fat as a little porker they said he was, Phillie could barely buckle up the girth. But he was a stayer and came in first, beating Sloan by a narrow margin."

Old Ben lit his pipe. "So Sloan was furious and stormed into the jockeys' room. When John Thompson came in, Sloan started shouting and cursing that he had cost him a small fortune and that he'd tell the stewards what to do with their stupid warnings. But he didn't reckon on the stewards actually being in the room. What with all the complaints about his rough riding, they'd been watching him. So the stewards called him in and asked him if he had betted on his own horse. He admitted he had and couldn't see why not. The stewards told him it was against Jockey Club rules and that they would have to take his licence. And that's what they've done, so there you are! Good riddance, I say."

"Well, it couldn't have happened to a nicer bloke," said Reg.

The Diamond gave a snort.

"He got in with the wrong sort, I think that was the problem," Mr Smallwood added. "All jockeys are prey to unscrupulous types."

"And once they get turned," Old Ben muttered, fixing his eyes on the younger lads. "There's no going back."

There was silence as they contemplated the sorry end to Sloan's career.

"Oh, and another thing," Old Ben added, checking to see who else was around. "I heard that when the Guv'nor gave in and let Sloan ride at Doncaster, there was a lot of rough practice. It was only because it was His Royal Highness's horse that no one complained."

"Come on now, that's quite enough tittle-tattle for one day." Mr Smallwood interrupted and waved them on, although Bertie noticed he'd waited until the end of the story. "It's like an outdoor meeting of the Mother's Union here, you'll be setting up a cake stall next."

"But what'd you say to it all, Mr Smallwood?" asked Old Ben not moving.

"Well, it's not my place to comment." Mr Smallwood paused for a moment. "I know that there are renewed efforts to ensure that racing is a respectable sport and we, as the Royal stable, have to be whiter than white in our dealings."

"Thank you, sir, most enlightening," nodded Old Ben, before jumping up and clapping his hands. "Right then, all back to work boys."

"Thank you, Ben," Mr Smallwood smiled.

Old Ben tugged at his hat. "Very happy to oblige, sir."

12

End of the season,
November 1900

THE DIAMOND LOOKED MORE beautiful than ever in his golden coat. Stretched tight over a form much finer than any marble statue, the precision of his proportion and the light in his face seemed to be a living presence of the divine. Under his palm Bertie felt the pulse of the veins weaving their way between flesh and skin. Large and strong, they spread out smaller and smaller, reaching every part of the body, until they existed only as tiny threads barely visible to the eye.

But beauty had its other side. The tormented soul that lurked behind the velvet eyes cried out. The sculpted jawbone swept from side to side, ready to bludgeon. The Diamond rocked himself up and down the stable box, lips rolled back to show yellow-brown teeth that chewed over and over again on invisible hay, until the scrape of tooth on tooth made Bertie wince. The same teeth had taken the finger of a young stable lad in one clean bite.

He took the brush and held it for the Diamond to see.

"Now then, old friend, let's calm you down."

The horse paused, his eyes steadied though his breath was still heavy and froth gathered around his lips.

"It's only me and I've just come to give you a bit of a tidy up, see." Bertie reached for the Diamond's neck. "You've frightened off all the lads and so no one will come and groom you except me. But you'll be going to a new home tomorrow; no more racing for you, which is just as you want it. Had enough of the limelight, haven't you, Diamond? You'll be able to take it easy now."

The cold glint faded from the animal's eyes to be replaced by a softer light. Bertie knew that he was listening by the low sounds. Gently, the Diamond buried his nose in Bertie's jacket.

"Mind you, it will be strange not to see you every day, and I'll miss you. We've been together a long time. All the things we've done, eh boy?" Bertie paused and looked at him. "But you'll be happier at Sandringham in the lap of luxury, lots of pretty ladies to admire you. I will come over to see you."

The Diamond was calm and perfectly still. He gave a little whimper and raised his whiskery mouth to Bertie's neck, twisting his head for his ears to be tickled. They stood together, the two of them.

There were footsteps in the yard and voices calling. The Diamond tensed up; his eyes rolled upwards, until the sockets were almost pure white. Bertie stepped back and wiped the tears from his face.

"You be a good boy for me, and don't let me down," he said and walked away, but the horse was no longer listening. The whinnying started, loud and piercing, like a child calling for its mother. The Diamond crashed his body against the door and tried to follow him. But Bertie kept on going and didn't turn back.

U U U

Bertie stood against the white railings of the gallop. The storm had brought down a lot of leaves and the turf was a patchwork of yellow and gold. It was a cold morning. Mr Smallwood approached.

"Morning, Bertie. The Guv'nor has asked to see you. He's in his private office."

Bertie swallowed. "Right, I'll come now, shall I?"

They walked back across the yard together.

"How are you finding things without the Diamond needing your attention all hours of the day?"

"It's only been a little while but it feels like months. Sometimes I wake up and I can still hear him calling. But I'll get used to it." Bertie stopped for a moment. "To be honest, I feel at a bit of a loose end. Don't know what will happen now, whether the Guv'nor will still let me ride."

"You are a funny one," laughed Mr Smallwood.

107

As they reached the office, Bertie brushed himself down, tapping his boots against the scraper and bashing his cap against the post to shift the mud, straw and horsehair. Walter Venn, the Guv'nor's new secretary, met them in the stone hallway. Walter was about Bertie's age. He was always so reassuring. Bertie liked him and was hoping to get him to join the cricket team.

"Don't look so worried, Bertie," said Walter. "The Guv'nor is in a very good mood, I'm happy to say."

As they walked along the wooden floor, Bertie's boots clattered as if they'd been iron shod. He tried to walk on his toes.

The Guv'nor's private office was more like a grand drawing room, with comfortable chairs and pictures of horses all over the walls. A big bay window gave a fine view of the gallops. In the corner, the Guv'nor was sitting at a large desk. He swivelled round in his leather chair and tossed the papers that he held into the scattered pile in front of him. Bertie hadn't seen him wearing spectacles before.

"Ah, Jones. Well, here we are at the end of the season. A time for reflection and planning, repair and preparation." The Guv'nor paused, clearly pleased at the words. "Now the Diamond has moved off to a carefree life at the stud, we have to think about your future."

Bertie stared at the fine woven rug with its patterns of zig-zags and colours that were rich like the leaves blown to the ground. He tried to conceal his panic. He wouldn't mind going back to the stables, riding the gallops, mucking out, anything. He didn't need to race in fancy clothes. He just wanted to stay at Egerton.

"Bertie? Bertie?" The Guv'nor appeared quite put out. "Well, have you no comment?"

"I'm sorry, sir, I, er, didn't quite catch what you said."

Mr Smallwood gave a quiet cough, while Walter pretended that nothing had happened. Bertie racked his brains; he couldn't remember. He frowned with effort and looked blankly at the Guv'nor. The Guv'nor took a deep breath and spoke to him very slowly as if he was a small child, and a rather stupid one at that.

"His Royal Highness wants you as his first jockey, Bertie. John Watts has retired, the Prince needs a new royal jockey and he has chosen you. Now, what do you say to that?"

Bertie heard this time, but it didn't help him to speak.

Mr Smallwood stepped in. "It is a great achievement at such an early age."

"And of course it is an endorsement of Egerton, so it all ties together very neatly," said Walter.

"And Bertie, I've more good news for you." The Guv'nor stood up and scrabbled around in the papers on the desk. "Now, somewhere, I've a letter from Lord Marcus."

"There you are, sir, I think this is the one." Walter stepped forward and passed over the letter. The paper made a satisfying rustle as the Guv'nor held it out in front of him.

"Now then, his Lordship says, 'I have got one thousand pounds for Bertie Jones, which is a big sum, but HRH gives it to him on the condition that he receives only the interest for a certain number of years. I shall consult with the finest financiers in the City to get the best return I can for the money. Will you kindly inform Bertie Jones of this.' "

The Guv'nor paused. Bertie blinked. "A thousand pounds, sir?"

"Indeed, Bertie. And very prudent of his Lordship to suggest investment," said the Guv'nor. "But you realize that means that you can't actually have the money as cash. Of course, you will be earning riding fees now too, so you will find that your circumstances will be quite altered. Venn here will do all he can to help and advise you."

"But things don't have to be so very different even if I am the royal jockey, do they, sir?"

"Well, no, of course not," said the Guv'nor, "But obviously you have the means now to have set up your own household, things like that."

"Yes, sir, but I don't see there's any point in changing. I mean, there's no sense in moving out of Egerton, or anything, if I'm mostly here or racing."

"No, Bertie, of course not."

"And Guv'nor?"

"Yes, Bertie?"

"Well, there is one other thing."

The Guv'nor narrowed his eyes. Bertie took a deep breath and continued.

"You have always been very kind to all of us, the Jones family, that is. Well, sir. I wondered if there was some way I pay you back. Not that I ever could, of course, but, you know, now if I am earning a bit more."

The Guv'nor held his hand up for him to stop.

"Oh Bertie, Bertie," he sighed and put his arm around his shoulders. "Your father was my dear friend. I've only kept an eye out for his family, the same as he would have done for me and mine. Anyway, the best way you can repay me is to keep winning. So no more talk of this. Agreed?"

Bertie nodded.

"Right then, back to work for us both, I think," said the Guv'nor.

PART III
CELEBRITY

13

Paradise in the Strand,
London, May 1902

"THERE'S ALWAYS FUN TO be had at Romano's," Danny said to Bertie. "And there are no trains for a good few hours tonight, so come and enjoy yourself."

As they arrived, a group of young officers were hanging over the balcony. Champagne showered down into the street and cigar ash fell like snow. It didn't seem Bertie's sort of place but he followed Danny through the door.

Inside it was a great gilded pit, more like a theatre than a restaurant with its galleries and ornate carvings. The rich smell of lobster and roasted meats mingled with smoke and perfume to fill the air with a decadent incense. Soft lamps flickered on the round tables arranged along the rectangular lines of the room. An orchestra with strings and shiny brass played in an alcove to one side. Couples danced across the central space. Paradise in the Strand, they called it.

Diners in their finery paused to see who the new arrivals were. Bertie felt underdressed in his travelling clothes; he had expected to go straight back to Newmarket. A neat man with a waxed moustache and a black suit waved at them, then made his way over, pausing only to pass instructions to the waiters.

"A pleasure to see you, Mr Maher, sir. I am just preparing your usual table."

Bertie could see a young couple being moved from their cosy table in the corner to one by the service entrance. As soon as they left their seats, a flock of waiters got to work with fresh tablecloths and glasses.

"I have a special guest with me tonight, Luigi."

The man clicked his heels. "Mr Jones, we are honoured to welcome you. Of course, we know very well your great horsemanship. The famous horse, Diamond Jubilee, was the source of many celebrations here."

"Blimey, that's putting it mildly, Luey." A stout woman who had swept in behind them broke into the conversation. Her loud Cockney accent made heads turn. Accompanied by two men who hung on her every word, she wore a black cloak and a hat of many feathers. "Luigi collected a small fortune that night and heaven knows what the others won, God bless them."

She threw off her cloak and glittered in an extravagant dress with sparkling jewels.

"Aren't you going to introduce me, Danny boy? I been wanting to meet Mr Jones for some time."

"Of course. Miss Lloyd, may I present Mr Herbert Jones?" He bowed very low. "Bertie, this is Miss Marie Lloyd."

Bertie shook her hand. He had never seen her perform, but everyone had heard of Marie and she was a regular at the races.

"It's an honour, Miss Lloyd," he stammered.

"And for me too, Bertie. May I call you Bertie?" She didn't wait for an answer but swept them all along. "Come and join us. I know we are going to be good friends."

Danny seemed put out but didn't argue. Bertie took a chair on the edge of the table, facing out and with a line for an easy exit to the door.

"Perhaps a little champagne?" asked Luigi.

"Excellent, bring us a bottle of your finest." Danny sat back and pulled out a cigar.

"Just soda water for me," said Bertie.

"Relax and have a proper drink," said Danny.

"Leave him alone and let him have what he wants." Marie slapped Danny on the shoulder. "I think I'll have soda water too."

Her two companions exchanged glances.

"Oh, and while you are about it, Luigi," she called out. "Give that nice young couple back their corner table and send them over a bottle too, with Danny's compliments. I saw you moving them on, you old scoundrel, and Danny's so keen to get everyone drinking."

Bertie smiled at her. She might be loud but her heart was in the right place.

"Did you go to the coronation, Bertie?" Marie settled herself in her seat.

"No, I was working, but we had a good celebration at the racecourse and later back at the stables."

"Me, too. I did see some of the procession, though. Lovely it was."

A group of bookies in the corner kept glancing over, like foxes picking out a rabbit. One of them caught Danny's eye. He saw him give them a wink. Some brother jockeys joined them. Not his usual crowd, but they were nice enough lads. He shook his head when offered a menu.

"Are you bored, Bertie love?" asked Marie.

"No, just thinking that I ought to get back to Newmarket. An early start again tomorrow."

"It's a tough life. My brother-in-law was a jockey. A lot of hard work to get to the top and then to stay there. It's the same in every profession, I suppose." Marie grinned at him. "You're quite a sportsman, I hear. Football, cricket, as well as horses."

"Reg, my brother, tells me I'm a fanatic, but I enjoy my sport and try to get a match in whenever I can."

"And you are a very generous young man, I understand."

Bertie started to feel he was under interrogation.

"Now, don't look like that, these things get round." She patted his hand. "I also know you sing in the choir and run yourself ragged getting back for practice on Sundays. I may not go to church much these days but that's where I started singing. And, like you, I believe in helping those who are less fortunate."

Marie wriggled closer.

"In fact, Bertie, we are setting up a few matches over the winter to raise funds for poor children. It will be me, and some members of the theatre, journalists, sportsmen, we'll all take part. Then there's the pantomime. Would you be interested in joining us? I know the punters would love it."

"That's a nice thing to do. So, yes, I'd be honoured." Bertie stopped himself. "Although I would need to check that it's alright with my guv'nor."

"Ha, bless you," Marie laughed, and her whole body shook. "HRH won't mind. He'd join in like a shot if he could."

A young woman with a tight dress and a bold stare fixed on Bertie and sauntered towards their table. Bertie spotted her and was about to take evasive action when Marie intercepted her.

"Now don't you be bothering Mr Jones, dearie." Marie spoke to the girl kindly. "There's plenty of gents over there who will be only too pleased to see you."

"We certainly will." Danny pulled the girl on to his knee. "Come and see Uncle Danny if you want some fun."

The girl giggled. Bertie looked on, lost for words.

"Poor Bertie. You looked like a frightened rabbit," said Marie. "The girls don't mean any harm. It's hard for them, they're just trying to make the most of what they have while they can, like we all are really. Danny, too. He's easily led, but good none the less, so don't be too hard on him. Anyway, I'm here to look after you. I'll be your big sister."

"You know, you remind me a bit of my sister Jess. She always looked out for me," said Bertie.

"Yep, everyone's big sister, that's me. Eldest of eight." Marie smiled. "And you remind me of my little brother, Syd, so there you are."

Danny moved the girl and stretched his arms. "I might indulge in a little game of cards. Care to join me, Bertie?"

"Not me, thanks, not my sort of thing." Bertie stood up. "In any case, I'd better be off."

"Really, Mr King's Jockey, leaving us already." Danny was so angry, jabbing his finger into Bertie's chest and spitting the words out at him. "You'll have to try harder than this."

Bertie took a step back. Danny had been in a strange mood all evening.

"Things have changed, Bertie, it's a new time. People expect certain behaviour from their sporting heroes."

"What does that mean, gambling and race fixing?" Bertie was tired. He wanted to go. "No Danny, I don't think so. The public deserve better than that."

Through the smoke, the table of bookies beckoned him over. He shook his head.

"I may be young and stupid, but at least I'm honest. You're a good jockey, Danny. Sloan was a good jockey. Don't end up like him." Bertie stopped and tried to calm himself. The room had gone very quiet. "You know, I'm just not much good at all this high life."

"Well, I'm not sure that it's all it's cracked up to be myself," Marie interrupted and signalled to Luigi. "It would be a good time for some music. It will cheer us all up."

Luigi clicked his fingers and the orchestra started playing a slow ballad.

"Something more uplifting, I think," called Marie. "Off you go, Bertie. We'll talk again soon. Come on, Dancing Danny, let's see your fancy footwork."

As the floor filled up, Bertie took his chance to slip away.

14
Reg: Newmarket, 1906

O N THE CRICKET PITCH, the teams were getting impatient.
"Come on, Reg, you're miles away," called Bertie, eventually marching up and waving his arm in front of Reg's face. "Wake up, Reg! You are supposed to be bowling."

"Bowling a maiden over more like," laughed Charles, who was home on leave from the Life Guards and had turned out for Egerton.

"You do talk a lot of nonsense, Charlie Marsh."

"True, but on this occasion, see for yourself." Charles pointed along the line of Reg's gaze.

Over by the pavilion, a motherly figure was laying out the tea. Her light-brown hair was pulled back quite severely and an expanse of white apron covered her dress, but there was a serenity about the way that she placed the dishes and arranged the plates that was almost hypnotic.

Reg saw them looking and quickly took his post.

"He'll have no time for you now," said Charles. "Seen it a thousand times before. The daft smile, the distant eyes. That's love."

"I'm sure I know her from somewhere." Bertie racked his brains as he tried to place her. "Vic, the farrier – is she his niece?"

"Don't know about that. I know her from the Rutland Arms. She's the head housekeeper there. I have a, er, um, friend who works there. Anyway, this friend is terrified of Nell, who runs a very tight ship, so I understand. Obsessively tidy. Ha! So you would like her." Charles ran off to the boundary.

At tea, Reg hardly left Nell's side. Bertie had never seen him so attentive to a woman. Usually he could take them or leave them, and he often did. She did make a good cake, though. Bertie had just managed to grab the last piece of Battenberg before Old Ben had cleared the plate.

"Lovely tea," he said, joining Reg and Nell. "And we put up a good show, don't you think? Shame about the business with Charlie and the vicar though. They've never really got on."

Reg didn't seem to hear him but just stared at Nell.

"We really ought to go and check the horses. There's just time before choir practice." Bertie wanted to shake him. "And Old Ben's waiting."

The church clock struck five. Nell nudged Reg. "Your brother's talking to you, dearest."

Reg nuzzled up to Nell. Bertie curled his lip and was about to say something when Charles came along.

"Told you, your big brother isn't listening to you any more." Charles drained his tea, clattering his cup into the saucer.

"Anyway, if I were you, Bertie, I'd enjoy the perks of your fame, not tuck yourself away in the stable dorm and live like a monk."

"Good job you're not me then, Charlie, or I'd never win any races for your father," replied Bertie with a smile.

"Ouch, we are sharp today. Think I'll need another cake after that." Charles returned to the tea table, deciding what to have next.

Nell frowned at Charles and nudged Reg. "You see that young Mr Marsh there? You tell him to keep his sister away from my girls. That Miss Flora stood in the courtyard last week, with her sash and her placards, just when we were in the middle of doing the changeovers." Nell spoke louder and faster as she got more worked up. "Giving them pamphlets, she was, and telling them they should ask for more money. All the time my girls were struggling past, hardly able to see over the top of their linens."

Charles hesitated, then continued his contemplation of the cakes. His face had turned quite white.

Nell took another breath. "They listened to her, oh yes, but because she's a lady, not because they want a vote. It's not right to give those poor girls such ideas. They'll lose their jobs if anyone sees them talking to her sort. Tell him, Reg, go on, tell him."

"I don't think you need to, Reg," said Bertie. "I'm sure that Charlie has got the message."

Charles picked up a large slice of jam sponge. "Certainly have, old chap, but don't know why anyone would think I have any influence over my sister. Bertie would be the better man to talk to."

Charles took a large bite of cake, dropping crumbs everywhere, and walked away.

∪ ∪ ∪

The last race of the season was over. Bertie tidied himself up and headed out. He found Reg sitting on the wall by the woods, enjoying a quiet cigarette.

"Ready for the big day?" asked Bertie, taking a seat in the space that Reg had made for him.

"I am. Nell's told me to take it easy on the ale, though. She doesn't want me to be breathing beer all over the vicar tomorrow."

"Already acting like a wife, I see, but a very sensible one."

"She certainly is, and a very pretty one too."

Bertie wished that Reg wouldn't say things like that, it didn't seem right him being so soppy. But he supposed that he was allowed to, given that it was the eve of his wedding.

"It was nice that you were able to take Nell to meet Mum," said Bertie. "And that she knew, well, that you were settled."

"I was just thinking about her, Mum, I mean." Reg relit his roll-up and puffed at it. "She was so excited about coming down for the wedding. It's always been so hard for her, what with Dad and us lot to sort out."

"I don't think she was ever the same after we all got split up. She didn't know where she was after that." Bertie took out his handkerchief. "Just wish I had been able to see her more often. I couldn't even get there in time for the funeral."

"Come on, Bertie, you did your best. It was sudden, no one expected it. In any case, you were on the other side of the country riding for the King. Mum would have understood, and you did such a lot for her in the last few years. She was very, very proud of you."

Bertie thought of his mother and tried to transform the terrible events of the past few weeks into something good and meaningful.

He had to believe. He had to have faith, otherwise what was the point of it all?

"You know, I was hoping that she might move down here and we could have a place together, with Jess and Bill, and the rest too, if they wanted." Bertie sighed. "We could all be under one roof again. Mum could have seen Lily properly, not just a short visit now and again. Poor Lily, she was so young when she went to live with Aunt Mary. She doesn't remember anything much about Mum and Dad, or Epsom."

"But you know, Bertie, Mum would never have left Epsom. She'd lived there all her life. Ethel and the grandchildren, her friends, they were all there. She didn't really know us any more."

"Do you remember that saying of Dad's? If wishes were horses, beggars would ride. We can't change what has happened now, but it doesn't stop me wishing."

"I know," said Reg. "Although would you really want our Perce under your feet?"

Bertie grinned. "Well, perhaps you have a point there."

They sat quietly for a while. Reg and Nell had thought about postponing the wedding, but everyone said that Mum would have wanted it to go ahead. Bertie vowed to make it as happy as possible for them.

"So, then Reg, what about Jess? Have you seen her yet?"

"Yes, I met her at the station this afternoon. She came down with Bill, the others are coming tomorrow. Anyway, it seems she's got the best room in the Rutland Arms. I think Nell must have put in a word. Very pleased she was, even though she moaned about how much it must be costing us."

"Well, that's alright. She can be a princess for a night and Lord it over us tomorrow."

They both smiled as they thought of Jess.

"You know, Nell's a funny girl." Reg leaned back against the tree. "I wanted to buy her a fur coat as a wedding present. That seems to be the done thing, doesn't it?"

Bertie agreed, but in fact had no idea, even though he had been the best man at many weddings.

"Well, she wouldn't let me. A waste of money, she said, what would I want with one? What do you make of that?"

"There's not many women who'd turn down a fur coat, that's for sure. Although I've never seen the attraction of wearing some poor dead creature around your neck."

"Nell wants me to stand down from racing. We are thinking about getting a little pub. Nell can run the rooms and the kitchen, and I'll do the rest."

"But you'll still play cricket?"

"You and your sport, Bertie. Of course I will, and Nell will still make her lovely cakes."

"Now, Reg, I'd better get you to that keg of ale that's in the lad's room or I'll be failing in my duty. There are a lot of thirsty men waiting down there."

He jumped to the ground and put his hand out to Reg.

ʊ ʊ ʊ

Running a finger under his collar, Bertie moved through the tightly packed groups that filled the front room of Reg and Nell's new house. He wandered into the dining room, where there were fewer people. Jess had already been round and tidied away the wedding breakfast, leaving just the cake. Nell insisted on preparing everything herself. Reg had wanted them to have a proper function room at the hotel, but Nell thought that this way she could get used to her kitchen before they started married life.

Bertie raised his glass in a private toast to the happy couple. He had waited until after he'd made his speech before having anything to drink. But now he'd discharged all his best man duties, telling a few yarns about Reg, praising his choice of bride and remembering to compliment the bridesmaid, not that he could have easily forgotten as Lily fixed him with a steely glare to make sure she had her moment of glory.

Settled in his corner, Bertie was about to raise the glass to his lips a second time when the Guv'nor came over.

"Good speech, Bertie. Well done."

"Thank you, sir."

"Very touching what Reg said about your dear mother. I knew her when she was just a girl. She and my late wife … " the Guv'nor stopped and cleared his throat. "Yes, such a terrible loss, and so close to the wedding. I'm sorry about you and the funeral, Bertie, if I could have done something I would."

"It's alright, Guv'nor, I understand."

"Well Bertie, all this got me thinking, and I've a suggestion. The new villas between the stables and the house are nearly finished. Venn will be having one, and I wondered if you would like to take the other. What with Reg moving out of the dormitory, it would be more fitting for you to have your own place."

Bertie went over things in his mind.

"Well, sir, I had wondered about getting a place and bringing Mother and Jess down, but now ... " he paused. "Then there's Ben, he is getting a little old to live in the dormitory. I could look after him, make him more comfortable. Perhaps this would be a good time to make a change."

The Guv'nor nodded towards Jess, who was talking to Reg and Nell.

"Have you considered that Jess might be willing to come and keep house for you for a while? It might be just the thing for her to make a fresh start."

The Guv'nor seemed to have it all planned out, but he had a point. Young Bill would need somewhere too.

"Well, my boy, think it over and let me know." The Guv'nor patted him on the back and moved off to find his wife.

Bertie walked out into the yard and admired the garden. Nell had already planted a variety of vegetables between the flowers, and pots of herbs lined the brick path. The hedge made it all nice and private. He breathed in the quiet and went to take a sip of his champagne.

"It's a lovely cottage, isn't it?" Flora slipped her arm through his.

Her hat sat at an odd angle and she looked very pink. An empty wine glass was in danger of slipping from her hand.

"Doesn't it make you want to settle down, Bertie?"

Bertie put his champagne down on the water butt.

"You look tired, Flora. Shall I find you a seat?"

"Oh come on, Bertie, when are you going to make an honest woman of me?" She shook herself away from him, swaying from side to side.

"Flora, really. I've never," he checked himself and looked around, lowering his voice. "You really should be more careful what you say. People might think you are being serious."

"But I am being serious, Bertie, and I've got to speak out if you won't." She threw her arms out, sending her wine glass flying. Bertie reached out and caught it in mid-air. "After all, I'm not getting any younger. Father is always trying to marry me off. That's why I hate coming back from London. Well, that and, you know, Grace and the babies. The whole happy family thing, which frankly makes me want to be sick."

"Flora, stop this. You're not yourself." Bertie wanted to hold her, but that was something he dared not do. "Look, Flora, think of your father. He cares for you and wants you to be a lady. He's been so good to me, and to my family. If he thought I had intentions towards you, well, it wouldn't be right, you see?"

"No, I don't, I don't see at all. You are one of the most successful jockeys in the country. Father used to be a jockey, just like you and your father. What's the difference?"

"The difference is that he was always an officer, a gentleman jockey, a gentleman trainer. And Charlie, he's an officer now too. My family, we're just grooms and horsemen. That's the difference," Bertie spoke softly to her.

"And Grace's father, isn't he just a horseman?"

"Oh, Flora, I don't know, but he doesn't work for your father."

"You just don't care for me enough to want to change things, do you?"

"Flora, please, don't say that, but I don't want you to spend your life waiting for me. You can do so much better."

"Flora? Flora?" Charles was calling.

She reached out for Bertie's glass of champagne, drank it in one gulp and handed him back the glass. With a toss of her head, she walked rather unsteadily inside.

15

Derby Stakes,
Epsom, June 1909

"GOOD SIGN, JONES, WE'VE drawn number one," said Lord Marcus.

"But there's a lot of support for St Martin, I heard," Bertie replied.

"I don't understand it myself," the Guv'nor glanced across at the American colt. "He doesn't appear so fine."

"Whereas our boy looks splendid, even in this downpour," Lord Marcus smiled at Minoru, who was being led round the parade by one of the stable lads under the close supervision of Old Ben.

Bertie made his way through the mud as the bell rang. Minoru greeted him with his usual sweet-tempered expression.

Old Ben was soaked, but held out his hands. "Ready, Bertie?"

Taking hold of the reins, Bertie jumped up, only lightly touching Old Ben's palms.

"Much obliged, Ben." Bertie raised his whip to his cap. "But please go and get yourself in the dry now. You'll catch cold."

"Don't you worry, Bertie, plenty of time for all that when I'm in my grave."

Bertie shook his head, he didn't like it when Old Ben said things like that but he wasn't going to argue with him.

The crowd applauded as Bertie moved out with Minoru. He gave them a wave and cantered off.

At the start, Louviers was up in front early, keeping close to his stablemate Brooklands. Together they sped up the hill. St Martin was gaining on them. Bertie held Minoru back. He kept there. A nice even pace. A good rhythm. Steady, boy. The horse felt strong. As they turned into Tattenham Corner, Brooklands was flagging and falling behind. A group swept up on the right. St Martin moved forward but the pack crowded him in. Tildy's warnings about the Corner came into his head, the Corner, always the Corner. Bertie swerved to the left, very close to the barrier. He heard the thud of the collision. The ground shook and the shouts told him someone had fallen, poor devil. Urging Minoru along the inside, Louviers was in their sights up ahead. Three horses were on their heels, but St Martin was not one of them. Bertie shifted forward. Minoru responded with determination. They were level with Louviers, but that colt wasn't done and Stern, as a skilled jockey, kept pace. Bertie could feel Louviers' breath on his neck. Minoru, so keen to please, accelerated and pushed himself ahead. As they got to the finish point, Minoru had managed to keep a nose in front.

Black objects rose up from the stands until the air was thick with them. At first Bertie thought they must be crows frightened by the noise, but as they tumbled down, he could see they were hats. People ran from all sides, closing in on them. He tried to walk Minoru to the enclosure, but the crowd swept them back on to the course and across in the other direction. Minoru became disturbed, crying as hands reached out and plucked at his mane and tail.

"Stand back!" Bertie shouted, but he couldn't hear his own voice against the cheers. Soothing Minoru as best he could, Bertie feared that they would both be pulled over. The Guv'nor forced his way through. Bertie prayed that Old Ben would stay away but, of course, there he was, standing next to the Guv'nor, head down like a charging bull. Old Ben got to them first, somehow opening up a channel to lead them away.

As they reached the enclosure gate, King Edward was waiting. He seemed frail despite his joy. The Prince of Wales stood close by. Rings of policemen tried to keep order as people rushed to congratulate him. The All Right was called; a man started singing God Save the King. The Guv'nor handed the reins to His Majesty so that he could hold his Derby winner. Everyone joined in the national anthem, over and over again they sang it.

King Edward turned to Bertie. He was very out of breath. "Good race, Jones. It was so exciting the Queen thought it would do for me. She's called for the doctor. Ha!"

"Oh no, sir. I'm sorry. Are you alright?" Bertie stood up in the saddle to check on the King.

"Just joking, Jones," he roared. "Just joking."

Everyone around them cheered and the King proudly led them in.

"Vive le roi," shouted a group of Frenchmen.

"You hear that Jones? Even the Frenchies love us today," said the King.

A man broke through the line. "Yes, Teddy, we all love you today," he shouted as half a dozen constables bundled him away. "But we won't tomorrow unless you do something about your bloody parliament!"

16

A day out in London,
November 1909

"IT REALLY ISN'T LIKE Percy to want to introduce us to one of his young ladies, is it Bert?" Lily had been going on about this all the way up on the train. "I mean, he hates it if we come across any of them."

Bertie lowered his newspaper and looked across at her as she rubbed a clearing on the window. The fog was getting worse. They swayed in their seats as the train lurched and wobbled; there were no other passengers in the first-class carriage.

"Well, perhaps he thinks more of this one and wanted her to meet the family, only not all of us at once," Bertie replied.

"But she's bound to have met Jack."

"Exactly, and now he's trying to put that right," laughed Bertie. "So introducing his sweet little sister and one of his more well-behaved brothers will, of course, do the trick."

"Famous brother, you mean."

Bertie went back to his paper.

Lily huffed loudly. "I was so looking forward to going down to London with you for the day. And the chance to wear my new hat and jacket." Lily stroked the dark green velvet of her sleeves. "But the thought of having to put up with another of Perce's simpering girls and him acting like an idiot as usual, well, it rather spoils things."

Bertie put his paper down again.

"We're only meeting them for tea. Then we can go and do something else, see a show or something. Whatever you want. I don't get to take you out that often, so let's enjoy ourselves." He smiled at her.

"Oh you are so nice, Bertie."

Bertie shook his head to himself and returned to the sports page. He could hear Lily's glove squeaking on the window again.

"Not far now. You can just make out all the buildings," she squinted out and reported back.

"Good," murmured Bertie.

Lily started rifling through her bag. "Like a barley sugar? I thought I had some in here somewhere."

"No thanks, I'm fine."

She drummed her boots against the floor, then started clicking her tongue against the roof of her mouth.

"Where are we meeting them, then?"

This time Bertie folded his paper up neatly and placed it on the seat beside him.

"Alright, Lil. You have my attention. We're meeting them outside the British Museum and then we'll find a teashop nearby. That is, I believe, the plan."

"The British Museum? Percy? Blimey!"

"Some of the words you use Lil, what would Aunt Mary say? As I understand it, this was his young lady's idea. Perce was all for going to the Ritz but she thought it was too flash."

"I'd have quite liked to have gone to the Ritz. Perhaps this mysterious woman has hypnotized our Perce and turned him into a decent human being."

"Well, that's a bit strong, but be kind. You're not to tease him."

"Me?"

"Come on, you know what you can be like."

"I didn't tease Reg, did I?"

"Only because you were too scared. He'd have told you what for."

Lily glanced slyly at Bertie. "Of course, I would tease you," she said slowly. "But then you don't have any lady friends, except of course Flora. Do you?"

Bertie turned to the window himself and started scrubbing at it. Lily watched him carefully.

"Seriously, Bertie, do you think you and Flora will ever … ?"

"Now Lily, you stop that right now. Saying things like that, you could cause no end of trouble. You hear me?" Bertie shook his head at her.

"Crikey, touched a raw nerve there, didn't I?"

Bertie didn't reply.

"It just seems so silly when you both, you know, like each other," Lily persisted.

"Now Lily, remember she's my guv'nor's daughter and you don't want to go saying silly things that could upset people. There is no more to say. Understand?"

"You tell her that," Lily muttered to herself.

"What?"

"Pardon," she replied

"What?" Bertie said again, sharply.

"It's 'pardon' not 'what'. And nothing."

Lily crossed her arms tightly and stared out of the window. Bertie followed her gaze. It was only early afternoon but outside the lamps were a sulphur-yellow haze through the mist. The metal creaked and groaned in the dampness.

"It's a real pea-souper out there. Do you think we'll even find Perce and his young lady?" Lily spoke in her sweetest voice.

"Well, it's hard to miss him really. His stands out like a copper-coloured beacon."

"I'm so sorry for upsetting you, Bertie. I've made you cross and you're never cross." Lil rushed forward and flung herself at him. "Thank you for taking me out today. I will behave, I promise."

"It's alright, Lil. No need to overdo it." Bertie grinned at his sister's impulsive display of affection. He stood up and placed her back in her seat.

"I'm being serious, Bertie. You know when I got sent away to Aunt Mary's after Dad died, I was so lucky that you and Reg were close by." Lily sniffed loudly.

Bertie passed her his neatly folded white handkerchief.

"It always made such a difference when you'd come and see me, or I'd go over to see you. Aunt Mary's always been very kind and all that, but you know it's not the same."

"I know, Lily." He patted her hand.

"I just want you to be happy. You work so hard all the time," Lily's voice almost disappeared and her face wobbled as she tried not to get upset.

Bertie tucked a loose strand of his sister's hair back under her hat, and sat back to look at her.

"Lil, really, I'm very happy. All I've ever wanted is to be around horses, and that's what I do. Now come on, pretty one, cheer up, you don't want to look all red and blotchy when you get off the train, or we'll be letting Perce down."

After that, Lily spent of the rest of the journey delicately dabbing her face with Bertie's handkerchief and rearranging her hat.

ᴜ ᴜ ᴜ

At the station, there was no queue for a taxi and the traffic was light, so they arrived at the museum early. Lily took Bertie's arm and they walked up the stone steps into the grand entrance hall. People were milling around, talking in hushed voices that echoed around the polished marble. Lily nudged Bertie and pointed.

"Can that really be our Perce?"

"Believe it or not, I think it must be," said Bertie.

They stood and watched as Percy, standing by one of the huge pillars, gently helped a tall, elegant, dark-haired lady into her coat. He buttoned it up for her with all the care of a mother sending her little one out into the snow. She talked non-stop and he listened attentively while trying to untangle the bag and scarf he held.

"Hell's bells, what's happened to Percy?" Lily couldn't take her eyes off them.

Bertie resisted the urge to comment again on her blasphemy and steered Lily back towards the door.

"Come on, let's wait outside. It doesn't seem right to stare."

"They seemed very, you know, close. Don't you think?" Lily whispered and gave a knowing look.

"Really Lily, you shouldn't talk like that." Bertie was shocked.

"She's very pretty though, like a Spanish princess." Lily was off on one of her flights of fancy. "I wonder where she got that coat?"

"Come on, look, there they are."

Bertie called out to Percy, who bounded over to greet them.

"Hello, hello," he shook hands with Bertie and kissed Lily. "Back in a tick."

He bounced back to the lady they had seen him with earlier, and guided her over towards them with the greatest of care.

"I do believe he's nervous," hissed Lily.

"Remember, you promised!" said Bertie, only too well aware that her memory was selective at the best of times.

"This," said Percy, "is Miss Beaumont. Miss Clara Beaumont."

"He sounds as if he's naming a ship. I don't hold with all this 'Miss Beaumont' nonsense, so please call me Clar." She spoke very clearly and with confidence, as if she was used to being introduced to new people. "Clara always sounds rather alarming; my parents named me after the musician."

Lily looked blank.

"Clara Schumann," Clar explained.

"Ahh!" Lily nodded and was about to ask a question, but Bertie cut her off.

"How do you do, Clar? I'm Bertie, Percy's brother, and this is Lily, our youngest sister."

Clar shook hands with great enthusiasm.

"I'm so pleased to meet you at last. Percy has told me lots about his family. And, of course, everyone knows you, Bertie."

"Yes, everyone knows Bertie." Percy looked pleased.

"You are taller than I thought you would be though." Clar looked him up and down.

Lily opened and shut her mouth, like a goldfish. It always meant trouble.

"Well, probably about average for a jockey, I'd say," said Bertie.

"It seems funny that Percy is so tall, and you being brothers," Clar continued.

"Percy takes after our mother, so does Lil, and Reg. Most of us are small though, like our dad."

"But you do look very dapper. And, I expect you earn pots of money," Clar carried on as if he hadn't spoken.

Lily gasped.

"Now, now, don't be coy, Bertie. I believe in honesty. There's far too much embarrassment about things like money, love and politics. Wouldn't you say?" Clar added with a wave.

"Well, I'm not sure I'd say that at all." Bertie felt himself getting cross at all her remarks. She was much too forward, and not at all ladylike. He took a deep breath and thought of Percy. "But I would say that it is probably a good time to go and find some tea."

"Well, I have a suggestion," said Clar.

"Thought you might," muttered Lily.

"There is a meeting of the WSPU just round the corner that starts shortly. You get a free cup of tea and biscuits, and you get to hear first-rate speakers, perhaps even Mrs Pankhurst. It should prove most enlightening," Clar enthused.

"The WSPU? Er, is that the women's suffrage people?" asked Bertie.

"That's right, the Women's Social and Political Union," Clar puffed out her chest. "I am impressed with you, Bertie."

Lily giggled.

"Well, I was thinking more of a tea shop." Bertie felt himself wishing he was back on the train. "I mean, I'm not sure a meeting like that would be suitable for Lily."

"Nonsense," insisted Clar. "Lily, how old are you? Nineteen, twenty?"

"Eighteen."

"Well then, you're old enough to make up your own mind. Wouldn't you like to find out about the rights and demands of all modern women?" Clar asked.

"Well, yes, I suppose I would."

"Rubbish, she'd rather be shopping in Oxford Street, wouldn't you Lil?" teased Percy.

Lily shot him a glance. Bertie sighed to himself; now Perce had done it.

"Actually I would be very interested in finding out some more." She stuck out her chin and looked dismissively at Percy. "Would that be alright with you, Bertie?"

"Er, I'm really not sure. Wouldn't you prefer to go somewhere posh for tea, with a nice piece of cake?" Bertie was starting to despair.

"It's alright, Bertie, don't worry, I know just what you're thinking," Clar chipped in using her most understanding tone. "Men are very welcome too, you know. We have lots of male supporters who are keen to help the cause, I can assure you."

"Right then, that's settled. Good plan, Clar!" Percy rubbed his hands together with what Bertie thought was a little too much enthusiasm.

"Come along then, this way," Clar set off with Percy following behind.

"This is so exciting, isn't it, Bertie?" Lily took his arm and walked as fast as she could to keep up with Clar and Percy. Bertie didn't reply.

They turned off the main street and into a small road, then through some railings and down several steps to a vestry behind a large church. The hall was decorated with banners and flags: green, white and purple. Everyone there was busy, putting out chairs and setting up stalls selling ribbons and rosettes.

"Claa-ra, how lovely! And what a group you've brought with you. Well done!" A large lady wearing a wide sash came up to them. She kissed Clar on both cheeks and with a "Welcome to you all", waved them towards the tea urn and then wandered off arm in arm with Clar. Lily followed Clar.

"Bit like a church bazaar, don't you think, Perce?" whispered Bertie.

"To be honest Bert," he whispered. "I think you're right."

"How long do these things last?"

"Hours sometimes," Percy sighed. "Sorry, Bertie, but once Clar has an idea in her head, well. Anyway, you might find it interesting. They do have a point, you know."

Bertie ran his hand across his face. "Well, I'm not sure that my guv'nor would see it that way and we really ought to keep an eye on Lil, you know what she gets like."

"Good old Bertie, always taking care of us." Percy slapped him on the back. "Well, let's get a cup of tea."

The tea looked weak and milky, but at least it was warm. Just as Bertie raised the cup to his lips and took a sip, someone tapped him on the shoulder. He gulped, catching the tea right at the bottom of his throat.

"Flora!"

"Bertie, what on earth are you doing here?" Flora seemed different in her London clothes. She wore a purple, green and white sash with Votes for Women written on it. "I didn't know you were a supporter of women's suffrage."

Still spluttering, he took the time to recover himself. "Well, it's a long story, but it involves Percy and a young lady he seems particularly keen on."

Bertie looked in the direction of his brother. Percy was fussing around Clar again, who was still holding forth. Flora followed his gaze.

"Umm," she said slowly. "Not his usual type from what I remember. I do know her, though. She's started working on the magazine at headquarters. Rather Bohemian and a bit bossy, but a nice girl, very enthusiastic. Oh, isn't that Lily there?"

"Yes, Lily came up with me. Percy invited us both up and I wanted to give her a nice day out, but … "

"Well, she looks as if she is enjoying herself. Don't worry, she'll be fine." She put her hand on his elbow. "Anyway, how are you?"

"Oh, I'm alright," said Bertie. "Anyway, it looks as if life away from Egerton agrees with you. You look very smart, Miss Marsh."

"Why thank you, Mr Jones." Flora did a mock curtsey. "But all this, it's a serious business, Bertie, really it is. I want to do more. I'm just too cowardly and then it's difficult with Father. As it is, he doesn't approve of my coming to live on my own and getting a job. So you won't tell him you saw me here, will you?"

"Not if you don't tell on me," smiled Bertie.

They stood quietly.

"Flora!" Lily burst over. "How lovely to see you. Bertie and I were only talking about you earlier, weren't we, Bertie?"

"I think we're supposed to taking our seats," said Bertie quickly, as people started to move towards the chairs.

"Oh, and here's Percy," Lily said. "Now, Flora, I think you've met my brother Percy. Percy, you may remember Miss Marsh."

"Very good, Lil. See, you can be very grown up when you want to, can't you?"

Lily poked her tongue out at him. Percy turned to Flora.

"Miss Marsh, how lovely to see you again. I'd like to introduce Miss Beaumont." Percy turned around but Clar had walked away with some other sash-wearers. "But I think she has committee duties. Perhaps later?"

"Come and sit with us, Flora," said Lily, pointed at some empty chairs towards the back.

"But there aren't enough seats."

"That's alright, Flora, you sit with Lily." Bertie motioned for them to go ahead. "I can sit just here."

Bertie sat down. He was happy. Flora was directly in front of him, so he could watch her: the curve of her neck, the set of her shoulders, the way she held her head. He was so close; he could almost feel the heat of her body and smell the scent of her hair. He could watch her and no one would know. Except Lily, who turned around for a moment and caught his eye.

The hall was warm. As the talks started, Bertie started to feel sleepy. The words of the speaker faded. Just as his eyelids started to fall, movement in the shadows to the side caught his attention. He sat up. Figures crept around the edge of the hall, some bulky, some tall. They signalled to one another and moved in a coordinated way, as if they were about to round up a herd of horses. A light caught the badge and buttons on a uniform. Bertie knew without doubt that something was about to happen. He tapped Percy on the arm.

"We've got to go."

Percy grinned, just as he used to when he was a boy and he was playing a game.

"Now, Perce." He pointed at the side door, where there was no one about. "Use that door. You look after Clar, I'll take the others. Meet outside, as near as we can to where we came in. Alright?"

The woman on the stage finished her talk, and the audience stood and clapped. Using the noise as cover, Bertie moved Lily and Flora towards the door. They didn't question him, thank goodness, although he heard Clar arguing with Percy. Police whistles started up suddenly from all directions, followed by a clatter of falling chairs and the screams of women.

"Keep going, keep going!" Bertie pushed them on, until they were well away from the entrance. "We'll give Percy a few minutes, then we'll move. It might not be safe when they start bringing people out."

"What's going on?" Lily clung to him, shivering.

"Well, I suppose, a raid of some sort. I don't know."

"It has started to happen more often, although it is the first time here," said Flora. "I don't like abandoning them."

Bertie peered into the fog for Percy and Clar. People, mostly women, were being bustled out on to the street.

"Come on now. Haven't you got homes to go to?" A police sergeant steered people out. "Please leave of your own accord, ladies, or we'll have to help you on your way."

Black vans drew up, but in the main, the women scurried off. Bertie caught sight of Percy and waved them over. Clar's hat was lopsided and her hair was falling down.

"I could do with a drink after that," she said.

"So do I," said Percy, holding his eye.

"What happened? Did you get hit?" asked Lily. "Policemen shouldn't hit innocent people."

"It wasn't a policemen, it was me." Clar look embarrassed. "I caught poor Percy with my elbow when he was trying to get my bag."

"Come on, let's go somewhere smart," said Percy. "Take us to Romano's, Bertie. It'll cheer us up and you'll be able to get us in."

They all agreed it was just what they needed.

"You don't want to go there." Bertie glared at Percy. "It's miles from here and I'm really not sure that it is a suitable place at all. Let's find somewhere closer."

"Rubbish," said Percy. "It's only a ten-minute walk."

"Oh, please, Bertie," Lily jumped up and down. "I've seen pictures of it in my magazines. They say everyone loves Romano's."

"Everyone except Bertie, so it would seem." Flora slipped her arm through his and marched him towards the Strand.

∪ ∪ ∪

"Bertie, what on earth are you doing here?" Danny circled round and smiled at Lily in a leering way that Bertie did not like. "And with such a bevy of beauties."

Lily blushed. Bertie took a step between them. "Really, Danny. This is my sister."

"Sorry, old chap," said Danny, but Bertie saw him wink at her.

Marie was at her usual table. Alone for once, she beckoned them over. She threw her arms around Bertie and gave him a big kiss on the cheek.

"Good timing, Bert, I was going to get in touch," she said. "Puss in Boots! Will you ride the horse again?"

"Pantomime time already? Just tell me where and when, Marie, I'll be there."

"This I must see." Flora took off her glove and put her hand out to wipe the lipstick from his cheek.

"It's alright, I'll do it," said Lily, taking out her hankie and pushing Flora to one side.

"And Clar? What are you doing here?" Marie patted the chair next to her. "Well, this is turning into an interesting evening. Come and tell me how it is all going with the magazine."

Percy was talking animatedly with Danny. Lily sat staring at Marie, who was listening attentively to Clar. Flora stared gloomily from the other side of the table. Bertie sighed and signalled for Luigi to come over with some menus.

17
The end of an era,
May 1910

WITCH OF THE AIR was saddled and waiting in the paddock. The Guv'nor and Old Ben walked her along. As Bertie arrived, a hush fell over the crowd. He heard a few quiet shouts of "God Bless King Edward", but they all kept a respectful silence. The news had travelled fast.

"How is His Majesty, Guv'nor?"

"Not good, Bertie. I called at the Palace on my way here and the reports are true. The doctors say that it won't be long now, even though he refuses to stay in his bed. But the King has particularly commanded that his horse should run today."

Bertie got straight on with the business of getting the Witch down to the start. Good as gold she cantered off, sleek and neat. It was a small field of just five horses. Queen Tii was favourite and looked in fine form with Steve up. Bertie had seen Queen Tii's father and siblings race many times. Danny was riding Wooden Wedding, not a very popular horse but still better rated than the poor little Witch. But Bertie knew that the Witch had heart.

Queen Tii got off to a good start but the Witch kept up, light and pacey. They could have pressed harder, but Bertie kept back, waiting and watching. About halfway round he saw the sign. Queen Tii started to shorten her stride, just as her father used to do when pressed. Bertie let the Witch go. Daintily she increased her step and they floated to the front.

It was a strange reception as they passed the post, winning by a good half a length. The crowd cheered, but there was a sadness that put a lump in Bertie's throat.

The Guv'nor ordered them all back to Egerton as soon as the racing was finished. It was a quiet and sombre trip home. Not even Old Ben could think of anything to say. Although it was late when they returned, no one felt like sleeping. They gathered in the office, where they made tea and talked about old times. The Guv'nor joined them. He had received a call to say that His Majesty had died around midnight.

It was a strange time, but the routine of the days carried on as usual. The horses still needed to be fed, watered and exercised. The stables and yard had to be cleaned. But all racing events for the next few days were abandoned.

There was a special service at the estate chapel on Sunday. The flag had flown at half-mast since Saturday morning. Jess had organized black armbands and sewn them on to their jackets. Across the pews the women were dressed in their mourning and held handkerchiefs to their faces. In the front stall, Mrs Marsh dabbed her eyes beneath her veil. Only Flora sat there calm and unmoved.

"It is like we have lost the sun," said Old Ben afterwards, "and we don't know if we will ever feel its warmth again."

"There will never be another like him for us. All through my racing career, he has always been there," said the Guv'nor.

"Very true," Old Ben nodded.

"But we mustn't forget that the new king is a good man and shares his father's passion for the turf," added the Guv'nor.

"So we won't be put out to grass then?" asked Old Ben.

"I trust not, Ben, not just yet anyway."

∪ ∪ ∪

A few weeks later, they were having Sunday lunch at the cottage.

"Well, that was a fine meal, Jess," Bertie put down his spoon, savouring the last mouthful.

"But you've hardly had enough to keep a bird alive, just a morsel of chicken and vegetables, and half a dozen raspberries." Jess picked up the blancmange. "Are you sure you won't have some?"

"It looks lovely, Jess, but not during the season. It's getting harder to make the weight." The pink pudding trimmed with fruit and cream looked very tasty. "Best not. Thank you."

"Well, Jess," Old Ben pushed his plate forward. "Don't let it go to waste, me and Bill, we'll finish it up."

Jess tutted but gave them healthy portions of seconds.

"Now who's for a cup of tea? Bertie?"

"Yes please, Jess, but I just want to go and check on something at the stables. I'll only be half an hour, so I'll be back in plenty of time to get ready for the match."

Bill gave a thumbs up, his cheeks bulging with pudding.

"Are you and Ben coming down to the cricket later?" Bertie asked Jess. "It's a lovely day. Reg'll be there and Nell's doing the tea."

"Sounds like just the thing. I'll fetch a rug once I get all this lot cleared up."

"We'll have a nice bit of cake down there too, Jess," Old Ben smiled at her.

"I don't know." She whipped the bowl away from Old Ben as soon as he'd finished the morsel. "One of you won't eat anything, the others won't stop."

"Ah but Jess, it wouldn't do for us all to be the same, and what did the vicar say this morning? All God's creatures in their glory."

Bertie left them to it. At the stables, it was all quiet. With the horses fed and exercised, the stable staff had gone off for their dinner. He just wanted to check Minoru's foot; he'd given it a good clean, but needed to be sure that this had done the trick.

There was a car parked outside; a driver waited. It appeared to be a Sandringham car; perhaps someone had come over from the stud. Inside the stables there was a man in a tweed jacket and a deerstalker peering into Minoru's stall.

"Excuse me, can I help you?" called Bertie.

The man turned round, he seemed hot and embarrassed. He also looked suspiciously like the new King.

"Your Majesty?"

"Ah, Jones. Good to see you. I, er, just thought I'd pop over and see the horses. I brought them some carrots." He held a small wicker basket containing some washed and trimmed carrots. "I usually take some of these to the mares and foals at the stud as a little treat – they enjoy them very much. But then perhaps Mr Marsh wouldn't approve, I mean he may have them on a special diet."

Bertie had never seen such perfectly presented carrots.

"Yes, sir, you're right. They are all on special diets. So perhaps best not to," Bertie said gently.

"Very good, yes, of course. A bit like you jockeys, eh? Only allowed special food." King George laughed.

"Yes, sir, but I think the horses do rather better than us jockeys," smiled Bertie.

"Yes, I'm sure it is a hard life in the saddle. Do you find, Mr Jones, that you are happier here in the stables than out on display at the racecourse?"

"Well, Your Majesty, there is nothing like the feeling of the race itself. The way it's just you and the horse finding your way through, riding together. But all the fancy bits. I'm not really one for all that, sir," Bertie stopped himself carrying on too much.

"It's alright, Jones, I know what you mean only too well."

The King seemed to drift off, even the horses were quiet. Bertie waited. King George took a long breath.

"Well, well, I am hoping that you will ride for me as royal jockey, Jones, just as you did for my late father."

"Thank you, Your Majesty. I am very honoured." Bertie swallowed. It sounded as if things at Egerton would continue as they were, that would please the Guv'nor.

"And you promise me you won't be disappearing off to Russia? I know my cousin made you a very generous offer and I know how loyal you are to your horses."

"You heard about that?" Bertie cleared his throat. "No, sir, I won't be going to Russia. Even if this young man is."

Minoru knew he was being talked about and peered out of his stall. He took a liking to the royal hat. In an instant he had snatched it and was chomping on it.

"Oh no, Minny, how could you?" Bertie leapt in to retrieve it. He held it out in front of him, all wet, slimy and dented with tooth marks. "Your Majesty, I'm so sorry."

"Ha! No, I should have known better." The King laughed as he took the hat back and shook it. "Look, Jones, no need to mention my visit to Mr Marsh. Don't want him to think that I'm going to be interfering in his good work."

"I'm sure he wouldn't think anything of the kind, sir."

"Well, even so." The King paused and looked around him. "It is good to know that things here, at least, can stay the same."

"Certainly is, sir, I'm not one for change myself." Bertie thought for a moment. "Perhaps if you have time, sir, you might like to see the horses? I'm not as knowledgeable as my guv'nor, Mr Marsh, but I can give you some idea of how they are all coming along."

"Oh, yes please, Mr Jones. That would be very kind." The King brightened up no end.

An hour later, Bertie ran back to the house. He was clutching a large basket of carrots.

18
Lily in Cambridge, November 1912

"BERTIE, MAY I HAVE a word?" Mr Smallwood came into the stables and beckoned him away from the others.

"Look, I've just got back from Cambridge. Saw your Lily in Market Street, dressed up as one of those suffragettes and selling leaflets. Standing in the road she was; nearly got herself killed." Mr Smallwood took off his driving gloves and shoved them into the pocket of his greatcoat. "It's none of my business really, but I thought you should know. It's dangerous for her."

"Of course. You were right to tell me."

"You know how the Guv'nor is about these things," Mr Smallwood continued. "And my little Doris is at an impressionable age. She thinks the world of Lily but I don't want her getting involved with that sort of thing."

"Yes, thank you, Mr Smallwood. I understand." Bertie looked at his watch. "Look, I'll drive over now, while it is quiet, and talk to her."

Since he'd first had a go at the wheel of Danny's Bugatti along the long stretch of Six-Mile Lane, Bertie had loved motoring. It was almost as good as being on horseback and more sociable than motorcycling, so it wasn't long before he'd splashed out and bought one of his own. Something sporty but not too flash. The Guv'nor let him keep it in the large garage space and John, the chauffeur, had taught him how to care for it.

"Trickier than a thoroughbred," Bertie would say as he came home in oil-spattered overalls.

Jess would tut, but she enjoyed a spin on Sundays. On one occasion Bertie had crammed six of them plus two of Reg's toddlers into the car and driven down to Southwold for the day. That had been an outing and a half, even allowing for the incident with the pothole and Old Ben's souvenir keg of Adnams.

Bertie had a clear run into Cambridge. Passing a park and two colleges on his right, he turned into Market Street. Just as Mr Smallwood had said, standing a good foot from the pavement, there was Lily in the road. She was trying to engage a passer-by in conversation, waving her newspapers and smiling. Several times, the man lifted his hat and tried to move away, but Lily was not one to give up. A number of men stopped to watch her. Bertie cringed at the thought of what Aunt Mary and Jess would say if they saw her out like this talking to strangers in the street. Lily looked so small, with a big Votes for Women poster tied around her neck and an enormous purple, green and white satchel across her shoulder.

Bertie thought for a minute about the best approach. If he told her to do one thing, she'd just do the opposite for certain. He pulled over.

"Lily?" He tried to sound surprised.

She turned and jumped when she saw him, the shock making her drop a pile of papers into a puddle. Bertie hopped out and retrieved them.

"Horrible day to be standing around." He tidied the papers and tucked them neatly back into her satchel. "Have you got time for some tea? You look like you could do with warming up."

"Well, I'm supposed to be on duty. Trying to do my bit, you know, for the cause, but I've been here for hours and no one seems interested. In fact, one woman told me I should be ashamed of myself and I was behaving like a, well, I can't tell you the word she used." Lily stopped to draw breath. "There was supposed to be another girl with me today, but her mother came and marched her home before we even got started. And, Bertie, they even told me to be sure to keep off the pavement or I'd get arrested for obstruction. But when I did that, I got hooted at."

"Don't get upset now." He felt cross that she had been left to fend for herself, anything could have happened. "Look, Lil, I'm interested in what you are doing. Why not come and tell me all about it over tea? That way you'll still be doing what you are supposed to be doing, but in the warm and dry?"

υ υ υ

"So, when did you get involved in all this?" Bertie asked, after Lily had finished her toasted teacake and made short work of his fruit scone too.

"About a year ago, I suppose. I'd been going to meetings since we met Clar and Flora, but I felt I should do something, so I volunteered at the local branch. Up to now, I've just been working in the shop, selling scarves and bits and pieces. That was fine." Lily paused to top up the teacups. "But, if I'm honest, I'm not sure about some of it. Maybe I'm just not brave enough. I truly believe that women should have the same rights as men, but I agree with Clar that peaceful persuasion is more powerful than violent outbursts. But others feel it is too slow and nothing changes."

"Well, I'm not sure violence ever solved anything, but there seems to be a lot of it around these days and I don't want you to get hurt."

"You are an old worrier, Bertie, but you can't wrap me up in cotton wool. I'm a big girl now, and you have to trust me."

"I do trust you, Lil, it's just other people I'm not so sure of."

"In that case, perhaps you could drop me off at the office and I can get rid of that damn satchel. And please can you buy some of my blasted papers? I can't go back with all of them and no money."

"Alright, just this once, but no more swearing."

Bertie left Lily and drove home, wondering how he could dispose of thirty copies of Lily's newspapers without anyone seeing.

19
Morning of Derby Day, Epsom, 1913

F ROM THE HIGHEST OF the low to the lowest of the high, that's what his dad would say as they walked the course in the early morning and watched the day-trippers arrive. Bertie smiled to himself as he watched the people making their way from the stations. The words never did make much sense but the hill on Derby Day had always been the place for a mix of folk, and nothing had changed.

The steward stood next to him. They watched the open-topped omnibuses ferry parties precariously along the grassy tracks. The passengers jostled and swayed on the top deck, holding out their glasses in beery salutes to the Temperance Society members waving placards below.

"Are you sure you want to go out there, Mr Jones? It's a rough old crowd today."

"Don't you worry, Sam," Bertie patted him on the shoulder. "I'm back on home ground. Nothing is going happen to me here."

The road ahead was black with the tops of the taxicabs crawling along in a juddering convoy dropping off their fares.

"Look at all these motor vehicles. There's not a single one left in London, they say," said Sam. "It's only an hour away now, so every villain and ruffian can get here in no time."

"You've been reading the papers too much, Sam. They're all just here for a good day out." Bertie checked his watch. "Anyway, I'd best be off. Shan't be long."

Bertie tucked the brown-paper parcel under his arm and pulled down his hat. He walked through the gate and out into the crowd. The air was full of carbolic and perfume, masking layers of less attractive smells. People were all dressed up in their Sunday best: shiny boots, polished faces and holiday grins. A family stopped without warning, arguing about where best to make camp. Bertie niftily avoided the pram, umbrellas, baskets, rugs, chairs and other assorted essentials carted along to make a home from home for the day.

It was good to be on this side of the fence. Here he could disappear into the crowd and imagine he was a boy again, flying down the slopes after Reg with the littler ones hanging on to his hands pretending they're racing, pretending they're Dad or Uncle Dick or the Great Jockey himself. But their old vantage point was a railway station now. Why did things always have to change?

Bertie cut away to the left towards the fair. Something sparkled on the white terraces of the grandstand. There was little wind, leaving the flags to twitch rather than fly. Notes faded in and out like a tuneful weather vane, until the booming of the military band caught up with itself and reached right across to the coloured tents. It could have been the National Anthem, but Bertie wasn't sure.

The steam engines were powered up ready to drive the big wheel, merry-go-rounds and more exotic boat swings. They smoked and sighed. They whistled and sang. Hot oily vapour hissed up into the sky and sooty clouds puffed out without warning, so that the light summer clothes of any passers-by soon got a dusting if they were unfortunate enough to get too close at the wrong time. Bertie knew to keep well clear.

He cut past the food stalls, hot fat spitting and sizzling as concoctions fancy and familiar were stirred, chopped and spread. A circle of people gathered as the candy-floss machines whipped up pink fluff that made the air taste sweet and sticky. Toffee apples with their blood-red sugar coating stood lined up on counters like uniformed lollies. Bertie could almost taste the crisp sweet shell shattering under his bite to give way to the sour flesh of the apple inside. This was not the place to linger when you were due in the weighing room in an hour.

Tildy was where she always was. He caught sight of her, out doing the morning rounds before taking refuge in her booth. Her outline was even rounder than last year, a rolled-up hedgehog without the prickles, although some would say that while you may not be able to see the spikes, they were there for sure. Her back was hunched under her layers of shawls, her battered hat tied on with a broad faded ribbon that somehow found a ledge between chin and neck. Bertie watched as she peered through the threadbare weave, glimpsing a smiling young couple walking hand in hand in her direction. She selected her prey like a fox in a field of sheep. Searching out the susceptible, the weak, the ones with preoccupations, she could smell them a mile off.

"You've got a kind face, dear; buy some lucky heather for your pretty lady." She thrust her old willow basket in front of them and held out a little sprig of white flowers. The young man smiled and in response to a prod from his companion, searched in his pocket for some coins. Squinting at the girl, she moved on to the second stage of her patter.

"I can see you've had your troubles, deary, but things are changing. I can see it all written in your face."

"How strange. Can you really? What else do you see?" the girl gushed. She was caught.

Bertie slipped back into the shadow of a deserted Punch and Judy stall that stood to one side, but Tildy saw him.

"I have some business to see to now, but come back later, pretty lady, and I'll tell your fortune."

The girl was disappointed but the couple ambled away.

"Hello, my lovely, you up to your old tricks again?" Bertie joined her.

Tildy turned around and opened her arms.

"Bertie, it's my little Bertie!" Air caught in her throat and the sound came out as a wheezy cackle and cough.

He lifted her up and swung her round.

"Put me down. You in your smart clothes, and all. I'm too heavy for you to be lugging about," but she chuckled.

"There you go. Light as a feather." Bertie put her down gently. "How's my favourite girl?"

"Oh, I'm getting along alright, and always better for seeing you. But shouldn't you be getting ready for the racing, young Bertie, not wasting time with old Tildy?" She gasped a little for breath, puffing in and out.

"Now, Tildy, when have I ever been down here and not come to see you? You know that's the real reason I come." He paused. "Now Reg said be sure to send his best. He can't get down this year what with the new baby and everything."

"I knows. Saw your Ethel the other week. She'd had a letter from Jess. Told me Reg'd given up riding now and was having a bit of a time of it. Seems only yesterday the lot of you'd be charging around here, making such a noise. Your poor mother, she is watching over you, Bertie, she wants you to know that. And didn't I always tell her that you were destined for great things?"

Her gaze was drawing him, but he fought its power and produced the brown paper parcel he had been carrying, all carefully tied with string.

"You open it for me, Bertie. My fingers are not so clever."

He pulled the string and shook out a black silk shawl embroidered with deep pink roses and sage-green leaves.

"Thought you'd be needing a new one for the summer and this will keep you nice and cool in the sun. Our Lily chose it for you."

"That's very kind. Very kind." She held the shawl and stroked it. "So soft. And with tassels. It's so fine. Too fine for an old diddy like me."

"Don't talk so daft, Tildy. Nothing is too fine for you."

"Your dad and ma was always good to me, Bertie. Your dad looked out for us, unlike some of the folk round here." She placed the shawl around her shoulders on top of her old grubby one. "So pretty. I'll never take it off."

"You always say that, but you don't have to wear them all at once," Bertie watched at her as she ran her hands over the material. "But you do whatever makes you happy."

Tildy smiled at him and touched his face. A troubled look came into her eyes.

"There's something I wanted to say to you, but it's gone from my mind. I'm old, getting old, too old. An old, mad woman, that's what I am."

"You talk more sense than most, so don't you be saying otherwise."

They stood quietly for a moment.

"Do you have to ride today, Bertie?"

"Yes, of course I do."

"In purple and green?"

"No, Tildy, purple and red, the King's colours, you know that."

"Well, you be careful. There's strange folk about."

"It's all alright, Tildy. Don't worry. Anyway I've got to get to our Ethel's in time for tea, wouldn't dare be late for that now, would I?"

The young couple had returned and were standing watching them, their mouths slightly open.

"Look, these good people are waiting to see you." He jerked his head in their direction. "I'll leave you to get on."

Tildy put out her arm and held on to him. An overwhelming feeling of sadness and love tugged at his heart as he looked at her lined face. Bertie kissed her hand.

"I'll see you tomorrow." He'd make sure then that she had everything that she could possibly need. "And don't overdo things today."

As he went to leave, the young couple held out a racecard. "Would you sign this for us, Mr Jones? And do you have any good tips for us today, sir?"

Bertie smiled. "Oh yes, indeed I do, a very good tip."

"Are you able to share it with us, sir?"

"Certainly I will, young man."

The young couple licked their lips.

"Keep your money in your pocket, that's my tip!" he laughed and gently patted Tildy on the arm as he walked away.

ᴜ ᴜ ᴜ

The crowd huddled in and cheered as he walked towards to the parade ring. Bertie smiled and waved, signing more cards.

"How do you fancy your chances, Mr Jones?" A small red-headed boy with a face full of freckles wriggled his way through several pairs of legs to appear right in front of Bertie.

The stewards closed in around him.

"It's all right," Bertie put out his arm to hold them back, then crouched down in front of the boy. "Well, me and the horse, we'll do our best. Will you keep your fingers crossed for me?"

The boy nodded. "Will you see the King today, sir?"

"Well, I expect he'll want to come and say hello to his horse at some time, so I'd better go or I'll be in trouble if I'm late." He stood up and patted the boy's head.

"Oi, Bert!" a familiar voice called.

Percy stood out above everyone else. Even though his hair was neatly cut and smacked down with Macassar, it still shone gold.

"Hello there! Do you know, I was just thinking about you."

"Blimey, I won't ask you for a penny for them."

"Ha! Oh, and, Perce, while you are on about pennies, can you give that little lad there a few for some sweets?"

"Leave it with me." Percy looked at the boy and back to Bertie. "Bullseyes, eh?"

"Bullseyes would be just right!" Bert called back, catching the boy tugging at Percy's jacket out of the corner of his eye.

Bertie reached the jockeys' room. There seemed to be double the usual number of police and officials.

"All rather heavy handed today, isn't it?" Bertie spoke to one of the stewards.

"Them upstairs are nervous, rumour is there could be trouble."

"Well, if you listened to everything they said, we wouldn't get anything done."

"You're right there, Mr Jones."

In the parade ring, Anmer was spruced up and smart. He certainly looked handsome enough to be a winner. In an unusual display of temper, Anmer twitched and stamped his hooves as Bertie approached.

"Don't know what's got into him," said Nick, the stable lad, as he tried to calm the horse. "Perhaps he's missing Old Ben."

"Well, I can understand that: so am I. It doesn't seem right without him, but I'm sure he'll be better soon and back keeping us all in order."

Bertie jumped up into the saddle. "It's alright, Anmer, not long now and we'll both be back before we know it."

Craganour, the shipbuilder's horse, walked past, looking fine. Booing broke out nearby. Reiff was up and glaring at everyone.

"So much bad feeling everywhere this year." The Guv'nor looked around. "I think you should lead them out now, Bertie, the stewards are getting worried."

Anmer shivered. Bertie reassured him and they set off for the start.

PART IV
AFTER THE FALL

20

Going home,
June 1913

A KNOCK ON THE DOOR. The sharp pain along his left side told him not to move. The bed felt strange. The height and shape of the room were unfamiliar. Chinks of light coming through the heavy curtains put the sun in the wrong place. The window should be on the other side. Mothballs and stale tobacco lingered in a way that they never did at home.

Moving his head to one side, the room started to spin. Queasiness rippled along his stomach. Strange shadows faded in and out. Sounds tumbled and clattered in his brain as he tried to recall the tucked-away images that he knew were there but just couldn't reach. He thought he heard Flora calling, but then Tildy was lulling him back to sleep. With the ripe soft ground under him, he disappeared.

"Bertie, are you awake?"

He opened his eyes as best he could. Heavy and sticky, the lids barely moved.

He knew the voice. It took him a long way back. He turned, not so bad this time. Jess stood solid against the white-painted doorframe.

"Where am I?" The words felt far away. He wasn't sure if he had said them.

"You're in London, Bert, in a hotel right by the station, so it'll be easy to get the train home. You came here from Epsom yesterday." Jess's skirts rustled. Her step was steady and firm. "You took a bit of a fall in the race."

Clenching his jaw, Bertie inched up the bed. Jess stood over him.

"Stay still, Bertie love. The doctor will be here again soon." She smoothed his hair. "Oh, your poor face. I can't see you under there, you're so swollen up."

He heard her stifled sobs and he could smell the lavender water that she always dabbed on her handkerchief. Bertie tried to reach out to her.

"What's all this then, Jess?"

"Nothing, just a bit of hayfever." She started to straighten the bedding. "It's good that the bruising is coming out. It means you're getting better, see?"

"This takes me back to when I was little, you'd always look after me if I was poorly."

"And you were always so brave, not like that Percy."

Another knock on the door. A tall figure beamed at him from around Jess's shoulder. Bertie knew the man but had to trawl his mind to find a name.

"Walter?" he said at last. "Why are you here?"

"I'm under strict instructions from the Guv'nor to look after you and not to come back until accompanied by your good self."

"Bertie is still very tired, Walter," Jess interrupted, "so I think we shouldn't trouble him too much just now."

"I want to go home, Jess." Bertie said, but the drowsiness was returning. "Can we go home?"

ʊ ʊ ʊ

Quiet voices, whispering, echoed through the darkness.

"What do we tell him? I don't want him upset and he doesn't remember ... "

Remember? Doesn't remember. Doesn't remember. His thoughts swam through the words, but he was far away. *What don't I remember? Tell me, Jess?* He tried to open his mouth to call but his mind could not control his body or reach out to his sister. He saw himself lying there on the bed. A dim outline of a face, all eyes and white skin, hovered above him. *Who are you?* Her mouth opened, black nothingness behind it.

Walter's voice entered his thoughts.

"Better he hears it from us, Jess. The press will be waiting, I'm afraid. I've tried to keep them at bay and the hotel has done its best, but they will be around."

"Newsmen? Bloodhounds more like! Well, let him sleep for a bit more, the doctor said that it would do him good, then we'll talk to him."

Bertie's heart began to pump harder, beating in time to a gallop, in time to the hooves as they hit the ground. His ears buzzed with the sound of drumming, a backbeat to the breeze hissing a tune as horses and men curved and dived among it. One long baying body blurring around him. A fluttering bird swooping down, pulling him out from his saddle, so he too could fly, taking him up, up and then dropping him floundering towards the earth. Dim in the background he could hear the voices, but they no longer troubled him.

∪ ∪ ∪

A rattle of crockery woke him. Still here, Bertie thought. He tried to sit up and although it was painful, at least the room wasn't spinning like it had been.

"Hello there, Bertie, I've made you some tea."

Jess held out the cup for him. Swallowing was hard but the tea tasted good.

Walter pointed at a chair on the other side of the bed. "May I, old chap?"

Bertie tried to nod.

"Well," Walter started, glancing over at Jess. "I'm not sure how much you remember about yesterday?"

"Not a lot. Maybe a bit more than earlier?" Bertie's voice felt stronger. He thought back. The Derby. Coming down the hill. He looked into the distance, trying to picture the race.

"I must have been thrown. Nothing, nothing. I don't remember anything until I woke up here." Bertie thought of the horse. "But Anmer? Poor Anmer? Is he alright?"

"Anmer's fine." Walter spoke quietly. "But a woman ran out from the crowd and into your horse."

The clock on the mantelpiece ticked steadily. Bertie took another sip of tea.

"What happened to her?"

Walter watched him. "She's in hospital. Still unconscious, I understand. They say that her recovery is likely to take some time."

"I see." But Bertie didn't see at all. How was it possible not to remember? "And the others?"

"They managed to swerve round. Miracle really. Young Snowy was right behind you. No one else was hurt though."

"Well, that's a mercy." Bertie's eyes closed, without him being able to stop them. "Home, I just want to go home."

ʊ ʊ ʊ

Jess retrieved the old leather case, running her hand over the grain and unclicking the locks.

"This has certainly seen some use, eh, our Bert?"

The neatly folded clothes were shaken out and draped over a chair. Collar and studs, toiletries and brushes were neatly arranged on the dressing table.

"There, that should be everything. I'll get these pressed for you though." Jess held the jacket and trousers and went over to the bell. "Can't have you going home looking all crumpled."

"What with the rest of me being enough to frighten the horses, I'm not sure anyone will notice the creases in my clothes."

"Come on, Bertie, you know you like things all neat. It will make you feel better and they'll do it in no time for you."

ʊ ʊ ʊ

Bertie stood with his left arm strapped tight. For a moment he felt reluctant to leave the safety of the room, but his desire to get home was stronger than his need for comfort.

"It will be better to take the side door, it leads directly into the station." The hotel manager clicked his heels and bowed his head. "Please follow me."

Walter stepped forward. "Will you be alright walking?"

"I'll be fine, really. Thank you, Walter." Bertie tried to reassure himself as much as anyone.

Jess adjusted Bertie's jacket and secured his hat. They followed the manager and the manager's assistant along the trail of plush oriental carpet to the caged lift. The assistant manager pulled the wrought-iron door across. A second set of doors then came together automatically, sealing them into a cube of shining copper. The lift creaked down to the ground floor.

The luggage boy was already waiting for them.

"Mr Jones, I wish you a speedy recovery and hope that you will return to our hotel under more favourable circumstances." The manager and the assistant manager bowed in unison. "Jimmy will look after you."

"This way, sir." The luggage boy went ahead, checking they were still behind him. It was quiet in the station. The boy whistled over a porter and gave him instructions.

"Give the lad a sixpence, Jess. It's a bit awkward for me," Bertie whispered.

"Sounds rather a lot, Bert. Thruppence would be more than generous."

"Jess, please. Just do it for me."

After much huffing, sixpence was found in pennies and handed over.

"Thank you, ma'am. And hope you feel better soon, Mr Jones." The boy ran off back to the hotel.

Walter had been checking the departures. "The train will be leaving in ten minutes, so we can go and take our seats."

"Mr Jones! Mr Jones!" A small man in a tweed suit and worn bowler hat came rushing towards them. He waved a card at them. "I'm from the Press Association. Might I trouble you for a few words, sir?"

"Really, I don't think Mr Jones is well enough for this." Walter went to shoo the man away.

"Well, if you don't mind me saying, sir, better Mr Jones speaks to me and I can hold off the others. They'll be along in a minute when they sniff out you've left the hotel."

"It's alright, Walter. He's just trying to do his job and I have to do mine." Bertie looked at the man. The press had always been very kind to him.

"Thank you, Mr Jones, much appreciated. How are you feeling, sir?"

"Much better, thank you."

"And do you remember anything?"

"Very little, I'm afraid. I was thrown and woke up very stiff and sore."

"Don't you remember the woman?"

"Bertie, we really must go and get the train," Walter intervened. "We don't want Mr Jones to tire himself, do we?"

Bertie's head was starting to ache again. "Very unfortunate. I hope she recovers soon. Terrible accident," he said.

"But, Mr Jones, it wasn't an accident." The man looked straight at him. "It was a suffragette. She was protesting. What do you think about that?"

Bertie put his hand to his brow. "I, er, I don't know anything about that."

The man stood to one side. Jess glared at him. Another man holding a camera appeared. "One quick picture, Mr Jones."

"Well really," Jess started. "I think this is too much."

The photographer's lamp flashed white. Shining stars fluttered down from the glass roof, a sparkling kaleidoscope in a giant greenhouse, an airless chamber. Bertie swayed. Jess was there, her hand was strong under his elbow and supported him.

"Will you be alright a minute, Jess, I'll get help." said Walter.

A man's voice cut in. "May I offer my assistance, madam?"

Cool air moved across over Bertie's face. The photographer was fanning a newspaper in front of him.

"Does that feel a bit better, Bert?" asked Jess.

"Yes, yes, I just came over a bit odd there."

The man looked at Jess. "Is there anything I can get you at all?"

"Thank you, but we're fine now, really," said Jess.

"Well, keep the paper, it is as hot as hell in here." The photographer turned to Bertie, hesitating for a moment. "You probably don't remember me, Mr Jones, but I've been taking your photograph for many years, right back to the days of Diamond Jubilee and all his pranks."

Bertie managed a smile. "You know I think you do look familiar. I'm sorry, but I'm not quite myself at the moment."

"Don't trouble yourself, Mr Jones. You get yourself better and I'll be seeing you from behind my lens again in no time."

The photographer raised his hat and picked up his case to go. He looked at Jess. "You best get on the train, though. That boy at the hotel has been tipping the wink to anyone who'll pay him. That's how come we got here first, bought an exclusive, but it won't last."

"That cunning little devil, I told you not to tip him so much." Jess sighed.

Walter Venn rushed over with a railway official.

"Mr Jones, sir, I'm the guard on your train. Very sorry to hear about your, er, accident." The man's jacket puckered around his stomach as he stood to attention. "We'll find you a quiet carriage. I won't let anyone near, don't you worry. Terrible business, my brother-in-law was down at Epsom on Derby Day. He saw what happened."

Walter interrupted "If you would be so kind, I really think that Mr Jones should get settled now."

"Oh yes, yes, of course."

They helped Bertie up on to the train and into the carriage. Bertie wanted to ask the guard what his brother-in-law had seen, but part of him was too tired to ask and part of him didn't want to know.

υ υ υ

Flashes of memory came back to Bertie as they travelled home. The jerky rhythm of the train became the movement of the stretcher as it rattled over the turf, the squeaking wheels, the jolting as the sides banged against the doorframe of the jockeys' room. So many hands, so much noise. Faces leaning in and peering at him, the feeling that he was different, part of himself was gone, disappeared, replaced by something other, foreign, like a piece of patch sewn into his soul. It must be the medicine giving him strange thoughts, that's what Reg would say.

"Just a few minutes to go, Bertie." Walter was busy taking the bags down from the luggage rack.

Outside, the layers of sooty grey buildings had been replaced by the vast skies and billowing trees of home. It was early evening but the sun was still strong through the glass. He squinted and his face felt like it would burst. The pain made him break into a sweat.

A voice called out the station name in the familiar Suffolk drawl. The uniforms of the local constabulary stood out among the passengers lining the platform. Bertie picked up the newspaper given to them by the photographer and tucked it under his good arm. Putting one leg down awkwardly after the other, he followed Walter. Jess stayed close.

The guard and the stationmaster rushed over with a porter in tow. John, the Guv'nor's driver, was helping Old Ben along. Old Ben looked older and smaller than ever, all dressed up in his Sunday best and scuttling along as fast as his rheumatism would allow.

"Bertie! Bertie! How are you, Bertie?"

"I'm alright, Ben, see?" he said. "You shouldn't be coming all the way out here."

"We had the devil of a job keeping Old Ben away." John spoke to him quietly "He's been very upset about it all, so Mr Marsh thought it best he came."

"Speak up, John," called out Old Ben.

"Very pleased to have him back, aren't we?" said John, much louder this time.

The station was busy for this time on a Thursday. People stood around, talking behind their hands. Some, at least, pretended not to stare. "Three cheers for the King's jockey!" shouted a man in the crowd and they all joined in. Bertie put his hand up to them, but the noise and the bustle were making him feel light-headed.

"Come on, Bertie, let's get you back," said Jess, guiding him by the elbow.

The car was parked just outside the station. Two policemen stood guard.

"Mr Marsh sent the Bentley. He thought it would be more comfortable." John said, opening the door.

Old Ben fussed around. "See this, we're very honoured, Bertie. The Guv'nor's pride and joy this is. He treats it almost as well as one of his thoroughbreds."

The spicy scent of polished wood and baked leather was inviting. The seats felt like hot-water bottles, just right for sweating out a fever.

"And I'll sit next to you, shall I, Bertie? We can a bit of a chat then," said Old Ben. "Do you want me to move over for you, Jess?"

"That's alright, Ben. You stay there with Bertie, I can sit up front with John."

"And I'll take the dicky seat so you don't get squashed," Walter called out.

John drove off gently and Old Ben brought Bertie up to date with all the local goings-on.

"A lot of people wanted to come and see you, Bertie, but me and Reg spoke to the Guv'nor. We thought it best to just have a few of us, only close family, as it were."

The car almost came to a halt as it turned into the lane. Bertie opened his eyes. Everything around him seemed so alive. Poppies, blood-red this year, fluttered along the verge among the cow parsley and moon daisies. Birds dipped in and out of the stick-dry hedgerows, some caught up in a courtship dance, some burdened with moss and twigs to shore up their nests, some defending their spot with a sweet-sounding song deceptive in its beauty. A blackbird paused, checking for prying eyes while a clutch of pink-bellied worms writhed helpless in its orange beak. The yellow light of evening cast freckles through the trees and diamonds in the emerald shade. The white gates and picket fencing stood pristine and neat. Everything was just as he'd left it just a few days ago; but then again, somehow it wasn't.

John tooted the horn when they passed the stables. The lads lined up in their shirtsleeves, fresh from their afternoon chores, caps pushed back, hot sticky hair plastered to their shiny faces. Bertie thought of himself and Reg, and of all those years they had stood there. For a moment he saw them, the two of them boys again, staring back at him.

"They've come out to welcome you home, Bertie." Old Ben's voice was thin and cracked, his chin trembled and tears were on his cheek.

Bertie gave them a thumbs up; it was all he could manage. But Old Ben more than made up for it as he waved in a very stately manner.

The black and white timber framework of Lodge Villas came into sight, standing out against the red roof tiles and brick walls. The gables towered above, offering shelter under the geometric shadows thrown down on to the spotless courtyard. The windows were open and the front door was propped ajar.

Lily, Reg and Bill were standing on the path to the front cottage, Nell behind them. Lily ran ahead and got to the car just as Walter jumped off the dicky seat and opened the door. Bertie got out slowly, uncurling his limbs and straightening himself out, glad to feel a breeze after the stuffiness of the car.

Lily stopped in her tracks, looking first at Bertie and then at Jess, then back to Bertie again. She covered her face and sobbed so much she shook from head to foot.

"There, there, Lil," Bertie tried to put his arm around her shoulders, but the pain was too sharp. "I'll be right as rain in a few days."

"Now then, Lil, Bertie doesn't want to hear you carrying on. Come along with me," said Jess.

Bertie turned towards his brothers, who stood back waiting their turn.

"Thank God you're alright, Bert," Reg cupped both his hands around Bertie's uninjured one. "We've been so worried about you."

"Ah, it looks worse than it is." Bertie noticed that Reg's fingers felt cold, almost icy, even though the day was warm.

Bertie tried to give him a mock punch. "Have you been looking after things for me, Bill?"

"Tried to, Bert," Bill scuffed his boots in the dust. "We've got a match on Sunday if you're up to coming. I've got the pitch all good and ready."

"Perce and Clar are coming up Sunday," Reg said. "And the rest of the boys too if they can get away."

Bertie swayed and his knees buckled. He grabbed hold of Reg to steady himself.

"Come on now, Bert, I think you should be inside and sitting down," said Jess.

Lily came over to him and kissed him lightly on the less bruised side of his face. "Jess said that would be alright as long as I didn't crush you with my enthusiasm."

"Me and Bill have got the cases. Haven't we, Bill?" called out Old Ben, snatching a bag from John's hands and hobbling off with it.

"He shouldn't be doing all this, but it's no use arguing with him," Bill muttered as he took the other bag and followed Old Ben.

Bertie watched them and turned to Nell.

"Those two, eh? I don't know how Jess copes with us all. Thank you for looking after them, Nell."

"It's you that's needs looking after now, Bertie," she replied.

Old Ben came rushing back down the path.

"That tea is looking very tasty, Nell. We don't want to let it spoil though."

ʊ ʊ ʊ

Bertie was installed on one of the big chairs in the parlour. He had his cup of tea by his side and was listening to them all talking around him. There was a loud rap on the door. Old Ben got up and looked out of the window.

"It's the Guv'nor, Bertie. I knew he'd come."

Bertie went to prise himself up. The Guv'nor was still in his work clothes and his presence made the room seem small.

"Bertie! No, no, don't get up. You stay right there. I don't want to interrupt. Just wanted to see how you were doing."

"Not too bad, thank you, Guv'nor. Glad to be home."

The Guv'nor leaned towards him, there was a faint smell of whisky on his breath. The thread veins on his face stood out more than usual, making his skin appear particularly puce. "We'll take care of you now, Bertie. Don't you worry."

The Guv'nor gazed out of the window and took a deep breath, sucking the air in until it looked like his buttons would burst. He thumped his right fist hard into the palm of his left hand. The loud clap made them all jump.

"Intolerable. That's what it is. Intolerable," he shouted to no one in particular. "I just can't believe this terrible business. How dare she, that woman, how dare she do this to you, to us, to the King! His Majesty has made it quite clear that this will not be tolerated." The Guv'nor beat his palm again and again. "God knows what is happening to this country when you can't even hold a race meeting, let alone the Derby, without it being jeopardized. I tell you, if she was my daughter or my wife, I'd give her a damn good hiding."

Lily gasped and started to cry. Jess tried to comfort Lily. Bertie put his hand over his eyes. Old Ben went to the Guv'nor.

"It's alright now, Master Dick."

The Guv'nor stopped suddenly and looked surprised to see Old Ben standing there.

164

"I'm sorry, I don't know what came over me. This isn't the time or place for this." The Guv'nor took out his handkerchief and wiped his face. "It's just that I am so, so outraged."

They all sat in silence. The throaty coo-coo of a wood pigeon echoed down the chimney.

"Cup of tea, sir?" suggested Jess.

"And a bit of cake, Guv'nor?" asked Old Ben. "Come on now, Master Dick, you know you're fond of a bit of fruit cake."

Jess hunted around for another cup and saucer. Bill offered up his chair. Lily gave Bill hers and perched on the edge of Bertie's.

Later that evening, Bertie was sitting in the garden. Jess had put a small table next to the chair and left a jug of home-made lemon barley water for him. It was covered with a muslin circle, weighted down by beads that tapped against the glass in the breeze. He listened to the blackbirds rustling through the undergrowth around the trees. Shutting his eyes and raising his face to the sun, he could hear the horses calling in the distance. Shovels scraped on the cobbles of the yard, the odd shout broke the peace and quiet of his seclusion. Spots of cold came across him, as a wisp of cloud or breeze-blown branches intercepted the light. He wanted to be back with the others, back with the horses, back at work, back before all this, but his mind was tired and his body ached.

Jess came and sat next to him. She started to sort out her mending box.

"Jess?"

"Yes, Bertie?"

"If she dies, Jess, will I be a murderer?"

"What? No, of course not, Bert. What are you thinking? What could you have done?" Jess tutted. "The woman was deranged, mad. She nearly killed you. She wants locking up."

She stopped herself and patted his hand. "Anyway, no one could accuse you of anything, poor Bertie. But it makes my blood boil, it really does."

◡ ◡ ◡

Bertie was awake. It was completely dark in his bedroom. He could see nothing. All around him the warm summer mustiness seeped from the walls of the cottage. The frantic dreams had stopped. He could not recall them, but his body still shook with their memory. As his eyes began to adjust, he could make out the familiar shape of objects around his room. The solid blackness of the chest of drawers gave way to a grey glimmer of the mirror and his brush set, polished and clean. He imagined the washstand at the far end with its bowl and jug; shaving brush, soap and razor all neat and tidy with two crisp fresh towels folded to one side. The wardrobe was in the corner with his wooden valet stand next to it. Bertie fretted that he couldn't remember laying out anything for himself to wear the next day. Finally, there was a chair and table to one side of the window, where he'd sometimes sit and look out over the garden.

The need for some cool, fresh air became too much. Bertie levered himself upright, trying to avoid too much weight falling on to his ribs and shoulder. Slowing placing one foot down then the other, Bertie managed to stand and lumber over to the window. The floorboards creaked in places he'd never noticed before. His awkward gait and heavy tread made him a stranger to himself.

At the window, he drew back the curtains. A white moth fluttered against the pane. It kept missing the way out and stayed stuck on its path, trying to beat its way through the glass. Bertie managed to catch it awkwardly. He feared he'd hurt it, but the quivering tickle against his palms told him it was fine. With his good arm, Bertie elbowed open the casement as far as it would go and opened his hands. The moth stopped for a moment, tested its wings and made a bid for freedom.

The smell of warm dew-sodden earth mingled with the honeysuckle and the rambling rose that clung to the wall outside. There was no sign of dawn, and there was not even a trace of pale moonlight to turn the night into a cold shadow of day. "God, who made the earth and heaven, darkness and light;" the words of the hymn floated through his mind, balm to the fevered soul. Bertie looked at the black horizon where layer upon layer of silver dots bloomed still and silent. Frothy swathes of Milky Way weaved through the sky and the shape of the Plough shone bright, its crook reaching out in an invisible line to the Pole Star. Only the screech of an owl landing its prey and the willow tree hissing in the breeze told him that there was still a world alive outside.

What if it had been one of his sisters? But that would never happen; he'd never have let them. Bertie half smiled to himself at the thought of trying to stop Jess, or Lily, or even dear old Ethel, doing anything they'd set their minds to do. His thoughts went back to Cambridge, and Lily in her sash selling leaflets on the road. He shivered and walked slowly back to his bed, stopping to take a sip of the medicine that the doctor had left. Climbing in under the covers, Bertie shifted himself into a comfortable position.

A cold draught on his face woke him. It was still dark. He felt trapped in this eternal night. Goosebumps tightened his skin and the back of his neck tingled. "Hello?" he called, or at least he thought he did. Pulling himself up, he took a look around. All seemed in order, although it was too quiet; no clock ticking; no sounds of the house settling. He tried to clear his head and to settle back down; it must be the medicine playing tricks with his head again.

When Bertie woke he could hear the bell in the chapel ringing. He sat up in bed. It must be Sunday. The clock in the tower struck ten.

"Well, you look better today." Jess brought in a mug of tea and a plate of buttered bread and jam. "We thought you were never going to wake up, but the doctor said to leave you and that rest was what you needed."

Bertie tucked into the breakfast.

"I'll be off to church in a minute. Is there anything else you'd like before I go?" asked Jess.

The rough stubble scratched as he ran his hand across his face.

"No thanks, Jess, a good clean-up is what I need. Then maybe I'll take a wander up to the stables. I could do with a bit of exercise, otherwise I'll be seizing up."

"Don't you go rushing around too much, Bertie. Rest and quiet, that's what the doctor said."

Old Ben and Bill popped their heads around the door. Jess hurried them out.

"Don't you two start, else he'll be on the cricket pitch this afternoon." She clapped her hands. "Now, get yourselves ready or we'll miss the start of the service. Let's leave him to a bit of peace and quiet."

After they'd left, Bertie got up, shaved, washed and dressed. Grabbing his jacket, he walked out of the back door and headed off to the stables. It was good to be outside. He felt alive again as the movement made his blood flow and his nerves tingle. He looked at the living things around him, touching the wild flowers and running his fingers through the hedgerow still wet with dew.

At the stables, men were posted like sentries around the buildings and the lanes. Bertie could see Mr Smallwood talking to one of the young lads. The lad's shirt was torn and blood soaked, and he held a cloth to a cut above his eye.

"But I couldn't just let them say those things, sir, it wasn't right. They keep on and on at us every time we pass them."

"I understand that, Tommy, but it doesn't help the situation. They are trying to goad you into saying things, telling them things. That's their job." Mr Smallwood stopped as he saw Bertie. "Hello, Bertie. Didn't expect to see you up and about."

"Fancied a bit of air this morning. Jess told me I wasn't up to church, so thought I'd just take a look at the horses. See how Anmer was doing." Bertie looked at Tommy. "But what's happened here?"

"Well, Bertie, it seems that there are men from the press outside the gates. Pretty much camping there, I understand. Asking the boys all sorts of questions on their way in. It started a couple of days ago but seems to have suddenly got out of hand. One of them tried to stop young Tommy and this is the result."

"Surely it can't still be what happened at Epsom?" said Bertie.

Walter came over to join them, sending Tommy off with one of the senior lads. "Well, yes. It seems to be the case. It will all blow over by tomorrow, I'm sure. They'll get fed up, but in the meantime we want to make sure that everything is looked after."

"Do you want me to talk to them?" asked Bertie.

"No, no, Bertie, the Guv'nor was very clear about that," said Walter. "Anyway, I just telephoned Sergeant Green and he's sending out some of his boys. Sandringham have been very helpful too, they are drafting in some of their men as well."

"See, Bertie, there's nothing for you to worry about. Just get some rest," said Mr Smallwood.

"And it may be wise to stay on the estate for a few days too," added Walter.

Bertie turned to go. "I was hoping it would all blow over, but it's all a bit of a mess really, isn't it?"

At the cottage, Bertie went to his room and retrieved the newspaper that the photographer had left at the station. It was still in the pocket of his bag. He looked at the front page. It took him a few moments to take it in. A blurred image of the racecourse, with Anmer on his back, hooves in the air and a woman lying on the turf, her hat rolling away from her, the crowd several deep, most still watching the race up ahead. It was inset with small round portraits of them either side, the woman and him, as if they'd been joined in some unholy union. "Suffragette nearly killed by the King's colt," read the headline.

So that's how it is, then? Bertie closed his eyes and opened them again, as if trying to wish it all away. Furrowing his brow until the muscles in his face ached, he tried to think. The words said that they, he and Anmer, had nearly killed the woman. Was there something they could have done, or not done? Bertie sighed until he was hollow and empty, until he could feel nothing inside.

υ υ υ

"There are piles of letters here, Bertie. Walter's just brought them over for you," said Bill, bringing in a great basket full to the top with envelopes of all shapes and thicknesses. "Half the country must have written, I reckon."

"There's some from Sandringham too, by the look of it." Jess picked up a handful. "Don't know how some of them got here at all. Look at the addresses. This one says, 'The King's Jockey, Stables, Buckingham Palace'."

Bertie started to open them up and passed them round.

"This one is from a young lad in Yorkshire, saying 'Get well soon' with a picture of me falling off a horse, by the looks of it. Umm."

"Well, it's going to take a month of Sundays to reply to this lot."

"Don't worry. I'll help you, Bertie," Lily appeared behind him and gave him a light peck on his cheek.

"Lily, what on earth? How did you get through the gates? Mr Smallwood said that there were men from the newspapers surrounding the place."

"Yes, I saw, so I slipped round the back and climbed over fence, through the wood and over the lawn. I saw Mrs Marsh and explained. And I really can help with the replies if you'd like. I've been learning to type."

"You?" Bill laughed into his cup.

"Yes, I'm quite independent these days, Bill, thank you. And I'll need to get a job and support myself one day. I want to be like Flora, with a place of my own."

"Not find yourself a nice young man, Lil?" asked Bill.

"Well, I might do, if there are any left after Reg and Bertie have finished chasing them all away."

"Only the unsuitable ones, Lil. You know that we'd be pleased for you to settle down with someone respectable," said Bertie.

"What do you mean by respectable? I might not like respectable." Lily paused as Jess shook her head at her to get her to stop. "Anyway, I'm quite looking forward to going out into the world. Although, I haven't said anything to Aunt Mary yet, so don't mention it if you see her."

Lily carried on going through the post.

"Nothing from those suffragettes then," said Jess. "You'd think that Mrs Pankhurst could at least bother to send a note to see how you're getting along."

Bertie didn't particularly want to hear from them; after all, what was there to say? He just wanted the woman to recover and the whole incident to be forgotten, then things could get back to normal.

"The Pankhursts and the WSPU didn't have anything to do with it. She acted on her own." Lily pulled a chair up next to Bertie and sat down. "Or so they say."

"Well, they would say that, wouldn't they?" Jess clicked her tongue. "Anyway, they've got their martyr, so I hope that they're satisfied."

"Not yet they haven't Jess," said Bertie. "While there's life and all that. Let's hope and pray that she comes round."

"Well, they say she'll be charged if she does." Jess put down the teapot with such a thud that a wave of dark liquid dotted with leaves slopped out of the spout. "And she deserves it, if you ask me. Walter told me that even though she's in hospital, she is under police custody."

"Well, I think that the poor woman is a damn fool, but I just want an end to it." Bertie turned to Lily, who had appointed herself chief letter-opener. "Come on, Lil, read out another one."

Letters and cards were passed round; some were on crested paper, some on greasy scraps. There were more children's drawings of horses, knitted scarves, tins of sweets, and a pack of sugar knobs for Anmer, which Jess said would do very nicely in the house as she happened to know that racehorses were not allowed them.

"This one is very well addressed, even has the cottage number on it and such beautiful lavender paper," said Lily as she opened it. "It says, er, well, nothing really, just the usual, about getting better."

"Read it, then, we'll never get through this lot otherwise." Bill tried to grab the letter.

"I'll try and find a more interesting one." Lily riffled through the basket, but Bertie noticed that she slipped the lavender envelope into her pocket.

᪥ ᪥ ᪥

Bertie woke with a start. He felt cold and his neck was painful from lying awkwardly in the deckchair. He moved his head from side to side carefully to ease it, stretching out the rest of his body. The others had all gone in. The bell of the chapel struck up. Bertie looked at his watch. Evensong. A stroll across the meadow would do him good and some time in prayer would calm him.

He got up and brushed himself down, smoothing his hair, then putting back his hat. This would have to do and he felt sure that on this occasion the good Lord would forgive him. He called through to door to Jess, but she and Lily were deep in conversation. Bertie decided not to disturb them and set off across the paddock to the church.

It was only a small congregation and they were all seated when he got there. A quiet, solemn piece that he didn't recognize was playing on the organ. Bertie paused by the entrance and peered into the darkness. A woman was seated at the keyboard. Her clothes were black and she wore a hat. The hat was like the one that had flown through the air that day.

"Welcome, Bertie." The vicar guided him in.

"If it is alright with you, vicar, I'll just sit at the back and listen. Not much of a voice today."

Bertie slipped into a pew at the back. The choir started the low call and the singing soothed him. He knew the words by heart but did not try to speak them. The sound of the voices lifted him to a place of rest and he closed his eyes to feel the music better.

Something disturbed the stillness of the building. A shiver made him groan out loud. Beads of sweat made their way down his neck, settling in his collar. He mouthed the words of the Lord's Prayer and his breath lightened. The woman at the organ turned around. How could he have not recognized her? It was Flora.

At the end of the service, Bertie made his way to the entrance. Flora rushed to catch him up.

"Bertie, Bertie. Let me walk with you."

"I didn't realize you were back."

"I came as soon as I could. And I did go round to your hotel in London, but, well, it just got too complicated. I came to see you yesterday too but they said you were sleeping."

"That's very kind of you to go to so much trouble."

"Of course it's no trouble. Surely you knew, I mean, did you think I wouldn't come?" She looked at him and sighed.

Bertie felt tired, too tired to talk, and was relieved to see the garden gate coming into view.

"I'm sorry, Flora."

"It's me who's sorry, Bertie. You just get yourself well." She kissed him lightly on his bruised cheek and stroked it softly.

He watched her go back towards the big house, her step getting faster and faster until she was running. Poor Flora. He shouldn't let her leave like that but he didn't have the strength to follow. His head buzzed and he felt he was falling. He caught the gatepost and steadied himself. At the window, a head darted back behind the curtain. Then Jess was rushing down the path towards him. Walter and Bill were behind her.

"Bert?" she took his arm.

"It's alright, Jess." Walter stepped in front of her. "I've got him."

"I'm fine. I'm fine," Bertie protested.

" 'Course you are, Bert, here you go."

Walter and Bill helped him inside and into an armchair.

"There you go Bertie. Rest a bit now," Jess tucked a rug around him.

He looked at their faces.

"She's dead, isn't she?"

ひ ひ ひ

Bertie caught up with Walter as he walked from the Guv'nor's office to the stables.

"Walter, can you tell me what's going on? People are being very kind, but they don't tell me what is happening."

"No one's trying to keep anything from you, Bertie, and even if they are, it's only because they don't want you to worry." Walter fiddled with the edge of the brown leather document case he carried under his arm.

"But sometimes, feeling you're being kept in the dark is worse than knowing. And I do want to know."

"Quite right, Bertie. I do understand." Walter looked at him. "Well, the inquest has been set for tomorrow, but you are not fit enough to attend. The doctor will contact the coroner, and they will understand."

"But nobody asked me. I should like to be asked," Bertie said.

"I know, but we thought in the circumstances you wouldn't want to be reminded."

"Yes, but it might have shed some light on what happened. Given me some answers." Bertie took off his cap and scratched his head. "Still, there will be a funeral. I ought to pay my respects."

Walter paused. "The trouble is that it isn't as simple as that, old chap. I know that you want to do the proper thing, but, you see, others may try to use the situation and it could be, well, be difficult. To be honest, it has been made very clear to the Guv'nor that you are not to go."

Bertie walked back to the cottage, trying to make sense of what Walter was trying to tell him. Jess's voice rang out loud and clear as

173

he approached the front path; something had got her into a state. Reg and Lily were with her in the back garden.

"Ah, Bertie, look at this." Jess waved a letter. "I was just saying, there's a letter here from a bishop who thinks you should go along to the funeral. Why would you want to pay your respects to someone who could have killed you? Why?"

Bertie looked at her. "Well, I can think of a number of reasons. How about human kindness for a start?"

Jess threw the letter down. "For heaven's sake, Bertie. Only a few days ago, you could hardly walk. And you were lucky. There wasn't much kindness in all that."

"Come on now, don't upset yourself, Jess. Where would we be then?" Reg tried to steer her towards a chair. "Lily, can you get a fresh cuppa for Jess? Her tea has gone cold."

Lily jumped to it.

"No, no, it's alright," Jess brushed Reg aside and followed Lily into the kitchen. "I'll do it. Lily's tea is undrinkable."

Bertie sat down, moving the cushion to get comfortable.

"Am I a fool, Reg?"

"No, Bertie, of course you're not."

"I was talking to Walter about things, you know." Bertie spoke slowly. "He'd discussed it all with the Guv'nor. They all think that it would not be proper to attend and, in any case, the doctor says I shouldn't go anywhere for a bit. But I feel like it has all been taken out of my hands."

"It might seem like that, Bertie, but the truth is that there are other things at play. If you go, they, the suffragettes, will turn it against you. It will look as if you are apologizing, as if you agree with them. Can you imagine the headlines? You are the King's jockey, you represent the King. That is why you can't go."

"But it seems wrong. It feels as if I am hiding away."

"No one would think that, Bertie, but sometimes you have to put your own feelings aside. It is hard for you but it wasn't your fault and you have nothing to feel guilty about."

"You mustn't go. Must he, Reg?" Jess came back to catch the end of the conversation.

"It's alright, Jess, no one is going anywhere." Reg tried to calm her down. "Alright Bert?"

Bertie didn't reply. His mind flicked from one thought to another as he struggled to work out the right thing to do.

"But it still seems wrong not to pay my respects," he said.

"Well, I can go," Lily piped up.

"You can't possibly," said Jess.

"Yes, I can. Clar will come with me. She knows the people there. I'll speak to her. After all what is the point of having a sister-in-law with connections if you don't use it? It's the perfect solution, don't you think Bertie?"

∪ ∪ ∪

A letter arrived from Lily. Bertie took it to his room and settled himself into his chair.

London, 14th June 1913

Dear Bertie,

I hope that you are feeling better and doing well. Clar and I have just got back from the memorial service for Miss Davison in Bloomsbury and as promised I am writing to give you an account of the day.

The service was held in the church next to that hall that we went to a long time ago, the day we first met Clar. Do you remember? Gosh, she's changed so much since then, hasn't she? But then I suppose everything has and, in any case, perhaps that's marriage for you.

It started with a big procession, like a military parade or a state funeral, like it was when the King died. Apparently the procession had come all the way from Victoria Station and was going on to King's Cross, where the coffin would go to Morpeth in Northumberland for burial in the family plot.

Clar and I watched the procession from a balcony overlooking Hart Street. A friend of hers has a flat there and didn't think it would do for us to get crushed in the street, which was very thoughtful as the crowd completely filled the pavements. The police had a job keeping everyone back and the cross-bearer, who was a girl in white, had to practically force her way through.

175

It was very impressive. Clar's friend said that members had been sent instructions to dress in white or purple or black. Those in white had to carry Madonna lilies, those in purple had to carry purple irises, and anyone wearing black had to carry red peonies. The procession was divided up by colour.

There were lots of bands. I heard them play the Death March and the Marseillaise – I did wonder why the Marseillaise as it is the French national anthem, isn't it? Clar thought it was something to do with revolution. Many in the procession carried large banners. Four black horses pulled the hearse and the coffin was covered by purple cloth with large silver prison arrows and laurel leaves upon it.

I felt sorry for her family who were in the carriage behind the hearse. It must have been awful to have all those people around. Someone said that there was an empty carriage and that this was for Mrs Pankhurst, but she had been arrested and so couldn't come but the carriage stayed, so that she wasn't forgotten and there in spirit.

We couldn't watch it all as we had to go down to the church when the coffin arrived. Clar said we'd never get through in time otherwise and it was a real job. Generally people in the crowd were quiet and respectful towards the coffin. Not everyone was sorry though. I heard some shouting out against her and the suffragettes, some called out about you and Anmer. It was a strange sight. I heard that Flora was there somewhere but we didn't see her.

Clar had invitation cards with directions that sent us to a side door. We then went up to the gallery and were able to sit on the benches. The church was packed, mostly with ladies, although there were a few men. They seemed to know that I was your sister, although I think that many people there thought that Clar, being Mrs Jones, was your wife, but anyway it caused a bit of a stir when we arrived. There was a lot of whispering.

To be honest, I thought that some of the people looked down their noses at us, but perhaps that's their way. They weren't at all like the swells at the races who are always so friendly, even the famous people and the ones with titles. But I suppose in the circumstances, they were upset and that made them act oddly.

I did get cross, though, when one of the ladies looked at me over her glasses and said, "Oh, the jockey, well, it wasn't as if he was badly hurt," as if that made it all right. I was going to give her a piece of my mind; I mean you just can't go round causing other people harm and then say things like that, it doesn't seem a very Christian way at all to me. But, don't worry, I didn't disgrace us, Clar shut me up, telling me that it was best not to say anything and they didn't mean it. She says that many of them had been very badly treated themselves and that that made them hardened to things, so they forget that other people can get upset by their remarks. I wasn't completely sure about all that, but it was probably the right thing to do.

Leaving the church was quite frightening, as the crowd seemed even larger and there was more of a crush. The people in the crowd, men and women, were rough to anyone wearing the colours of the suffragettes. I was glad we weren't wearing anything like that, Walter was very clear that we shouldn't and it meant we were able get away without trouble.

So, at least the Jones family were there, we showed our faces. We paid our respects to the poor woman, brother dear, and please be assured that it would not have done at all for you to go yourself.

I am staying up with Clar for a few days, Aunt Mary said that she felt quite well and that it would do me good to get away for a bit and have some young company, which was kind of her.

Percy, Jack and Mark, or 'The Tribe' as Clar calls them, are fine and send their best. I haven't seen much of them as they work such long hours, but we're all planning to go on a proper Sunday outing together tomorrow. Clar is marvellous with them. She really keeps them in order, quite a task as you can imagine. Actually Clar has stopped working at the magazine now. There has been a disagreement between the publishers and the organization and so it's moved out of HQ. It is still published but much smaller. Clar says it is just as well as she has her hands full and that she doesn't need to have babies as she has three full-grown ones in the house and that is quite enough.

Anyway, I'll say goodbye now, brother dear, and get this in the post. Tell Jess that I'm going out now to get the bits and pieces that she wanted and I'll bring them over next Sunday.

Your loving sister,

Lily

Bertie folded up the letter and put it into his box of collectables under the bed. It was a weight off his mind that it was all over, perhaps now things could get back to normal. He went downstairs and put on his jacket.

"Where are you off to?" asked Jess.

"Off to the stables. Best get a bit of training in. It's Ascot next week."

"But surely it's too soon?"

"Get straight back in the saddle, that's what our dad would say, and that's what I'm going to do."

21

Royal Ascot, July 1913

IT WAS A FINE evening out by the teahouse. The jockeys sat in rattan garden chairs overlooking the lawns that swept down to the untidy muddied edges of the riverbank. The water meadows shimmered orange in the last hazy rays of the dipping sun. Moorhens peeped to their young as they clambered out to find shelter in the gnarled trunks of the old willow trees that stood silhouetted against the sky with their spindly branches drifting nowhere in the gentle babble of the river. But to Bertie, the babble became a roar, the birds screeched and the sky wept blood. What if it happened again? He went over each step in detail. The figure on the course darting among the horses. The reins cutting into his hands as he tried to pull up. Her face. Anmer's cry. The thud and falling. Was there something else he could have done?

A slight pressure on his arm made Bertie jump.

"Another drink?"

Bertie sat up and looked blankly at Snowy.

"Another soda water, Bertie?" Snowy asked again. "You were miles away there. Everything alright?"

The others stopped talking.

"Oh yes, I'm fine," said Bertie. "Just thinking what a fine evening it is. Don't you think, boys?"

"We're a fortunate lot," said Steve, "A fine place like this, just up the road from the racecourse. A few evenings ahead of us where we can enjoy the company of our comrades on horseback and put the world to rights."

They tapped the table in approval.

"Almost like a holiday, I'd say," piped up Fred junior.

"Well, it would be if it wasn't for the bloody scales," said Danny.

"Fred junior doesn't need to worry about that for a while," Steve replied.

"But your day will come, Fred, my boy, just ask your dad and your uncles." Danny wagged a warning finger.

"Well, he has got a point, and your father was as thin as a whippet in his youth, wasn't he, Fred junior?"

"He was."

"You see, before long you'll be worrying about how much water you can wring out of a lettuce leaf, just like the rest of us."

"Or worse, still roller-skating like a mad American," said Steve, "or is it dancing like a turkey?"

I think you mean the Turkey Trot, dear boy." Danny adopted his best English accent. "An excellent way to keep off the pounds."

"Old hat now, Danny. Forget turkeys, you need to tango. That's what they are all doing in Paris," laughed Steve.

"Of course, you should know with all this your time in gay Parree. I must be getting a bit behind the times," replied Danny.

Bertie turned back to the sunset.

"Have you heard the latest about Steve's ma, Bertie?" asked Snowy.

Their voices sounded far away. Bertie looked at Steve and shook his head.

"What about my ma?" Steve asked, playing to the audience.

"I heard she beat some poor woman with an umbrella, just because she made a less than complimentary remark about her boy," said Danny.

"Oh that." He pulled a face.

"Go on Steve, tell us what happened," Danny egged him on. "Hold on to that bad rib, Bertie, you'll love this."

"Well, as you know, she is a very spirited woman, my mother." Steve looked at the ground and shook his head. "Thank goodness the woman didn't press charges. In fact she said she was very sorry for causing offence."

"Well, that's mothers for you," said Snowy.

"Perhaps we should set her on to those lunatic suffragettes, don't you think, Bertie, like that one that nearly did for you?" said Danny.

"Nearly did for the lot of us," muttered Snowy.

"Ma would put them straight. She doesn't hold with that nonsense, not at all," said Steve. "And she was very sorry to hear what happened to you Bertie. She asked particularly for me to send you her best wishes."

"Very kind," said Bertie adjusted the cushion as his rib twisted uncomfortably.

"You know, I thought it would be me," Danny said.

"Could have been any of us, they've been threatening for long enough," added Snowy.

"They're dangerous. One of them attacked some poor vicar thinking it was Lloyd George, so I heard," said Wilf. "It was your woman at the Derby, I think, Bertie. She must have been out of her mind."

Bertie rested his elbows on the arms of the chair and linked his fingers before him. The sun had disappeared and he shivered in the twilight.

"Look at Hurst Park. The grandstand there was burnt out," said Fred junior.

"At least no one was hurt and the fire didn't get to the stables," said Frank. "So that was a blessing."

"And you, Bert. You getting on alright?" Wilf asked.

"Oh, I'm fine, boys. Very lucky, I count myself very lucky," he replied, but wished they would stop asking.

"Expect you'll be glad to get out there tomorrow, won't you? It'll help you to get it all behind you."

Bertie sat silently.

"Anyway, it'll be good to have you back with us, old Diamond Jones himself," Danny added, standing and raising his glass. "Gentlemen, to Bertie Jones, the finest man in racing."

The others joined in the toast.

"And I'll tell you all something right now," Snowy's Lancashire accent thickened as his voice grew louder. He slammed his glass down on the table. They all sat back with surprise. "If anyone tries anything like that tomorrow, I'll ride right over them. I will, I will, and I don't care who they are."

Snowy sat down again, his hands in tight fists making small punching movements into the air.

"It's alright, lad," Bertie looked over at him. "It's alright. It can't happen again."

ʊ ʊ ʊ

Coming out from the weighing room on the first day of Ascot, Danny was slightly ahead of Bertie but stayed close, all the time keeping up a stream of chatter.

"The going is too hard, we really could do with some rain. It would be nice to freshen things up a bit – this humidity is enough to drive you crazy."

Steve walked, silent and grim faced, on his right. Bertie didn't dare slow down as Snowy and Fred junior would have stepped on his heels. The crowd clapped and cheered him. All the people milling about made him uneasy but the feeling of their goodwill touched his heart. He tried to give them a smile, if only to make up for the glares from his fellow jockeys as they looked around suspiciously.

At the parade ring, the Guv'nor left Anmer with the groom while he came over to greet Bertie himself. Lord Marcus and Sir Dighton rushed towards him too, pursued as usual by a clutch of puffing courtiers. The other jockeys gently slapped him on the back as they walked off to find their own owners and trainers.

"Good to see you back out here, my boy." Lord Marcus took his hand and shook it warmly.

"Their Majesties said to be sure to let you know that they are watching over you," added Sir Dighton.

"Anmer looks none the worse for all that's happened,' said Lord Marcus. "Like his rider, thank God, eh, Bertie?"

Bertie touched his cap but didn't comment. He knew well enough that Anmer was putting on a good show. His attention was taken by the groom holding Anmer. The figure was familiar. The Guv'nor saw him looking.

"It was supposed to be a surprise. He wanted to come."

For a moment, Bertie felt his nerve falter. He swallowed and strode over. It was Reg.

"Hello, Bertie. I came down this morning. The Guv'nor said it was alright. Old Ben is furious about being left behind though, Jess had to bribe him with strawberry shortcake." Reg stopped. "You don't mind?"

"Mind? Of course I don't mind. Have to admit though it gave me a bit of a turn, I thought it was our dad for a minute."

The bell rang.

Anmer stood placidly while Bertie jumped up from Reg's upturned palms.

"Look after yourself, Bert. See you at the other end!"

Bertie left the parade ring. As he cantered up to the start, the rows and rows of people lining the course appeared closer than usual. He felt them pressing in around him, crawling, ready to swarm. The sweat ran in a cold line over his hot face, breaking out along his neck and down his back. Get a grip, he told himself.

Anmer was as good as gold, walking straight up to the line without a murmur. Now and again the horse looked at him for reassurance. Horses have long memories, better than most humans, he'd always thought. Anmer would remember, just like he remembered. He'd feel the blow of flesh hitting bone. He'd smell the iron heat of warm blood soaking into the clodded earth. He'd see the face in his dreams.

"We'll get this one over, boy, then we'll be back on form."

Reg would be waiting at the finish. It was good of him to come down today, what with the family and running the pub. He pictured Nell and the little ones waving Reg goodbye as he got on to the train. No, he mustn't let Reg down. Bertie thought of the Guv'nor and Lord Marcus, even the King and Queen. Everyone had been so kind. He mustn't let them down.

Anmer gave a shudder, he seemed to read Bertie's mind.

"Sorry, boy, I'll be alright now."

Anmer twitched his ears and moved his head up and down in reply. The starter's flag came down and they were off. Bertie didn't allow anything else into his mind. It was just him and Anmer. He made himself look ahead, ignoring the barriers, letting the shouts pass over him. The physical effort needed all their energy and he felt a surge of relief at the burn in his muscles and the ache in his lungs. He felt alive again. Anmer held his tail high and purred like a cat.

It wasn't one of their best rides, for certain, but he and Anmer had proved to the world they could race again.

U U U

Without looking at the clock, Bertie could guess the time. It was the same every night. Through the open window the far-off bubbling of the river and the cries of its creatures carried over the night. The unfamiliar surroundings and the strange room disturbed him. Then he remembered that Reg was there. Listening closely he could make out his breath from across the room. The sound, rhythmic and dependable, had always been there, soothing him through childhood fears and the worries of growing up.

Reg could sleep through anything, always had, flat out. Sound asleep, peaceful sleep, the sleep of the good. The raspiness of his breath was new, rattling the air down deep in his lungs, but the stillness, the restfulness, was the same. Bertie pulled the sheets right up to his neck and drifted off.

As the sun rose, Bertie opened his eyes. This time he felt awake and refreshed. That was the best night's kip he'd had since, well, certainly for a long time. A run down to the river, that's what he'd do.

By the time he got back, Reg was up and about.

"You're not racing today, Bertie?" he asked.

"No, day off today, then just the one race tomorrow. Thought I'd go down and be a spectator for a bit. Not sure I've done that since we were kids."

Reg paused. "Very proud of you yesterday, Bert. Getting back up like that can't have been easy."

"Glad to have got it out of the way, that's for sure."

"But take it slowly, little brother. You know, you've been through a lot."

"Stop worrying, Reg, I'm fine. Now, you go on down to breakfast. I'll just get cleaned up and be there in a minute."

"Righty-ho."

"What time's your train?" Bertie called after him.

"Thought I'd get one before midday, see if I can miss the crush."

"I'll come down to the station with you."

"Don't be daft, Bert. I'll see myself there. You need a bit of peace. I should think you've had enough of crowds."

"Shame you can't stay. Snowy'll have an easy run in the Gold Cup, Tracery is in fine form. Do you want me to put a fiver on for you?"

"Better make it five bob." Reg popped his head back round the door. "Nell is a bit strict about that sort of thing."

"Very wise woman," said Bertie.

ပ ပ ပ

Bertie had found himself a quiet spot where he could watch the race in peace and as far away from everyone as it was possible to be. He'd seen many old faces and had chatted to them. Their Royal Highnesses asked to see him. Now he wanted a bit of time to himself. But he felt restless. Perhaps he was just missing Reg? He had been thinking a lot about his dad, remembering how he had come to the station when they left for Newmarket with Old Ben. They never saw their father again. He wanted to talk to Reg about it, but he didn't. "What's made you so bleeding cheerful all of a sudden?" That's what Reg would say. Then of course all the way back Reg would have worried about him. "What's up with Bertie? It's not like him ... "

And it wasn't like him. He looked out into the distance, over Ascot Heath with its bushes and copses. Something lurked there, he was sure, hovering, waiting. Bertie closed his eyes and opened them again. Maybe he was imagining things, seeing things that weren't really there. The hubbub around him carried on as if nothing had happened. The sun was giving him a headache. He needed some water but his body felt heavy, rooted to the spot.

The flag came down and the Gold Cup started. Bertie trained his glasses on Snowy, who was waiting at the back, biding his time. The horses were coming round the far side, the pace increased. Snowy had found a good line and lightly encouraged Tracery through. Bertie felt his heart beat faster as he urged them on. Snowy and Tracery moved up, looking strong. The horse lengthened his stride and quickened his pace. He took the lead. Nothing would stop them now and Bertie was already congratulating Snowy in his mind.

Something moved on the far side of the lens. Bertie swung the glasses round and saw a man climbing over the fence and walking on to the course. The man was holding up a flag. There must be something wrong. It was odd though, Bertie had never known the stewards do that before. The man raised his arms and rushed right into the path of the race. Tracery's head hit him straight in the chest. The man recoiled like a dummy in target practice. As Tracery tumbled, legs flaying out at all angles, Snowy was thrown to the side. The other horses jumped over them or swerved sharply. One clipped the man with its hoof. The body twitched violently. Tracery righted himself, getting up to rush after the others.

The crowd booed and shouted, ignoring the finish of the race to concentrate on the scene in front of them. Snowy staggered up. Stewards came out to help. People were all over the course. Bertie let his glasses fall. A gunshot echoed around. It jolted him, spooked him, sparking a bloody anger that he could not control. His jaw set so hard that his teeth ached. The rage numbed his brain and sent him running along with the others who were baying like hounds. He watched as people spat and cursed and kicked the limp body sprawled in the mud. A revolver lay to one side. Bertie wanted to grab it, to shoot and shoot until there was nothing left. Instead he seized the man, pulling him by the jacket so that his upper body dangled like a dummy, head lolling. Bertie clenched his fist and drew back his arm ready to land a blow. The man opened his eyes, hideous blue against the bloodshot white. In that vacant stare was the half-chewed remnant of a tormented soul.

"No, Bertie, no!" Reg grabbed his shoulder and dragged him from the scrum. "Bertie, what the hell are you doing? Remember who you are."

Just as Reg pulled him away, the whistles and cries of the police formed a ring around the crowd.

"What are you doing here?" Bertie shook from head to foot.

"I had a feeling something wasn't right," Reg said. "Come on, let's get you off the course."

Reg practically carried Bertie back to the jockeys' room.

"You're not looking too good, Mr Jones," said one of the valets, fetching him a chair.

The room lurched from side to side.

"Bertie, you are not well. My driver is just outside, please allow him to take you back to your hotel." It was Mr Rothschild, Snowy always rode his horses.

"Oh, I'm fine, sir, thank you, just too much sun." Bertie sat down. "But Snowy and Tracery … ?"

"Please don't unsettle yourself, Bertie. I was just sending someone to see how Snowy is doing. Poor boy, he went off in an ambulance but I think they took him back to the hotel." The old man patted his hand and turned to Reg. "Talk to your brother, he really should rest."

Lord Marcus and Sir Dighton arrived with some of the stewards and a number of policemen.

"There you are, Bertie. We were worried about you. It is looking quite ugly out there."

Bertie was bundled into Mr Rothschild's car and soon they were back at the hotel. Bertie's tongue felt swollen and his mouth was dry. He held on to Reg.

"Mr Jones, is there something I can get for you?" Miss Everly from the reception came out to meet them. "Perhaps some tea, or a cold drink?"

"Thank you, but I'd like to see how Mr Whalley is."

"I can check on Snowy, Bertie," said Reg. "You get settled somewhere quiet and have a nice cup of tea. I'll be back in a jiffy."

The waiter led him to a shady spot, a table under the willow trees. There was hardly a soul in sight. Bertie lay back in the white wicker chair and closed his eyes. At home when he was a boy, he would dangle his feet in the brook. Even in the summer the water was icy cold, so cold that it made your tummy tingle. Maybe he should take his boots off and sit by the riverbank.

"Tea, m'lord?"

Danny stood there carrying a silver tray, much to the distress of the young waitress who was trying to reclaim it.

"When did you get back?" Bertie sat up.

"Oh, just a few minutes ago. I saw this lovely young lady bringing your tea and thought I'd assist." Danny put the tray down and pulled up a seat. "This place is crawling with plain-clothes policemen, I'm sure of it. And did you see all the press by the gate on the way in?"

"Can I get anything else for you, sir?" the girl asked, adjusting the tea things quite unnecessarily.

"No, thank you. Unless you would like something, Danny?"

Danny shook his head.

"Thank you then, that's everything."

"Would you like me to pour for you, sir?" The waitress hovered by the table.

"Er, no, thank you."

The girl took a sudden step towards him. Bertie ducked to one side.

"Mr Jones, sir, I just wanted to say if you need anything at all, you just let me know. Just ask for Elsie." She peered into his face. "You need looking after, what with all these goings on. I think you are very brave." She gave a little bob. "Pardon me for speaking out, sir."

She ran off.

"Made a conquest there, Bertie," laughed Danny. "Did you see the way she looked at you? You could have been a bit more friendly."

"You do talk nonsense, Danny." Bertie wished he would go away.

"Still pining for Miss Flora, the boss's daughter?" Danny looked pleased with himself at the way he'd made it rhyme, beating out a tune with his fingers on the edge of the chair.

"Oh, for heaven's sake, don't you ever stop?" Bertie looked away.

"I'm sorry, ignore me. It's how I cope. I don't mean anything by it." Danny crossed his arms. "Don't let your tea go cold."

Bertie went to pour his tea. The china cup rattled in its saucer and hot tea splattered everywhere. He paused to try and steady his hands, conscious that Danny was watching him. First, a splash of milk and then a bit more tea, until the mixture was just right.

Elsie came back and laid a fresh linen cloth. Danny waited for the girl to go. "You're up tomorrow, aren't you?"

"Just the three o'clock."

"Look, I really don't think you are well enough to ride, Bertie."

"Oh, don't you now?" Bertie narrowed his eyes. The rush of heat that he had felt earlier in the crowd returned to him. "And I'm supposed to listen to a man who is a liar and a cheat?"

Danny looked at him in amazement. "Steady on, old boy, I thought we were pals, good friends. What's all this about?"

Bertie's voice didn't belong to him, it was almost as if someone else was speaking, someone he couldn't control. "I think it is about time that we were honest with one another. I saw you with Sloan all those years ago at Egerton. You were waiting by the car. Yes, you were a really good friend that night. I only kept quiet to avoid a scandal, but I've never trusted you since." Bertie stood up. His voice got louder. "So stay away from me. You hear?"

Reg rushed over. "What on earth is going on? I could hear you from the veranda."

"Danny's little secret is out. That night, with the Diamond. I told you I recognized some of them."

"Bertie, if only you knew." Danny was almost in tears. "Not everyone lives in a cosy world with brothers and horses. Some of us have had to fight for every penny we have and, yes, that has meant that I've had to do things that I'm not proud of. But I've tried to make amends, and particularly to you, because I thought you were my friend."

"You have no idea, Danny, do you?" said Bertie.

"Come on, let's sit you down again." Reg put Bertie gently back in his chair and handed him his cup and saucer. "He doesn't mean it, Danny."

"Yes, I do," thought Bertie, but he kept quiet and concentrated on not spilling his tea.

"He's not himself. None of us are at the moment with all this madness around." Reg stopped. "And you, Danny, you came through alright today?"

"Had to move out of the way pretty smartish, but yes, we were alright."

"I checked on Snowy," Reg spoke to Bertie. "He's bruised and a bit shaken up but otherwise he's fine."

ʊ ʊ ʊ

"Snowy?" called Bertie, tapping at the door of the room.

A nurse in a crisp white uniform answered the door.

"I'm sorry, Mr Whalley isn't receiving visitors."

"No of course, I just wanted to see how … "

Snowy appeared behind her.

"It's alright, thank you, nurse," he said. "Bertie, please come in, you're the one person that I would like to see."

"I just thought I'd check on how you were getting on."

"Oh, I'm coming along, Bertie. Shame about the race though, we had a good chance, I think."

"Yes, you were coming through nicely there."

"You saw what happened?"

"Well, I was watching though my field glasses, but saw enough."

"He came out of nowhere, Bertie. Had a gun, and a stupid flag. I thought he was a steward. But I saw his eyes, Bertie, he was mad. We hit him, but there was nothing I could do."

"Of course not, Snowy." Bertie tried to remember the man, but all he could see was that woman's face. He turned his attention back to Snowy, who was pacing up and down the room.

"I'm getting back tonight. I need to see Doris. She'll be worried out of her mind. She's been fretting no end about you, Bertie, so this will really, well, you know."

"Poor Doris. Yes, she'll want to see you for herself."

"Come too, Bertie. We'll be back in Newmarket tonight."

"No, Snowy, I can't. I'm racing tomorrow."

"No, not now, not after today." Snowy grabbed his arm. Tears were streaming down his face. "You can't, Bertie, you really can't."

The nurse came over and gently took hold of Snowy.

"I think we need to get him settled, Mr Jones, if you don't mind."

"Of course." Bertie went to go. "Look after him."

"Don't worry." She smiled. "And I'm sorry, I didn't realize who you were at first. I can get the doctor to come and give you something to help you sleep, you know, for the shock."

"No, thank you, nurse," he said "I'll be fine."

ʊ ʊ ʊ

Bertie was ready early the next morning. Reg was on the telephone to Jess. Walter had arrived at the hotel with a car to take him to the racecourse.

"We'll run just the one race as planned on La Marquise, Bertie," said Walter. "She's not got much of a chance but at least there will be a royal horse running and that's what is important."

Bertie nodded. Reg joined them.

"Do you really think it is fair to ask Bertie to ride today after what happened to Snowy?"

"No, to be honest, I don't." Walter shook his head, "The Guv'nor isn't happy about it either, no one is, but apparently the prime minister spoke to the King last night. The prime minister thinks it will be good for morale if the people see Bertie up, the King had no choice, so there you are."

"Stop worrying, Reg. I'll be fine. In any case, it's my duty." Bertie stood up and rubbed his hands together. "So come on, let's get going."

As they arrived, shafts of rain fell like bullets. People scattered in front of the car as they searched for cover, their summer finery all soaked and clingy.

Bertie set off to walk the course as he always did. Reg caught up with him, bringing along two large black umbrellas. "You can't walk a mile and three-quarters without one of these. You'll catch pneumonia."

As they were completing the circuit, Mr Smallwood came towards them. "Bertie, we thought we'd lost you. What's taken so long?"

"He's been checking all around the fences and the bushes," said Reg. "And more than once."

Bertie went to get ready. In the jockeys' room, no one spoke of yesterday. In fact, no one spoke much at all. As he and the others weighed out and walked to the paddock, it felt more like going into battle, soldiers on the front line.

There were few visitors in the paddock, but Lord Marcus and Sir Dighton were there. They looked solemn and cold, but they put on a smile when he appeared.

"Very kind of you to come out in this," said Bertie.

"We wanted to see you off, Bertie," said Lord Marcus. "Anyway, I'm not so infirm yet that I can't tolerate a bit of bad weather on parade, young man."

"Glad to hear it, sir," Bertie smiled as he knew the gruffness was just his lordship's idea of a joke. "Please thank His Majesty for his kind note, Sir Dighton. Much appreciated."

"Their Majesties are most concerned for you, and we all appreciate what you are doing."

There was a rumble of thunder. It was some way off, but the clouds in the distance were heavy and black.

The Guv'nor rushed over, brushing down his coat and straightening his hat. His face looked crumpled and lined. Walter was by his side, half-running to keep up.

"My Lord. Sir Dighton. I am so sorry I'm late." The Guv'nor sounded tired as he looked round at them all. "I had to go back to Egerton unexpectedly."

There was something in his voice that made Bertie feel uneasy. Why had the Guv'nor gone back? He wanted to ask Walter but he had slipped away.

"Anmer, as you know, Lord Marcus, won't be running today. It would be safer," the Guv'nor continued. "As for Jones here, I'd prefer that he didn't race today, but still ... "

"I think, Mr Marsh, that the King's jockey is keen not to disappoint the public. Is that not so, Bertie?" said Lord Marcus.

"Indeed, sir."

"I know, I know," the Guv'nor sighed.

Bertie and the Guv'nor took their leave and joined two of the stable lads walking La Marquise. Reg was with them. Bertie had ridden La Marquise before, but didn't know her well. Lightning flashed, the horse swung round.

"It's alright, old girl," he soothed and stroked her neck. "It's just the clouds having a bit of a disagreement."

Bertie remembered when he was a boy, counting the seconds between the flash and the claps to work out the distance from the eye of the storm. He would quiver under the horse blankets as the stable shook and the world got darker and darker until there were only shadows. But now there was nowhere to hide.

"Have you worked out if it is coming or going?" Reg smiled. "How many miles?"

"It's coming towards us and about four," Bertie replied with a grin.

La Marquise calmed down. Reg helped Bertie up into the saddle. The rain lashed at his face until the skin felt numb. Huddled people, neatly intertwined, lined the course like artificial tree trunks on a pantomime stage. He searched the rails for any signs of trouble, but the truth was that he couldn't tell today any more than he could yesterday or on Derby Day what was out there.

A crackle splintered through the air just as the flag went up. La Marquise jumped and shot off at a speed that took Bertie by surprise, but he held on and guided her forward. The rain was so thick that Bertie could barely see beyond the reins. But the horse knew where she was going; the determination in the little filly was clear in the confidence of her stride and the pull of her head. The light dimmed suddenly; Bertie couldn't make out where the sound from the heavens stopped and the sound from the turf started, there was just one low groan that shook the earth, no beginning and no end.

As Bertie leaned in, he saw that the ears of the horse were soaked black and glossy, pulled back in grim concentration. He was touched at her courage and tucked in close to her; she felt the comfort of his touch and sped ahead. The sound of the crowd became louder. They called his name. Bertie thought of the people standing in the cold and the rain, cheering for him, their money and their hopes riding with him. The calls became louder and he knew the post was close.

Another horse came alongside. Bertie saw Danny's colours and this made him urge La Marquise on with an aggression that he had never felt before. His whip arm was up and ready to strike before he knew it. Horrified at what he might do, Bertie dropped his arm quickly. He had never resorted to such a thing in his life. He despised the whip. Despite the blood rush of the finish, he would not push her. It would have to be as it would be. She had run her heart out.

It was a dead heat. Bertie patted and praised La Marquise, who looked quite bewildered at all the fuss. The crowd sighed loudly as the result went up for Danny.

"They're disappointed. They wanted you to win, Bertie," Danny called across.

"The odds were better, that's all." Bertie turned towards the paddock. The Guv'nor was there with Walter.

"Are you alright, Bertie? You are sure you're alright?" he kept repeating.

"I'm fine, Guv'nor, I'm fine. Bit surprised though, wasn't expecting much from her at all," Bertie put his head on the horse's neck. He felt her pulse, fast and strong, against his temple.

"Once you're done here, Bertie, head straight back to Egerton with Reg. Walter has organized it all, so you should be able to get back before nightfall."

22
Loss, July 1913

IT WAS DUSK WHEN they arrived at the station. They had all been very quiet on the journey home, which suited Bertie as he was tired and slept most of the way back. John was waiting for them with the Guv'nor's car. Bertie was surprised to see him.

"You didn't need to collect us."

"Mr Venn thought it would be better, sir." He was polite and, although always a man of few words, he seemed particularly reserved that evening.

"We didn't tell you before," Reg cleared his throat. "You had enough on your plate."

Bertie's mind flicked through the potential problems. What could be serious enough to cause the Guv'nor to come back during Ascot? His breathing became fast and shallow. "Come on, then, what is it?

"It's Ben," Reg answered quietly.

"Old Ben? What's he done now?" Bertie tried to laugh, wanting it to be another of those strange domestic dramas that really were nothing in the scheme of things. He wanted to cover his ears and not to hear because he knew in his heart that this would not be something good.

"He's in a bit of a bad way," Walter said slowly. "He had a nasty turn yesterday. He was as right as rain up to then. Wasn't he John, you saw him, didn't you? He was fine in the morning."

"He was, but the incident at the Gold Cup upset him. He wouldn't even have any tea, just wanted to go off for a walk, he said, to clear his mind. Anyway, they found him slumped over the fencing by the paddock. He can't have been like that long."

Bertie swallowed but he couldn't get rid of the tight knot that lodged in his throat.

"They carried him back and put him on to the bed. By then the doctor had arrived. But he said just to make him as comfortable as we could, and that at his age, well, you know." John paused. "The Guv'nor came back last night and sat with him for ages. He wanted to make sure he had everything that he needed. Jess has been looking after him. So he is as comfortable as can be. He isn't in any pain, you can be sure of that."

"We didn't think there was any point in telling you before. There was nothing you could do and you'd been through enough," said Reg.

Jess came out to meet them and bundled Bertie inside.

"Look at the state of you, Bert, worn out you look."

"Alright, Jess, but please don't nag. You look tired too. Anyway, how is Ben?"

"Very poorly, but comfortable. I think he's been waiting for you to come home. He fretted so much about that man on the course at Ascot yesterday, and what with it coming so soon after, well you know, the other business."

Bertie went upstairs and into Old Ben's room. The breeze ruffled the curtains and made the gaslight flicker. Bill was sitting in a wooden chair by the bedside, reading from the big Bible. He stopped as Bertie entered and closed the book.

"Hello, Bill. You've been looking after the patient, eh?"

"Poor Ben, stuck listening to me. My reading's never been up to much." Bill got up. "I'll leave you for a bit."

"Thanks. I'll have a chat with Ben and you could probably use a cup of tea."

"Can I bring you one up, Bertie?"

"No thanks," He looked down at Old Ben. "We're alright for now, Ben, aren't we?"

As Bill closed the door, Bertie sat in his place, moving the Bible to the bedside cabinet. Old Ben lay under the sheet. His hands were on top, pressed together as if in prayer. He looked as if he was made of marble and he was silent apart from the rusty sound of his breath pushing in and out of his chest.

Bertie took Old Ben's hand in his. He looked around, blinking hard to clear the tears from his eyes. He had rarely been in this room, and then usually just to rush in to close a window that was banging when Old Ben was out and Jess was complaining. The objects that were so familiar when they were with Old Ben, looked forlorn and out of place away from their owner. The watch and chain should be hanging from his waistcoat. The penknife, as sharp as a cavalry sword and useful for every occasion, should be safely tucked away in his trouser pocket. His well-worn baccy pouch and handsome new pipe from last Christmas belonged in the mysterious place in his jacket. Even that old bit of twine should be tucked somewhere, handy for all sorts of occasions.

On the dresser, there were a few picture postcards, old and yellowing. Bertie recognized one that he himself had sent years ago when the Guv'nor had packed him off to Brighton for a rest after they had won the Triple Crown. Bertie began to talk of their old times, repeating Old Ben's favourite stories. He knew the old man could hear him: perhaps he wasn't lying in the body on the bed any more but he was there with him somehow.

Old Ben died later that night. The Guv'nor arrived late from Ascot and came straight to the cottage. He spent some time alone with Old Ben, emerging red eyed and pale.

Reg had brought over a bottle of brandy. He poured a healthy glass and gave it to the Guv'nor. He held out another for Bertie.

"I know you don't usually drink, but this might help."

Bertie shook his head.

"Well, if you don't want it, Bertie, I certainly could do with it," said Jess, swooping it up and clinking glasses with the Guv'nor. She downed it in one draught.

The Guv'nor looked lost. "You see, Ben has always been with me. I don't know what I'll do without him."

They all stood still. The clock chimed one.

ᴗ ᴗ ᴗ

The church was packed. The whole estate had turned out and more besides. Everyone wanted to pay their respects and say their goodbyes. From his place in the choir stall, Bertie could see the coffin on its bier, decorated with just a few of the many wreaths and flowers that had been sent. The sunlight made a rainbow path along the nave, streaming through the stained-glass windows and disappearing into the pure white ray that reflected out from the polished brass of the handles.

All things bright and beautiful,
All creatures great and small.

As they sang, Bertie thought he could hear the voice of Old Ben joining in, slightly too loud and always out of time. It was Old Ben who had persuaded him to join the choir as a small, shrill-voiced twelve-year-old.

"Always wished I'd had a voice, Bertie," he'd said. "But these things are God given and the good Lord saw not to bestow this on me, but He did give me the gift of enjoying it. I am grateful."

The Guv'nor was there in the front row. He kept his hand across his brow throughout.

The bell tolled. One note calling out, followed by another. From when it was first put there, Old Ben had been one of the ringers. Church on Sunday, at Easter, Christmas, christenings, weddings and deaths, he had rung them all in. Now they rang for him, echoing across the countryside as the procession left the church for the private cemetery. Walled off and tucked around the back, it was a good spot. He'll like it here, thought Bertie. Still close enough to keep an eye on us.

23
A dry spell, September 1913

BERTIE RODE IN FROM the gallops. Over by the office a group of men gathered around Mr Smallwood and Walter. They stood very close together and there was a lot of pointing. Bertie passed the reins to a stable boy and sent him off ahead to see to the horse, promising to be along in a minute.

Outside the office, there were four burly types in caps wearing patched jackets that looked too small and trousers that flapped untidily around their ankles. A short fat chap in a big check jacket and a bowler hat was talking, every so often pausing to stab his finger into a wodge of papers that he was waving about. Walter looked at him and shook his head.

After a lot of shouting, the men got into a waiting cart. Mr Smallwood set off towards the stables, leaving Walter standing and watching them clatter down the lane. Bertie waved, but Walter pretended not to see him and ran towards the office. Bertie headed him off.

"What was all that about? And don't pretend to me, I can see that something is up."

"Bailiffs," he answered. "But keep it under your hat, don't want to alarm people."

"Again? Well, that's nothing new." replied Bertie. "I've known the Guv'nor all my life and he's never been one to hold back, particularly when it comes to looking out for people and horses. He's an honest man, which can be hard in this business."

"Well, it is serious this time," Walter sighed. "You know how it is, there is never any question of economizing."

"There's no denying that it has been a dry spell, we've just not had the horses."

"We need a break in the weather soon, Bertie, I can tell you."

"A winner, we need a winner."

ʊ ʊ ʊ

When the sun was at its hottest, Bertie took the thick rubber vest down from the coat hook. Danny always swore by Doctor Weiner's Trimsuit. "Desperate times call for desperate measures, Bertie my boy," he'd drawl in that odd English accent he had acquired. Well, things couldn't be more desperate. The Great Eastern was next week. He had to make a good show.

The garment was heavy and stiff. Just getting into it would shift a couple of pounds. Bertie rolled it up like he was making pastry, grey pasty pastry. Now what did Danny do? If only he'd paid more attention. Up and over his head. That wasn't too bad. Trying to get his arms in was harder. The material caught and buckled in on itself, rolling and riding up. Bertie wriggled and writhed, like he was wrestling a snake, one of those big thick ones at London Zoo, the ones that squeezed the life out of people and then opened their mouths to swallow them whole. Bertie had to admit that this snake was winning. Rubber snagged his neck, his arms, his body, sticking to the skin and pinching.

The sauna would have been easier. But it was too late, he'd got this far. Getting air into his lungs was hard, as the suit clamped into his ribs. He took a deep breath, the warm sweet chalky chemicals mixed with dried perspiration and coal-tar soap rippled down his nose and throat. With an almighty heave, Bertie gathered together his strength and tightened his muscles. The vest yielded reluctantly, staggering down his shoulders and torso, tearing at the flesh under his thin cotton undershirt. Relieved but not even daring to think about how he might remove it, Bertie grabbed a couple of old jumpers, put them on, wrapped a towel around his neck and face, then walked out into the yard and broke into a run.

He carried on at a steady pace for some time. The sweat worked its way from his head and neck, down into the suit. His body squelched inside the suit. It must be working. Bertie tried to sing to help the time pass, but the words blurred in his brain. He heard voices, angry voices. The Guv'nor was shouting. Bertie looked around but he couldn't see him. Perhaps it was the heat. But the Guv'nor was always shouting lately. The slightest thing would set him off.

"Get out! Go! Get out of my sight!" The Guv'nor's voice again.

Bertie ran faster, not knowing where he was, unsure whether he was going towards the Guv'nor or away from him. He stumbled. There was a smell of petrol, rubber and smoke, the squeal of metal. He collapsed on to the ground and lay blinking in the sunlight.

"Bertie?" A figure bent over him.

Sugar and spice and all things nice. Flora?

"Bertie, are you in there somewhere?"

He sat up.

"You almost ran into the motorcar." She fumbled to loosen his clothing. "You need some air."

"Don't come near me like this, Flora. Really, you don't want to spoil your pretty clothes."

"Don't be silly." She unravelled his head. "Now, let me just check you aren't hurt. I think Jack managed to stop in time."

Bertie tried to get his thoughts straight. His face burned and his throat ached. "Where am I?"

"Almost at the road into town." She looked him over. "Can you move your arms and legs?"

Despite the Trimsuit, Bertie managed to wave each in turn. "See, I'm fine."

"What's that strange corset thing you are wearing?" She pointed at his middle.

"Oh, I was trying to get a few pounds off. Got this American suit thing on, one of Danny's. Better than a sauna, they say."

"Well, Bertie, you should have some water. I know that's defeating the object of all this, but you'll be no good with sunstroke, now will you?" She called to someone in the motorcar. "Jack, have we got any water?"

"I heard the Guv'nor shouting at me. He sounded in a real state."

"No, not at you. It was at me." Flora shook her head. "He made it very clear that we weren't welcome."

The driver got out of the car. At first Bertie thought it was a man, but he could see now it was a woman in a skirt. She wore a peaked cap with an RAC badge on it.

"Here's some water, I always keep some in the motor." Jack held out a large can to Flora, who soaked her handkerchief and put it on his lips.

"Is he alright?" asked Jack. "He looks like a tramp."

"It's not a tramp. It's Bertie, Bertie Jones, the jockey," said Flora.

"Oh my God, the one who … "

Flora shushed her and Bertie heard the other woman walk away.

The water brought him round. Flora cradled him in her arms. A large rosette was pinned to her jacket. It crushed his face. The circles of purple and green and white filled his field of vision until he was aware of nothing else. He clambered to his feet.

"Let us drive you back." Flora put out her hands to help him.

Bertie drew back from her and ran towards home.

ʊ ʊ ʊ

Bertie sat on the scales, his saddle neatly placed on his lap.

"Alright there?" he asked as the stewards fiddled with the contraption.

George looked at him. "I'm sorry, Bertie, but you are just over. You can't ride."

"Surely not, I can't be," he protested.

"We've just checked again that it's all working properly. I can call a second over if it helps."

"No, George, no. I wasn't doubting you, it's just I wasn't expecting a problem." Bertie tried to calm himself down.

"We'll have to get another jockey organized." Mr Smallwood covered his face with his hands.

"But it's the Great Eastern. It's so important. We've have to win, you know we do." Bertie sat for a minute, wondering what to do. The jockeys behind him were getting impatient. He had a thought. "George, there's nothing in the rules about having to have a saddle, is there?"

"There must be," said George.

"Only I was thinking that if I got rid of the saddle and just had the pad, then … "

Mr Smallwood interrupted, "Oh no, Bertie, I don't think that's wise. You'd as good as be riding bareback. That's far too dangerous."

"Needs must and all that," said Bertie.

George called over a second steward, who called in someone else. There was no clear statement on this.

"Can we just try and see if losing the saddle would be enough?" asked Bertie. "Otherwise it may all be a fuss for nothing."

"Well, I suppose," George hesitated. "Alright then, let's see."

Bertie passed the saddle to Walter. George nodded at Bertie.

"Thank you, gentlemen," smiled Bertie and hopped off the scales.

"Determined little bugger when he wants to be," said Mr Smallwood, as he explained to Walter what had happened.

Bertie walked out as quickly as he could. The Guv'nor was waiting. "Where's the saddle?"

"No saddle, Guv'nor, I can't make the weight with a saddle, so I'm doing without. Nothing in the rules about it." Bertie spoke quickly.

"That's true, sir, they checked," added Walter.

The Guv'nor sniffed at him. "We'll have to find another jockey, that's all there is to it. I can't let you do this."

"There's no one else available that knows the horse and you know he's got a good chance this time. Guv'nor, there is no rule says you can't and you know I can ride as well with or without a saddle."

"No, Jones, I will not let you do this." The Guv'nor took off his hat and ran a hand over his head. "And you, Smallwood, what do you say?"

"I think Bertie knows what he is doing, sir. He's a master horseman on the rough, so he'll be fine as long as he stays out of the way of the others."

The Guv'nor paused. "No, Bertie, no, I can't risk it."

In a flash, Bertie was in the saddle and had set off to the starting line before anyone could catch him. Muttering broke out as he rode out of the paddock. He leaned over to the Anmer. "I hope I'm right, boy, or you and me are going to end up with more than egg on our face."

"What the hell?" Danny called out. "Are you trying to kill yourself?"

Bertie ignored him.

There were no delays at the start and Bertie set off with a good lead. The soft going had made it tricky with the slipperiness of the turf. Mud and sweat built up on Anmer's coat, but Bertie hung on. They kept clear of the pack, avoiding any swerving or bumping. Keeping their position, it was a quick, clean win.

Bertie's legs ached with the strain of the ride, but they'd done it. He could barely see for all the grime on his face. The Guv'nor was on the other side of the course, deep in conversation with the officials.

"Blimey, Bertie," said Walter, in a rare show of emotion. "I've never seen Anmer run like that before."

"Me neither. I think it was fear that egged us both on," said Bertie. "There's not going to be trouble, is there?"

"Well, there's a few that are not too chuffed, but, as you said, there is nothing in the rules. You won fair and square. Mind you, I think that they are practically rewriting the rulebook as we speak."

Bertie patted the horse. People stared. A man crossed his path and spat at the ground. Danny cheered, but was shushed down. George, the steward, came over.

"Alright, Bertie, we've allowed it. No one doubts your courage, but you weren't just risking your neck. You mustn't try that one again, though, or we'd have to take it further."

"Thank you, much appreciated, George. And you have my word that I won't."

The Guv'nor walked up behind him. "No, Bertie, you certainly won't try it again because I won't give you an opportunity. You've been a liability lately. You've become as mad as the stupid bloody woman that you ran over. Get out of my sight, Bertie, and I don't want to see you until you've sorted yourself out."

The Guv'nor swung round and stormed off. Everyone turned away, acting as if nothing had happened, leaving Bertie standing alone.

∪ ∪ ∪

Bertie crouched down by the side of Old Ben's grave, the little wooden cross the only marker until the earth had settled.

"Hear that, Ben?" Bertie felt his knees creak on the way down. "That doesn't sound so good, the old joints aren't what they were."

Chestnut leaves made a coloured patchwork over the grass. A jug of crisp chrysanthemums stood rust, gold and white, perfuming the air with the cool hint of autumn shows and bonfires.

"It's a lovely resting place, though. Not much trouble from the neighbours, I bet." Bertie tidied the flowers. "Oh, Ben. I wish you were with us. I'm finding it really hard without you, and now I've really upset the Guv'nor. He wants rid of me."

The temperature dropped as a cloud shielded the sun, but Bertie didn't feel it.

"You see, it's all my fault, Ben. I'm a cursed man. I carry the mark of Cain and must suffer. But so must all who are dear to me. I would have done anything to spare you, you know that, don't you?"

Rooks in the tall tree nearby flapped their wings and called to one another.

"I need to make amends, Ben, to serve my penance, but I don't know how." Bertie sat back on his heels. "I see her, you know, mostly at night in the dark. I'm hoping that the good Lord will guide me, but I can't bring you back and I'm sorry. So sorry."

A last ray from the dying sun touched Bertie's face.

"Best leave you now. I'll come back." Bertie stood and patted the earth. "Sleep well, Old Ben, sleep well."

24

Snowy's wedding, Newmarket, November 1913

IT WAS A LOVELY service. Jess was right.
"You have to go to Snowy's wedding, Bertie," she had said. "You've been moping around the house for weeks, not seeing people, not going out. I know it's been hard for you, but you can't let Snowy and Doris down. Anyway, it will cheer you up. I'm putting your suit out, then I'll get changed myself."

If Jess knew about the business about the saddle at the Great Eastern, she hadn't mentioned it, and it wasn't like her to keep quiet, especially about something so important. But she must have noticed that he hadn't returned the calls from Walter or Mr Smallwood. He couldn't even bring himself to talk to Reg, even though Reg had tried to broach the matter.

The joyful words and uplifting hymns were a tonic. Some of the more traditional members of the congregation, mostly Snowy's family down from Manchester, had been a little critical of some of the more showy touches: the printed service sheets with 'Doris and Albert' entwined in fancy lettering and the grand choir brought in from Cambridge had caused a flurry. But the young couple seemed so happy that it was hard even for the most dyed-in-the-wool Methodists to grumble, and those that did were inclined to blame the popish tendencies of the Church of England.

Bertie saw the Guv'nor in the congregation, but kept his distance. He couldn't face a confrontation today, and the prospect of Jess finding out that they would soon have to find a new home made him shake with shame.

The wedding breakfast took place at the Smallwoods' house. They walked there from the church. Some of the ladies ahead were complaining that their new narrow skirts would not allow them to step out enough to avoid the puddles and their fine silk shoes would be ruined. Danny was there, dressed in an extravagant snow wolf coat and an unsightly driving hood, offering to chauffeur them to the house. No one appeared very keen to take him up on this, though.

Ahead, the Rothschilds had arrived in a large black Rolls Royce. The driver had stopped and jumped out to open the door for them. But they had to queue outside with everyone else to be officially greeted by the couple themselves, as well as Mr and Mrs Smallwood and Snowy's mother. Mr Rothschild looked in his element as he chatted to the jockeys and trainers. His wife smiled sweetly, although she had a faraway look that was her usual expression, so Bertie had noticed, when forced to accompany her husband to the enclosures.

Mrs Smallwood whispered that she didn't expect to have to entertain the likes of the Rothschilds.

"I knew we should have booked the Rutland Arms, but Doris wouldn't have it," she said.

"Might I have a word, Jones?" The Guv'nor seemed to have appeared from nowhere.

Bertie fought a strong impulse to run away but he followed the Guv'nor outside, keeping his head bent to conceal the unmanly trembling.

"Bertie, I've been meaning to come and see you." The Guv'nor pulled at his cuffs. "But you know how it is."

"Yes, Guv'nor, I understand." His mouth could hardly move to say the words.

"You see, I was hasty the other week. Now I understand why you did it. And," the Guv'nor looked around, "well, it's been a terrible time of late, for all of us. So, I just wanted to say, take your time, get yourself well. We need to make ourselves strong for next season."

Bertie wanted to take the Guv'nor's hand and shake it heartily, but only managed a nod of his head.

"Excellent. We'll put this year behind us, Bertie, and make a new start."

After the speeches were all done, Snowy came to find him.

"How are you feeling, Bertie? I heard you'd not been too well." Snowy didn't wait for a reply. "I tell you, I'll be glad to get this over with, Bertie. Don't get me wrong, it's a lovely day, but all a bit too fancy for me."

Bertie smiled. "Where are you off to?"

"London tonight, then we get the boat across to France, a few days in Paris, then on to the south and the sun. It will be good to be back. I've missed it there. The French leave you alone, they don't take so much notice. And it'll be Doris's first trip, so she's very excited."

Snowy lowered his voice. "Look Bertie, I wanted to talk to you. I know my run-in at Ascot was nothing compared to all that business you had to go through, but I want you to know I can imagine what you are feeling. It's a terrible thing. I cut right back on my rides, just couldn't face being up."

Snowy took a breath and carried on. "Makes you feel like you've had enough. And, I tell you, I think I have. Now me and Doris are married, I'm going to find a tidy little yard somewhere and train my own horses. I've had enough of being up there, always in the front line, always on show. I love horses, they are my life, but there comes a time, Bertie, when you have to think about yourself."

"Trouble is, Snowy, I wouldn't know where to go or what else to do," he replied. "And the Guv'nor needs me."

"Well, I know all that, but I still think that you have to look to yourself, Bertie."

Doris came up to them, sparkling in her lace and diamonds.

"You two look very serious," she smiled.

"Not at all, Doris, I was saying what a lucky man young Snowy is," laughed Bertie.

"Dear Uncle Bertie, I don't believe you for a minute, but you are so sweet to say so." And she kissed him on the cheek.

25
Northumberland, November 1913

BERTIE HAD BEEN THINKING about the trip to Northumberland for some time and now that the season had finished, he could put his plan into action. Travelling by motorcar would be best. He could be alone, slip in and out quietly. It would be quite a challenge for the Sunbeam, especially in the short days, but the old girl would manage it somehow. He'd told the others he was off for a bit of a break and that he'd be calling in at some of the northern yards.

"It'll do you the world of good," said Jess. "I'll pack you up some supplies for the journey, just in case you can't get any proper food."

Only Reg knew where he was really going. "I should come with you," he said.

Bertie shook his head.

"Alright, have it your own way. But remember, you've done nothing wrong, nothing to feel bad about."

Bertie slipped into the garage. He would have to spend some time getting the motorcar up to scratch. A lot of dust had gathered these last couple of months. But there it was, all shiny and clean.

John came over from working on the Guv'nor's Daimler.

"Gave it a bit of a once-over for you, Bertie," he said. "There are a couple of cans of petrol and a spare wheel in the back too. So you're all ready for your grand tour."

ᴗ ᴗ ᴗ

The church had come up suddenly on his left, half-hidden by the blind bend and the sprawling greenery. The road leading into Morpeth from the south was spacious enough to turn the motorcar round in one go, even though the tyres spun on the greasy, wet surface. Slowly retracing his route, he pulled over into the lane that ran alongside the churchyard.

Bertie climbed out. His legs ached after the long drive. The drizzle hissed through the trees and the chill of the north wind cut through to his bones. Bertie pulled the collar of his mackintosh closer to him. The place looked empty; a blessing, as he didn't relish the thought of being seen. And while the press had pretty much lost interest now, he was anxious not to stir it all up again.

The entrance to St Mary's was back on the main road. Bertie walked through the lychgate. The stone of the arch disappeared under the clinging, coiled strands of dark green ivy. Yew trees lined the uneven path that led to the porch. The glossy needles held red waxen berries that threw a garish light over the sombre shadows.

Clinker-grey clouds gathered around the square tower that loomed overhead, meeting and merging into one swirling mass. Sightless eyes from gargoyle faces peered out at him, moving closer then retreating as his eyes blurred. Rest. He needed to rest, to sit, to find sanctuary. Bertie lumbered towards the porch, his hands trembled.

The heavy iron ring turned more easily than he'd imagined. The clunk as the latch lifted reverberated deep and low as if echoing from somewhere distant. Bertie felt the ancient carvings of the oak door smooth against his palm. One light push brought him into the thick silence of the gloomy half-light. The sound of his boots on the flagstones trampled the silence, so he lightened his step until there was almost no trace of himself. Removing his cap and goggles, he clasped them to him and bowed his head before the altar. The sun must have broken through the gloom as the colours from the stained-glass windows scattered beams of blue, violet, pink and yellow at his feet.

Slipping into the worn wooden seat of the nearest pew, he stared at the claret words woven into the cream hessian of the hassock on the floor: 'Nearer my God to thee.' Slowly he reached down and moved it closer to him. He knelt and, weary, rested his elbows on the ledge and brought his forehead into his hands.

It felt as if he had slept, as if he had been taken by the angels to a place of rest, where his fevered mind received the balm of benediction. After a while, how long he didn't know, he sat back and looked around. Had she worshipped here? Had she asked God to guide her? Had this led her to ... ? Bertie shook his head. Best not to dwell on that, better just to pray for her soul. The clamminess in the air, dusty from decaying stone and mortar, made him shiver. The damp was making his breath raspy and out of time. He wanted to do what he had come for and then head home.

Outside, Bertie wasn't sure where to start. So many souls and they all clambered to live again through his attention. The path was taking him round behind the church, up and back towards the lane where he had parked his motorcar. The crows cawed from their nests high in the cedar pines and a robin hopped nearby, stopping every so often to warble an autumn lament. A hedgehog looked right at him before scuttling for cover in a mound of leaves by the graveyard boundary. Bertie thought of Tildy and was sure he heard the whisper of her voice. The only other sound was a faint scraping. It came from behind a white stone monument topped with a carved cross and enclosed by wrought-iron railings. Wreaths and baskets garlanded with flags and ribbons in the colours of the suffragettes all but covered the gravel enclosure. The colours drew him, the purple, the green and the white. He saw them in his dreams, just as he saw her.

The scraping stopped. Through the haze of the wispy mist that had gathered about, a figure rose from the other side of the monument. A dark gabardine coat flapped around her bony frame as the wind tugged at it. Her head was down and covered by the wide brim of her black hat. She raised her face to him. The sight of the blood-drained skin and eyes that held no flicker of light brought a cry to his heart.

The woman stretched and bent down to retrieve a trug. Bertie saw now that this was no spectre, but an older woman with deep lines on her forehead and wisps of silver hair that caught her wind-roughened cheeks. She looked at him but her face moved not a muscle. Bertie stood his ground.

"Are you here to see my daughter's grave?" she asked. "It has become quite an attraction, you know."

"I just wanted to pay my respects. I'm sorry, I should have brought some flowers."

"Well, as you can see, there are plenty of those, and they keep coming," she waved her arm. "It's quite a job to keep it tidy. They made her a martyr and martyrs get a lot of flowers, or so I've found."

She looked at him, squinting through the half-light.

"You're the jockey, aren't you?" she said. "I thought you'd come eventually."

Bertie met her gaze. He owed her at least that.

"Well, I'm afraid that I can't give you any answers, Mr Jones, if that is what you were hoping for. I'm too occupied with my own questions. I still don't understand, but I pray, every day I pray for her."

"No, I don't think I came for that," he replied. "And I pray for her too."

The woman continued as if he had not spoken. "Much as I admired her conviction to her cause, I am not sure that I could ever condone her methods. I love her and I mourn her, and I believe wholeheartedly that she felt what she did was necessary. My sadness is that she suffered so greatly."

She took a step nearer until her shadow engulfed him. Bertie saw a black glint of malice come into her eyes. Her lips drew back and he saw the angry snarl of a cornered she-wolf. For a moment Bertie thought that she would leap at his throat and tear out his heart.

"Was there really nothing you could have done, Mr Jones? With all your talents, was there nothing that could have saved her? They say you have special powers, that you can tame the wildest of horses, but you couldn't do anything for my daughter. Surely there must have been something, something?" Her voice trembled, until it stopped altogether. She hurried away.

Bertie stared after her, wanting to call her back, to explain, but his body was numb. At the monument, the tributes in their multitudes cried out their messages of loss, accusing him, blaming him for depriving them of such a beloved sister. Stepping back, his foot slipped on the grassy bank. He righted himself and ran as fast as he could back to the motorcar, calling on all that was holy for the engine to start.

26

Christmas, December 1913

"Aren't you glad you came with me today?" Lily asked, breathless from trying to keep up.

"Yes, Lily, there's nothing I like more than watching you shop." Bertie slowed down for her.

"Be fair, Bertie, I have been helping you sort out your gifts, so it isn't just all for me. You'll still have to get something for me, of course. I've given Jess a few hints for my presents, in case you get stuck." She sighed. "I thought you were enjoying yourself. Seeing Percy and the others too, that was nice."

Yes, yes, of course." Bertie felt tired. "I just don't feel much in the mood for Christmas, that's all."

"You'll cheer up, Bertie, you know you will. Once the rest of the parcels are delivered, all nicely wrapped, you won't be able to stop yourself. You love Christmas more than all of us put together. The cards, the carols, the mince pies. You'll soon be out collecting holly and decking the halls." She caught her breath for a moment. "And you've got your West End pantomime next week. We'll be there to cheer you on, although you always do the same thing every year. Can't you ask for something different?"

"They like to see me ride the panto horse. It has become a tradition now, or so they say."

"Mind you … " Lily started again.

A dull thudding sound started up in the distance.

"What's that noise?"

"Probably a Salvation Army band. It's that time of year," she reassured him.

Drums, yes, it did sound like a military band, but Bertie had an odd feeling.

"We should have got a taxi earlier."

"But you like walking usually," she protested.

Bertie steered them off the main road and into a side street. Approaching them, half a dozen or so women marched along, huddled together. Some of them wore big rosettes. Two held poles joined by furled banners. One carried a large placard on a stick that read, 'Votes for Women'.

"Let's take a different road. I don't think this is the right way." Lily pulled Bertie back towards the way they had come. Turning suddenly, she knocked the bags and boxes that he carried. They flew up and out of his hands.

Lily put her hands to her face. "Oh, I'm so sorry, Bertie."

"It's alright, Lil, I'll get them." He spoke gently to her and crouched down to pick them up. "See, everything is all wrapped up tight and there's nothing here to break, so no harm done."

Dusty boots made of fine leather stopped in front of him. Bertie looked up and stared into the face of Flora. Over her coat, she wore a wide satin sash that fitted tight across her breast. The white, green and purple swam before his eyes even in the closing light of the dim afternoon. Every time he saw her, there were always those colours, and every time he saw those colours, he thought of the woman.

"Flora!" said Lily.

Bertie stayed kneeling, trying to remain calm while he gathered together the bags and parcels.

"You know these people?" asked one of the suffragettes.

"Er, yes." Flora turned her face from him.

"Aren't you going to introduce us? This nice couple, they may like to join us," the woman persisted.

"Oh well, I'm not sure," Flora stammered.

The women stood and waited. Lily's mouth twitched. Bertie returned to his packages.

"Even in this light, I can see you are blushing, Flora. What is wrong with you?" One of them laughed. "Come on, speak up."

Flora hesitated.

"Mr Jones is a jockey for my father. And this is his sister, Miss Lily Jones."

"Oh," they said in one very long note.

Bertie felt them gather like hens about a newborn kitten, their beaks all sharpened and ready. He sat up on his haunches and raised himself steadily.

"Well, Mr Jones, I don't suppose you are any the worse off for our poor sister's sacrifice," the older woman spoke.

Bertie didn't answer. He looked at Flora. She kept her head bent. Lily stretched the finger of her glove and wound it round and round until the flesh beneath it pinched and swelled with the pressure.

"You must be used to it, falling off, I mean," said one of the pole-bearers.

Bertie looked at her and shook his head. "No, ma'am, I wouldn't say that."

Lily snapped and stepped in front of Bertie. She pointed the end of her flapping misshapen glove at Flora.

"Tell them, Flora, go on, you tell them, you must. Tell them how hard it has been for Bertie."

Flora looked away and Bertie felt his heart rip.

"Come on, Lil, let's go. No one has to explain anything." Bertie wanted to grab her and pull her away but his arms were full with the now precariously balanced bags and boxes. "Come on, now."

The women turned and continued marching down the street.

"How dare they say that to you, Bertie?" Large tears rolled down Lily's face.

"It's not important, Lily, not any more. Let's find our way home."

ひ ひ ひ

Bertie hadn't spotted Reverend Wright and now it was too late.

"Bertie! How fortuitous. Jess said she wasn't expecting you back for some time, but here you are!" The reverend's voice was always loud, but today it made Bertie's skull throb.

"Evening, vicar." Bertie made a great effort to smile.

Reverend Wright stood over him.

"We've missed you at choir practice recently."

"I'm sorry," Bertie mumbled, and tried to say something about horses.

"Now Bertie. I won't beat about the bush. I, we, we all have all been most concerned about you. This unfortunate incident, you must put it behind you. I know that things have been hard for you, especially with dear Old Ben passing on when he did. But you can't let this ruin your life."

"I'm fine, vicar, really I am." Bertie squirmed under the vicar's gaze, and then was annoyed with himself that he had behaved in such a way, as if he had been caught out like some sort of naughty schoolboy.

"I may be wrong, Bertie, but I think that you are putting on a brave face. All the joy has gone out of your eyes. You rush here and there, like a ... ," he paused, searching for the right image. "Like a wound-up clockwork toy. You must try and find some peace."

Bertie looked round in the hope that someone would come and release him, but realized that there was little chance. He turned and faced the vicar.

"Well, I can't say that I'm finding it particularly easy at the moment, but I'm doing what I can."

"You've always been a good Christian man, Bertie. Now let God help you find forgiveness and reconciliation." The Reverend became more fervent.

"I thank you, vicar," Bertie said at last. "But surely the good Lord would understand that sometimes a man, Christian or otherwise, needs to be left alone. I have not turned from God, but I need some time to think things over."

Reverend Wright started to speak, but Bertie intercepted. "I won't delay you any more now, vicar. I know that you must be busy." Bertie waved as he went off in the direction of the stables.

"Oh, Bertie!" Reverend Wright called after him. "Bertie!"

"Yes, vicar." Bertie stopped and made himself smile amiably.

"Bertie, the, er, annual Christmas party for the children and the old people. Are you, I mean, would you be happy to sponsor it again this year?"

"Of course, vicar."

"Well, it will cost a little more this year, I'm afraid. The price of things seems to have increased so much, although we could of course leave out the roast dinner and have something simpler."

"Oh no, they can't go without their Christmas dinner. You just let me know, vicar, and I'll sort it out."

U U U

Bertie sat on the wall. The days were at their shortest and the wintry sky was already collecting the colours of dusk. From the field, a great gather of rooks took flight, swirling like black snow over the trees, their calls fading as they settled in the woods.

"Thought I'd find you here." Reg came and sat beside him. "You've been so quiet lately, everyone is wondering about you."

"Oh I'm alright. It's been a busy season, but that's good," Bertie replied. "Are you feeling better now? Jess said that you'd been quite poorly. I meant to call round."

"Yes, just a cold. Poor Nell, trying to look after me and the boys. Not sure who she would say was more trouble."

Bertie looked at his brother. Reg's face was flushed and his eyes glinted almost fever bright.

"Well, you look after yourself, Reg. Jess said that you've been working all hours. You are supposed to be taking it easier now, but I reckon that pub of yours is as bad as racing."

"Don't fuss so, Bert, you're as bad as Nell."

They sat for a while.

"Well, I have some good news." Reg spoke slowly and started to roll another cigarette. "I'm not supposed to say yet, but well, you're always the first to know about these things. We'll have another little one arriving come the summer."

"Ah, that is good news," said Bertie. "You know, if it's another boy we could be on the way to a Jones team in a few years."

"Perhaps rather than leaving it all up to me, you might like to settle down yourself and make your own contribution," laughed Reg.

"Well, I don't think so. I don't know. Perhaps one day, but not yet at least." Bertie got his words in a muddle and decided it was best to stop.

"It'll be odd at Christmas without Old Ben fussing round," said Reg.

Bertie didn't reply.

"You know, Reg. I've tried not to, but I blame that woman and I can't help it. If she hadn't, you know, if she hadn't run out like that." Pondering for a moment, he plucked a switch of grass from the meadow. It was almost dark. "Well, there wouldn't have been all that trouble and perhaps Old Ben wouldn't have got himself in such a state, and he would still be here. I can't stop thinking that."

"There now, Bert, don't take on so. You don't know that, none of us can say for sure that things would have been different. Old Ben was very old. And at least he went peacefully. That's how he would have wanted it."

Bertie tried to say something, but he couldn't. A tremor started first in his hand, then up his arm, then his whole body shook, even his teeth chattered. He drifted outside himself, watching as Reg leapt up and came towards him. Someone else was there, he was sure. "See what I see … " the words were loud in his head but unspoken.

"It's all right, Bertie." Reg held him close, just like he was one of his own babies.

27

London, February 1914

L ILY'S BEHAVIOUR STILL PUZZLED Bertie. She kept close to him, slipping her arm through his and holding tight. But all the way up to London she had been oddly evasive, which was strange given the efforts she had gone to in persuading him to meet her mysterious friend. Bertie hadn't wanted to come at all, he rarely wanted to go anywhere much these days, but this trip seemed so important to Lily. Danny's appearance at the station was even more confusing.

They walked in silence across Bloomsbury Square, past Percy's old lodgings, and along a street lined with wrought-iron railings that fronted sooty yellow stock-brick houses. The skeletal trees eked out shadows from the gunmetal light of the morning sun as it crept across the untidy winter grass in the square. They passed a muffled-up dog-walker dragging an irritable terrier. A couple of pigeons pecking at bits of bread under a bench and a squirrel early out of hibernation were the only other signs of life. It suited Bertie not to talk.

Danny dashed ahead of them, muttering about checking that everything was ready. Bertie watched him run up the small flight of steps to a three-storey terrace. The white-panelled front door opened before he had even reached the knocker. A Chinaman came forward and shook Danny's hand. As they spoke, Bertie saw the Chinaman glance over. He was young and fine featured. He wore an old-fashioned smoking cap and a dark tunic that was not unlike a long racing silk.

"Lily, what is this? Surely not, I mean, is this your young man?" Bertie's head ached.

"What? No, no, no, Bertie, nothing like that." She bit her lip and ushered Bertie along.

As they approached, the Chinaman put his hands together, as if in prayer. He bowed from the waist, keeping his back perfectly straight, then led them inside. The hallway smelt of incense and, although Bertie couldn't see any smoke, his eyes felt scratchy and raw. A maid took their hats and coats and they followed the Chinaman into a room that was shrouded in night.

Heavy curtains kept the outside world at bay. Bertie counted at least four three-branched brass candelabra arranged around the room, each burned bright, dribbling wax and sputtering tall reflections of the thin-leaved potted plants that sprouted from clumps of large brass holders. A stone statue of a cross-legged Eastern monk, one hand raised and his eyes downcast, sat on a large mahogany trunk. Perched on the mantelpiece, a white-marble elephant waved human arms and feet that glowed orange from the hot coals that burned in the fireplace. Even Jess with her fondness for knick-knacks would have found the decoration too elaborate. Centred in the room was a round dark wooden table that shone with wax polish. It was of a size to seat six comfortably. Seven well-upholstered chairs were evenly spaced around it. Bertie ran his finger around the inside of his collar as the heat of the room clung to his neck.

A portly woman stood before them. She dabbed at her hair, an unnecessary gesture as every strand was in place.

Lily gave a little cough.

"Bertie, I'd like you to meet Mrs Pemberton, Mrs Prudence Pemberton. Now, Bertie, Mrs Pemberton is a spiritualist and she wanted to see you. She has important information for you."

Mrs Pemberton. It sounded such a sensible name. And she looked like a sensible woman, with her tidy suit and reading glasses on a chain around her neck. Bertie looked around him.

"And your young man, Lily, where is he? The one you were so keen for me to meet. Or is there no young man?" Bertie kept his voice low but spoke right into her ear.

"I didn't exactly say that there was a young man." Lily kept her gaze ahead and smiled stiffly.

"No, but you implied it. You knew I only came because I thought it was important for you."

Lily turned to him. Her voice became louder. "It is important, Bertie, but important for you. We want to make things better."

"You stupid, stupid girl." Bertie turned to Danny. "And you. Did you put her up to this?"

"Come on, Bertie. Mrs Pemberton can help. Percy has known her for years. She contacted him so that she could help you. She knows about these things. She can stop all this nightmare for you. She can lay the spirits to rest."

"So, it seems as if you have all been in on this."

He shook Lily's hand from his arm and stepped away from her, astonished at the distaste that he felt.

Mrs Pemberton approached him. Her eyes glinted and flickered.

"Please, Mr Jones, please calm yourself. I know it must feel strange, but I can help if you'll let me." She spoke in a low tone, pronouncing every word with care.

Bertie turned away, almost bumping into a tiny serving woman who was carrying a tray heavy with teapots, jugs and cups.

"Come on, Mr Jones, let's sit down. Much cosier here, we can have some refreshment." She steered Bertie towards the low table in front of the fire. "Ang, we seem to have forgotten the Madeira cake. I'm sure that these nice people would appreciate a slice."

The Chinaman sent the girl off and then sat down on the chair to the other side of Mrs Pemberton.

Bertie pursed his lips, but took a seat. Mrs Pemberton presided over the refreshments, offering tea or coffee and cake. Bertie accepted a cup of tea, but it didn't taste like tea, it was smoky and bitter and there was no milk. Occasionally Mrs Pemberton stopped and stared over Bertie's shoulder. He brushed himself down.

"You have a lot of guides," she said to him.

Bertie wanted to cross himself every time she spoke. Prayer and the Good Book should be his guidance, not this mumbo-jumbo.

"Angels, guardian angels who watch over you," she paused for a moment. "You know you have the power."

Perched on his chair, clutching his cup, squashed between Mrs Pemberton and the fireplace, Bertie looked at the door. Fresh air and sunlight was what he needed, not this unnatural hot house with its strange objects and artificial smells.

"Now to business. Mr Jones, I have messages for you that will not wait."

The lights flickered and the door slammed shut. Lily jumped. Danny gasped. Bertie sighed, were there to be party tricks too?

The Chinaman started to sing in very deep, low sounds, repeating six words over and over again. They were in a foreign tongue, but had the rhythm of a lullaby. Bertie shook his head to get rid of the tiredness that drew him down to a place where he did not want to be.

"An old man who is dear to you is here." Mrs Pemberton frowned as if listening very carefully. "His name is Ben."

Bertie felt something inside snap. He stood up.

"Enough. That's enough." Teacups went flying, but Bertie was past caring. He pointed at Lily and Danny. "It is bad enough that you bring me here in the first place, but to drag in poor Old Ben, that is just too much."

"But Mr Jones," said Mrs Pemberton. "Please, I beg you."

But Bertie was not to be stopped. "Really Danny, I would have though that you had more sense. Can't you see this is all one big fake, just the smoke and mirrors that belong in the music halls?"

The heat, the smell and the dreadful tea made Bertie feel sick. He stumbled out of the house. They called after him but he kept on walking, faster and faster.

U U U

Bertie banged through the door of Romano's. He didn't look at anyone but walked straight to an empty table in the corner. A trio of waiters flapped around him and Luigi rushed over, haranguing the others for not looking after Mr Jones properly. Bertie handed over his coat and hat.

Luigi snapped his fingers. "Soda water for Mr Jones, *subito*."

"No, Luigi, brandy. I want brandy."

Luigi raised an eyebrow, but despatched a waiter with the order.

"Mr Jones, are you … ?" he started.

"That's all, thank you."

Marie swaggered over, but dropped her smile as she saw his face.

"Bertie? In all the years I've known you … What on earth is the matter?"

"Don't you start, Marie, please. I've just about had it."

The waiter placed a large balloon-shaped glass on the table in front him; an inch of thick, golden liquid glowed at him in the lamplight.

Cold air swept into the room as the door opened again. Danny and Lily stood there. Lily rushed to him, struggling to catch her breath.

"Bertie, Bertie, I know you are upset but something has happened. You must help."

"Well, perhaps we should all sit down, put out some cards and use the glass to see what the spirits spell out?"

"What on earth is going on?" Marie put her hands on her hips.

"There's a suffragette rally in Trafalgar Square but lots of bully boys have turned up as well as a big show of police." Danny spoke quickly.

"Well, I'm ready for a bit of a scuffle. Those bully boys will wish they'd stayed at home today." Marie rolled up her sleeves. "Dillon, you coming?"

Dillon staggered from a dark corner of the room, his eyes red and bleary. Bertie hardly recognized him: Dillon had gone downhill fast since his run-in with the Jockey Club but, despite the young woman in the shadows blowing him a kiss, he seemed to make Marie happy.

"This is what I have to put up with, Bertie. Why couldn't he be more like you?" Marie was even more fired up and gave Dillon a hefty cuff as she marched him out.

Or, why couldn't I be more like him? Bertie thought.

Lily moved towards Bertie, looking into his face and shaking him. "Flora is there. We passed her as we tried to catch up with you, but she wouldn't come away with us. They say it will be a bloodbath. She'll come away for you, Bertie. You can make her."

"Why should I make her do anything? After all, that is what she's fighting for isn't it? The right to be her own person."

"Poor Flora. She said that she wanted to start living a proper life, not just dreaming her time away in her head. I thought it was rather beautiful, although I wasn't sure what she meant." Lily stopped for a moment. "But we have to help her, she'll get hurt for certain. Please come, Bertie."

"Oh Lily, grow up will you?" Bertie snapped. "It's time everybody grew up."

She jumped at his words and began to cry.

"Come on, old fellow, you know you don't mean any of that," said Danny

"For God's sake, why can't you all just leave me alone?" Bertie shrugged him off and stood up, catching the table with his leg. The table toppled back and forward before righting itself, but the glass fell to the floor. "Can't you understand? I've had enough!"

Bertie walked out into the street. People scurried along the Strand, away from Trafalgar Square. He joined them, buoyed along by their panic. The chill of the air cleared his head. Above the shrill chatter and the rumble of the omnibuses, he could hear shouts and calls behind him.

An icy wet film of rain cut through the mist. In a corner by a shop front a girl sat with her knees drawn up under her chin. A cloak pulled over her head and with just a few golden curls caught by the lamplight, no one except him seemed to have noticed her. The memory of Flora on that late afternoon over twenty years ago came back to him. It was if he had stepped back into the wood and there she was, sheltered under the old oak tree like a lost fairy child. Every detail of that moment was clear to him: the smell of her hair, the sound of her voice, the smoothness of her skin as she took his own rough hand.

"Where to, mister?"

Bertie realized that the girl was standing close to him, sallow and weary, holding his hand with a papery touch that felt as if it would turn to powder under the slightest pressure. This was not his Flora.

"No, no. I'm sorry." Bertie took what coins he had out of his pocket and gave them to the girl. "Look, take these. Go and get warm."

She snatched the money and disappeared into the backstreets.

Bertie steadied himself. He must get back to Flora. Whatever had he been thinking? He could never abandon Flora. Passers-by knocked into him and complained as Bertie made a sharp about-turn. He took no notice. His pace increased as he thought of her alone and in danger.

The shouts and calls were all jumbled up and out of time. A police van rushed past them, then another one, almost shoving the omnibuses off the road and nearly injuring the pedestrians stuck halfway in the road. He broke into a run, weaving in and out of the crowd. Traffic was backed up bumper to bumper now. He cut across the stationary vehicles, passing St Martin's on his right. A quick scan told him that he'd get a better view by the stone parapet that circled the north side of the Square and stood above the main gathering points.

Trafalgar Square itself was black with people. Flags and banners swayed precariously. Whistles blew and marching songs were drowned by boos and cat-calls. Police vans encircled the perimeter. Mounted officers chivvied people away from the fountains, herding them towards the enclosed space directly below him.

Bertie looked into the scrambling mass below. It was difficult to make out people's faces in the dank light. Women screamed as they were dragged out from the crowd and tossed to waiting arms that bundled them away; some of women kicked, some dropped to their knees, some stood rigid, but all were roughly handled. Big thick-set men laid into anyone who tried to help, beating them with sticks as well as their fists until the defenders fell to the ground bent double.

Under the lamplight, three thugs tore off the sash of a suffragette. Laughing, they pushed her back and forth between them, pawing at her body. Then a large pennant declaring the Shorthand Writers of Great Britain held by a tiny lady in a large hat hit the men like a lance, knocking them out of the way. Figures flew like banshees on to the floored men, who disappeared from view.

The crowd was getting thicker. Bertie sighed. It was hopeless, he would never find her in this. In a last-ditch attempt, he climbed the parapet and called her name out through the rain and up into the sky. As the sounds echoed all around him, he was drawn to a figure buffeted to and fro below. She must have felt his presence for she stood still and looked right at him. It was Flora. Everything stopped. Bertie was aware only of her.

A shriek nearby brought him to his senses.

"Come to this wall!" He shouted to Flora and pointed at the stepped pillar directly beneath him. "I'll get you."

He climbed over the parapet and balanced on the ledge. The top of the balustrade was strong. Flora struggled through the thickening crowd, dipping and squeezing her way through. She reached the pillar and tried to heave herself up, but the stone was slippery in the wet.

"Don't worry," Bertie tried to reassure her.

Bertie hooked his foot through the carved stone and leaned down. Hanging almost upside down, he put his arms out.

"Jump, Flora!"

She made an effort, but it was nowhere near high enough. The blood rushed to his head. He brought himself upright again. A passer-by stopped and watched.

"This time hold up your arms too," Bertie shouted.

Flora jumped again. Bertie swung down again but missed her.

"You're like a monkey, you are." The passer-by came closer. "Are you in the circus?"

"Go away," Bertie hissed at him. "Go away."

"No need to act like that, you should keep a better eye on your wife, letting her mix with that lot."

"Again!" Bertie shouted to Flora and lowered himself once more.

He caught her arm, just above the elbow. His shoulders burned so much he thought they would melt his grip. A man below snatched at her skirt.

"Kick out," Bertie called.

She set her face hard and pounded her right boot into the man's head.

"Now push up against the wall and jump."

As her foot hit the wall, she used it to spring upwards. Bertie caught her, and unceremoniously bundled her over the ledge, then pulled himself up. Flora clung to him.

"You're lucky your man works in a circus, missus." The passer-by was still there. "You better get going though, the rozzers are coming up here now. There's more of them piling in."

Bertie scooped up Flora and ran with her all the way back to Romano's.

Luigi, discrete as ever, whisked them away to a quiet corner, clicking his fingers at the waiters. Flora was pale and silent.

"Hot sweet tea, I think," said Bertie. "Plenty of it. Then we'll get you home."

Flora sat up. "Keep the bloody tea, I need a brandy, and a large one."
Bertie smiled. She'd live.

Marie walked in, hatless, hair ragged, her face bruised and bloodied.
"I'll have the same," she said.

Danny followed, trying to brush down his clothes. "So Bertie, you
went back after all."

"I'm sorry, Danny, you were right. So was Lily." Bertie looked
around. "Where is Lily?"

"That's what we came to tell you. She went to try and find Flora.
We followed but lost her in the crowd. We think she's been arrested."

ひ ひ ひ

No one knew what had happened to Lily. Danny and Flora went with
Bertie to the police station at Charing Cross and then to Bow. They
tried the hospitals. Lily's name was not on any list. They walked the
streets for hours, tracing and retracing where she might have gone,
trying to find her.

"This is ridiculous, she can't have just disappeared into thin air,"
Bertie said. "I'll contact the Guv'nor, he'll know what to do."

Danny passed him a mug of tea from the stall on the corner. "I don't
think that is a very good idea. He's too mixed up in the establishment.
You are too mixed up in the establishment. They won't want to get
involved, Bertie. They won't want you to be involved."

"She's my sister. I am already involved. Well, I can ask Lord
Marcus. He's always been very good to me. I'm sure he'll be able to
find something out."

As he said it, Bertie realized that although he had known Lord
Marcus for nearly twenty years, he had no idea how to contact him.
Lord Marcus would arrive at Egerton, arrive at the parade ring,
arrive in the stables, lately they might even speak on the telephone.
Occasionally they would meet at an official function, but for all the
time they had spent together, Bertie realized that he knew nothing
about him outside racing.

Danny shrugged. "Up to you, Bertie, but it would be easier all
round if you let me help."

They sat side by side on the steps by Trafalgar Square and watched
the light creep in from the east. The stone was cold and damp.

"I'll go down to the WSPU offices." Flora brushed down her skirt. The streaks of mud had set hard and the seams of her jacket were torn. "They will have some information, I'm sure."

She leaned forward and kissed Bertie's cheek.

"Danny's right, you know. Don't ask them."

U U U

The next morning Bertie telephoned the Guv'nor from Danny's rooms. The Guv'nor had never let him down.

"For heaven's sake, Bertie. You shouldn't be doing this. Get someone to deal with this on your behalf. The press will have a field day if they get wind of this." The Guv'nor voice was loud and distorted.

Bertie moved the earpiece away in the hope it might make things clearer.

"Think of His Majesty, think of Egerton, you know how delicate things are." The Guv'nor paused for breath. "Stupid, stupid girl. She should have thought of all this before getting involved."

"It wasn't her fault, Guv'nor. She just got caught up in it." Bertie wanted to add, while trying to help Flora, but he held back. "She wasn't involved herself."

"Well, never mind that now. Get someone to speak to the police, but try and keep out of it. At least Jones is a common surname."

"Well, my main thought is to get her back safe and sound." Bertie felt his own voice rise.

"Yes, of course, Bertie, of course." The Guv'nor spoke more deliberately now. "But tell as few people as possible."

"Yes, Guv'nor," Bertie struggled to reply. His throat ached and, for the first time in years, he yearned to see his dad again.

"And Bertie, don't disturb anyone at the Palace or connected with the Palace. You hear me?"

"Yes, Guv'nor," Bertie cleared his throat, replying mechanically now.

"It would be very difficult for them to refuse. They hold you in very high regard. But refuse they must. You understand?"

"Oh yes, Guv'nor. I understand. I understand perfectly." Bertie smashed the receiver down.

The police made no progress. Bertie flitted back and forth to Cambridge, Newmarket and London, just in case Lily had made her way home. Bertie kept his word about keeping quiet but only to protect Jess and Aunt Mary. Danny took Bertie to see Lord Rosebery. Danny had been riding for Lord Rosebery and he had always been very kind to him.

Indeed, Lord Rosebery asked no questions but undertook the task discretely and more willingly than they had expected. "In 1908 I stood and watched from the Palace Yard as the suffragettes, thousands upon thousands of them, marched into Parliament Square begging Asquith for the vote. I did nothing," he said. "That day brought so much misery and suffering, perhaps this can atone a little."

It took three days for Lord Rosebery's men to find Lily. They tracked her down to Holloway Prison, where she was using a false name and serving a one-month sentence for breach of the peace because she could not pay her fine without revealing her true identity. Danny and Flora persuaded Bertie to let them collect her. They paid the five pounds and took her back to Flora's flat.

Bertie came as quickly as he could from Newmarket. Danny was already there and took him into the sitting room.

"Lily's been sleeping. The doctor gave her something and Flora has been watching over her," he said. "Look, Bertie, she's been through a lot, you know, so you need to prepare yourself."

But Bertie couldn't concentrate on what Danny was saying, he just wanted to see Lily.

The door opened. At first he didn't recognize her as she walked into the sitting room. Her gait was rigid, almost tipsy in its effort to stay upright. With her higgledy-piggledy clothes and hair half falling down, this couldn't be Lily. She seemed to look through him. The vivid blue of her eyes was veiled into a dull grey and black rings made her cheeks seem shrunken. Yellow streaks sallowed her complexion and the bridge of her nose was swollen. The twisted smile across her face from the red weal that ran from mouth to left cheekbone made her look like a painted puppet.

Flora came in behind Lily. She held her hands out ready to catch her.

"Oh my God, Lily. What have they done to you?" Bertie wanted to scoop his sister up and take her home, to safety, to peace. But Lily let out a scream and started to tremble.

"Please take me away, Flora. Please take me away," she said over and over again. "I can't see people. I can't."

"But, I'm not people, I'm your brother."

Flora shook her head at him. She took Lily in her arms, soothing her as if she was a child and led her back to the bedroom.

"I was trying to explain, Bertie, she has been through a lot. By the time we found her, they had been feeding her by force. She was in quite a state but the doctor has been here and examined her. He says she'll mend physically, but it is the shock that has taken its toll. I don't know all the details but gather that they couldn't get the tube through her teeth and so they rammed it down her nose. She fought fiercely."

"She would do, she's as stubborn as they come. Stubborn, but brave." Bertie sat down and put his head in his hands. He had let this happen. He should have taken more care of her.

"When can we take her home?"

"Well, it seems that she wants to be with people who understand, who have been through what she has experienced." Danny spoke slowly and quietly.

"But we're her family. She should be with us." Bertie paced up and down.

"Flora suggested taking Lily to Dorset Hall. It's a good place, a place of recuperation for the women, in fact the woman at Epsom, your Miss Davison, used to stay there."

"She's not my Miss Davison." The warm air was choking. "But Lily hates violence, why would she want to go and be among people who live by violence?"

"It's just until she feels able to cope with things a bit more," Flora walked in. "They are used to dealing with women out of Holloway, who have been affected by their experience. It really is the best place for her, but of course she can always stay here with me for a while."

"Well, it seems that you have it all worked out." Bertie struggled to keep his voice steady.

"No, Bertie, no, it isn't like that at all." Flora ran after him but he had gone.

ʊ ʊ ʊ

Despite the cold, Bertie's throat was on fire. His chest throbbed. He drove off with the engine screaming, weaving around other vehicles and nearly hitting an omnibus as he headed away from the crowded streets. It was a filthy night, the rain started before he got out of London but Bertie didn't stop to put up the roof.

By the time Bertie arrived at Egerton, his breathing had become short and he was running a fever. Jess put him to bed with a poultice and a hot-water bottle, but he couldn't sleep. The cries of Anmer in the stable woke him. He had to go to the horse.

Anmer jumped and kicked in his stall. His coat was lathered up and his eyes flashed with a wild light. Bertie picked up the brush and swept it across the horse's coat but it did little to calm him.

"I know, boy, I know. We need to clear our heads and cool our blood."

Bertie flung a saddle on Anmer and they bolted out into the night. The rain had cleared and the moon shone full as the clouds raced by.

Up on the gallops, a sudden change of pressure made his ears crackle. Bertie shook his head and tapped his ear. They stopped. Anmer sniffed the air. Wailing came and went, as if the crowds in the distance were calling to him. Bertie's skin prickled. Each nerve in his spine was alert and waiting. He called out but his voice scattered and was lost.

Something fluttered by. Anmer reared. Bertie flinched. Everything around them seemed to have been snatched away, leaving just the cries in the wind. They were back at Epsom. They galloped around the Corner. This time they saw her. The woman. They rode towards her, towards the noise, towards the light. This time they would not stop until they had atoned for their sin, until they were with her. An eye for an eye, he and Anmer must make their peace, so that she could have hers.

A bell rang out from the church on the hill. With each peal the pure sound fused into its own echo to form one long singing note.

A golden cross on the tower glowed and shone, sending its yellow light to his heart.

"No! Don't do this. Don't do this or you will make me a murderer," she called. "Don't make me a murderer."

PART V
RESURRECTION

28

Report of a death,
February 1914

B ERTIE OPENED HIS EYES. He lay flat on his back, looking up at the ceiling, light white, the curtains were drawn around him, bright white, tucked around him were laundry-fresh sheets, starched white. Nearby, the droning voice of a woman read snippets from the newspaper.

"Oh what a shame, listen to this." Her voice changed pitch. " 'We have just received news that Herbert Jones, the royal jockey, has died from the serious lung haemorrhage that afflicted him at home a week ago.' Now that's sad, such a gent, they say."

"The one that came off his horse at the Derby last year when the suffragette woman ran out?" a man spoke. "I'm sure someone said he was in here somewhere."

"She died," the droning woman continued. "Poor creature. Mad though, she must have been mad."

"Shouldn't think the jockey was too pleased neither," the man moaned with the pain of laughing.

"Sit still, Alf, for heaven's sake. Where's your respect?"

"It gets them like that, those types. Makes them neurotic; too much thinking and too much reading, it's not natural for a woman." The man sounded knowledgeable about the whole business. "But the poor old horse, and the poor old jockey. I knew a chap who was there. Saw the whole thing, he did. A miracle, he said, that more people weren't hurt. All the same, I'm sorry to hear about Diamond Jones."

Bertie blinked. He was still here, caught in a straitjacket of sheets and feeling what it must be like to be dead. Was this his tomb? Was this what people meant when they were illuminated? Slowly he moved his right hand. He touched his neck; it felt sore but the skin felt warm. He moved across and tried to grab his left arm. His chest felt heavy, as if a press was screwed down on it. Bits were sticking into him. The pain felt real enough. It wasn't how he pictured heaven, but maybe it was a like a waiting room; you had to stay put until He was ready. But then he shouldn't assume that he deserved to go to heaven.

Bertie tried to call out, but his tongue stuck to the inside of his mouth and only a half-choked gagging sound came out. After another few attempts, he lay back exhausted. Eventually a nurse came. She lifted him slightly and put some water to his lips. The liquid released the thick metal taste of blood. It made him want to retch but at least he could move the inside of his mouth.

"Am I dead?" he managed to whisper. "I just heard someone say it's in the papers that I've passed away."

She smiled at him and stroked his brow.

"Well, I can take your pulse just to check, if you like."

The nurse rearranged his bedding, tucking in the edges and folding the corners all nice and neat.

"Newspapers. They'll make up anything for a good story," she said. "My mother was in our local paper once for helping to make a citizen's arrest, they put ten years on her age, she was most upset."

Bertie fidgeted as he tried to think how it had all happened.

You are very lucky, though," the nurse tried to be encouraging. "You must have a guardian angel watching over you."

"Tildy? Where is Tildy?" he asked.

"I don't remember someone called Tildy. You've had a couple of sisters in and quite a few brothers. A lot of people have been calling in to enquire too. Of course, there were journalists, but we try to keep them away. But no, not a Tildy, but I can ask the other nurses, it may have been when I was off duty."

"But how did I get here?" he gasped, fighting for a good breath.

"Come on now, calm down, Mr Jones," The nurse put a cool hand on his forehead. "From what I understand you were taken ill at home. They said you had a bad fall from your horse earlier in the day, and that may have caused the haemorrhage. Your lungs are weak and so they would be the first things to collapse under that sort of pressure. But you have done remarkably well, so there is no need to fret."

Tiredness numbed his thoughts.

"Now I'd like you to get some more rest ... " but the nurse already sounded far away.

Later that day, Jess visited with Walter. She looked very smart in a new coat and hat.

"I've brought you some hot-house daffodils, to cheer you up." Jess unpacked her bag. "And some grapes and in this tin is a fruit cake, just as you like it. You won't get anything decent to eat in here."

"What happened?" asked Bertie. "I don't remember a thing."

"You were out riding, must have been very early in the morning. Anyway, Anmer brought you back, slumped over his saddle you were. Isn't that right, Walter?"

"We think you must have had a fall but managed to clamber back on the horse, something like that. The lads found you and got you in here. Not before time too."

"And Anmer?"

"Oh, he's doing fine. In fact, he seems much more like his old self again."

∪ ∪ ∪

Bertie had done a lot of thinking since he had been back from hospital. It was a lovely spring morning, a time for fresh starts. Up at first light, Bertie had already been down to the stable. Anmer heard him approach and was calling, stretching his neck over the stable door.

Mr Smallwood came over. "Good to see you up and about, Bertie," he said. "Anmer was a bit of a saviour, bringing you back like that."

Anmer nuzzled up to Bertie, giving his jacket a friendly nibble.

"Alright if I take him out for a bit of exercise?"

"Go ahead, Bertie, but take it nice and gently now."

"No need to worry, I'm as fit as a flea now."

They cantered off. Anmer held his tail high and there was a joy in his movement. They didn't stop until they reached the top of the

Downs. The air was fresh and the linnets twittered on the gorse flowers.

"Thank you, Anmer." Bertie leaned forward and spoke in the horse's ear. "I feel that I've been given a second chance."

Answering with a confident neigh that was as loud as a bugle call, Anmer was ready to go again.

Bertie finished up at the stables, then spent the rest of the morning at the barber's shop and having a bath.

"You look very spruced up," said Jess. "If I didn't know better, I'd say you were off to see a young lady."

"As it happens I am off to see Lily at Flora's flat."

"Really? Well, you never get dressed up like that to see me."

Bertie made a hasty retreat to the motorcar and set off for London. He stopped in Piccadilly to buy flowers and a large box of chocolate truffles. Holding a bouquet in one hand and the chocolates in another, Bertie rang the bell to Flora's flat.

"Bertie, this is a surprise," said Flora opening the door. "I'm afraid Lily has gone to a lecture. She won't be back for at least an hour or so."

"I know, something about social welfare, wasn't it?" Bertie took a deep breath. "Actually, it was you I came to see."

He handed her the red roses.

"Bertie? What's wrong?" Flora looked at him suspiciously. "You've never given me flowers before."

"Well, perhaps I should have done?"

"I really think you should come in, Bertie, and I'll get you some tea. You don't seem yourself at all."

Flora bustled into the small scullery area and came back with a tray of crockery.

"Lily seems a lot better now, don't you think?"

"Well, a lot of that is down to your care, Flora."

"She wants to study nursing, either here in London or back in Cambridge. I think it will be good for her." She knelt by the fire and set the small copper kettle down to boil. "We can toast some bread if you are hungry."

Bertie took her arm and helped her up.

"Come and sit next to me, Flora. I'd like to talk to you."

They sat side by side on the sofa. It had been a long time since they had been alone. He kept hold of her hand. Her face was flushed from the heat.

"You see, Flora, I've been doing a lot of thinking. And I know I've been slow and it has taken a time, but I am ready to make a new start, with you, if you'll have me."

"Why, this is so sudden, Mr Jones," she laughed.

"I'm serious, Flora. I'll talk to the Guv'nor, or I'll give it up, or we can go to Russia, I've good friends in the imperial stables. Anything or anywhere you want, Flora, I will give it to you. I will take you there." Bertie stopped. There, he'd said it. He had finally got the words out. He felt a sense of freedom, elation, joy. He got down on one knee. "You see, Flora, I'll even fall at your feet."

"You don't have to do that, Bertie."

Flora slipped down next to him.

"But I don't know what to say. I've waited so long, perhaps too long." She stared into the flames. "I'm such an old maid, Bertie, I'm not sure I can change, not even for you."

"Of course you can, Flora. It will be a new life for us both."

She was quiet. He stroked her hair, golden in the firelight.

"Bertie, I love you. I have always loved you and I will always love you. There will never be anyone else. But I'm not a young girl any more. I've changed and it is too late. I have my life now."

"I understand that it is all rather sudden. Would you, perhaps, give it some thought?"

"No, Bertie, it wouldn't be right. I'm sorry. But we will always be friends, good friends, won't we? Promise me."

Bertie took out his handkerchief and wiped the tears from her face.

"Of course," he said, and although his heart was sorrowful, he was glad that he had spoken.

ひ ひ ひ

It was twilight when he got home. He hadn't waited for Lily to return. The evening was crisp. Lilac and orange crocuses lined the path. The sound of Jess laughing made him smile. He hadn't heard her laugh like that for a very long time, probably since they were

238

children back at Epsom. Bertie walked round the side of the house. Jess was on a bicycle. Walter held on to the saddle and was running next to her. As he let go, she went on for a few feet, then wobbled and collapsed to one side. Bertie was about to dash over, but Walter caught her. He held her gently and righted the bike. Jess brushed herself off. She looked like a young girl, as she clambered back on. Bertie crept back to the front door.

A letter from Northumberland was waiting for him. He thought of the figure in the churchyard and of his own mother, how she would worry and fret over them. Mother always sent him and Reg a card with a prayer at the start of the season. Jess had told him how Mother followed their progress in the sporting pages, right up until she died. He remembered her delight at their arrival and her sadness at their departure. The mother of the suffragette would be no different to the mother of the jockey.

Bertie went to his room. He slit the envelope open with a paperknife and took out the woven cream sheets bordered with black. The scent of lavender filled the air.

Dear Mr Jones,

I wanted to write to you to apologize. I allowed my grief to overtake my better judgement. It was just the shock of seeing you that brought back the pain of my loss. I understand that, of course, you would have avoided this tragic outcome if it had been possible and it must be a hard burden for you to bear. Fate has forever entwined your soul with my daughter's through this unhappy collision.

Between Emily and me, there was a special bond. I always knew when she was in trouble. The morning she died, a robin flew into the house. I opened the window to let it out. The bird looked at me before flapping its wings and disappearing into the heavens. I like to think that it was Emily saying goodbye, but perhaps she lingers. Perhaps she lingers with you and in you, for you too now share the bond.

There were many things left unsaid when we met in the churchyard. You perhaps wanted to understand her, Mr Jones, to understand how she came to do what she did on that dreadful day.

Well, I am sure that she meant you no harm. Her mind had become confused and her body so brutalized that she no longer considered the implications of her actions other than to further her cause.

When people encountered my daughter in later life they saw the wild-eyed fanatic, but I knew the true woman, the kind intelligent spirit that lay beneath. I saw what she became through the treatment inflicted upon her.

I have spoken to many of the women who belonged to the same movement and they told of the punishments that they suffered. The authorities were harsh, Mr Jones. Society was, and is, harsh on those who will not fit neatly into its little boxes. Emily tried to keep from me many of the details of her experiences while she was imprisoned. But I know about the brutality of the feeding tubes. I know that she nearly drowned when they pumped freezing water into her cell because she refused to come out. I know that her misery was so great in Holloway Gaol that she threw herself down an iron staircase and narrowly escaped with her life.

So you see, there were many things that drove her to the episode at Epsom. You are a Christian man, Mr Jones, I saw it on your face when we met in the churchyard, and I would ask that you join me in praying that God will be merciful to her and that she will find peace.

Yours sincerely,

Margaret Davison

Bertie looked out of the window. He could feel someone standing behind him. There was that strange stillness that buzzed whenever she was there, as if they had both moved into a space that was neither for the living nor for the dead. He wondered if he had disappeared from the mortal world or still sat in his chair. He wasn't scared, just sad. He wanted to help her, to free her.

29
The Derby, Epsom,
June 1914

BERTIE WALKED UP TO the caravan at the far edge of the Downs. It was late in the evening but the midsummer sun had yet to disappear completely. It was so quiet, no birdsong, no people, no leaves rustling in the breeze. Tildy sat looking over the hills. Wispy curls from her clay pipe mingled with wood smoke from the campfire and drifted across his path. She had her back to him, lost in the hum of her chanting. He hesitated, wondering if he should slip away and leave her undisturbed.

"Look at the heavens, Bertie." Tildy's voice made him jump. "Strange. Strange and troubled times."

Streaks of orange and pink shot across the sky and engulfed the clouds.

"The world is caught in a madness," she shook her head and turned her face to him. "I've been expecting you."

Bertie knelt down beside her. "Thought you'd be out and about, I was looking for you on the Downs earlier."

They sat listening to the crackle of the fire and looking into the flames. Across the other side of the clearing, the rest of the campsite was empty.

"They're all down at the fair," she said.

Bertie returned his gaze to the fire.

"You seem troubled, my Bertie," she said.

He kept his head down and didn't answer. Tildy touched his arm. "She stays with you."

Bertie kept silent, although his throat ached with the burden of his thoughts.

"She stays with you," Tildy said again.

Bertie rocked over on to his heels and looked up into her eyes. Flashes of red and black brought a sorrow to mind that stretched beyond his own nightmares. He shivered and took a deep breath.

"I thought of telling the vicar. They can help sometimes, or so I've heard, but I don't think he'd understand. Lily even took me to a spiritualist, but it was all nonsense."

Tildy was quiet for a long time. He wondered if she had heard him.

"You have to help her find peace."

Bertie sank his head over his knees. "But how? How can I? She is always there, standing behind me, in my shadow. She is my shadow."

Tildy put her arm about him.

"You must send her to the light. She'll leave you then and you must let her go. Are you ready to do that?"

Bertie straightened himself up. "To be honest, Tildy, I'm not sure. But then I'm not sure of anything anymore."

Tildy gathered her shawl up around her and damped down the fire.

"Come with me." She walked off in the direction of the racecourse. Bertie followed. The sky had turned the colour of blood and Tildy looked as if she was walking up to heaven itself.

By the time they reached the Corner, darkness had fallen. There was no one about, just foxes barking in the distance and a pair of owls hooting from the trees. Bertie felt uneasy. He didn't want to go any further.

"Come on, Bertie. It's alright." Tildy spoke gently, like she used to when he was a boy.

Tildy took a switch of bushy twigs and a box of matches from her apron pocket. She struck a match and it glowed like a Christmas candle. The tinder smouldered. She waved the twigs back and forth. They did not flame but the bitter smell caught in his throat. Tildy chanted Romany words and took his hand.

"Now, hold on to me, Bertie. Keep your feet flat on the ground. Let the earth support you and the heavens protect you."

Moonlight struck the silver of her earrings as they dangled back and forth. The shadows bristled.

Tildy kept tight hold of his hand and they were in a tunnel.

"She doesn't want to hurt you, but she wants to show you."

Bertie felt himself fade away and he was looking out through another's eyes.

A paddock with rough churned turf. Plodding old horses ridden by farm boys galloped around. He heard a voice; someone else's thoughts were in his head.

White ox-eye daisies and crimson poppies peep above the green meadow fresh with early summer rain. They mock me with their fair faces. "Gather us up and make a dainty posy for your mother. Leave well alone. Come and play." I know they are there. I know they tease and test me, but I cannot dwell on them. There is much to be done and time is passing.

Quivering grey midge-balls hang in the air, the flies dart and dance in the watered-down sunbeams. They play in my hair and my eyes, hoping to divert me but I don't respond to their prodding little stings that prick my skin. My attention is focused on the horses cantering around the little makeshift exercise track that surrounds the field. Hunting horses, strong and sinewy. Slow and rhythmically fall their hooves. The thud is reassuringly even on the stodgy ground, it helps guide me to them.

The smell. I try not to think about it. Sweat from the horses and sweat from the men in shirtsleeves who ride them round and round. These people know me and think nothing of it when I ask them to help me in my experiments. Every so often, I dash out among them, seeing if it is possible for a woman to stop a horse. They think it amusing.

"You thinking of joining a circus then, Miss Emily?" one of them calls.

"Something like that," I laugh, "but be sure it is God's work and many people will be grateful for the help you are giving me today."

I know I look an odd sight. I see them exchange glances. Flicking and squelching, the mud gives way beneath my boots and my skirt slops heavily around my legs. I run in front of the horse and as it canters by, snatch at the cracked bridle with one gloveless hand. It is so strong, the force, that it drags the gnarled edges of the leather through the soft underskin of my fingers and palm. They bleed but the beast draws to a stop before me.

"Come on, Jed, go a bit faster this time. Don't spare the horses for me. It could be matter of life and death to a lady in the street," I call and bind my handkerchief around the wounded hand.

He stabs the heel of his boots into the horse's belly and it increases its pace. I wait for it to come round again and rehearse the scene in my head. As the lumbering grey animal approaches, I stumble out over the grass towards him. The horse knows I'm heading for him, I can tell. He stretches his neck out and increases his stride. Jed curses him and tries to pull him in. I cannot keep up but cut across in front. As I get alongside, I see my reflection in the animal's deep-lashed dark eye. He strains to get away, but I have the hard dry leather in my hand and pull. The horse draws up and looks at me, confused. I wave my free arm in a wide circle.

"He's worried about hurting you, Miss Emily. They'll always stop if they can. Horses are clever like that."

"Yes, thank you, Jed. I'm sure they are."

"Tildy? Tildy? Are you there?"

"It's alright, Bertie, I'm here. But you are the watcher. Just stay and wait."

The darkness lifted. He stood on the hill at Epsom. The sun told him it was the middle of the afternoon. People everywhere. They walked past him and through him. The bookies called numbers to the punters that flocked around them, exchanging dockets for coins. He was linked to her like one shadow to another. The voice came to him again.

This bloody wig is itching like hell. I'd like to rip it off and run, run until I find a cold clear stream where I could disappear. All these hot stinking bodies around me. My own hot stinking body. No room to breathe.

Stop being such a cry-baby. You've come this far. Anyway you've quite enjoyed it. You like a bit of a flutter. Think of this as just another one, a different sort of gamble, but one that can make a real difference. Those poor wretched souls condemned to invisibility, silence. You can give them a voice! Onwards now. There's no turning back.

"Go back. Go home." A hiss in my ear, a scaly, fat paw on my arm pinches into my flesh. "Go back to your mother."

An old gypsy woman, all rounded and hunched, puts her face to mine. The black soft silken shroud about her head and shoulders falls over my hands as she drags me down and nearer to her. The material is fine and soft, too fine for such a woman. The basket she carries digs heavily into my side. Beneath the smell of grease and wood smoke, I breathe lavender and roses, fresh and airy. Intense, her black eyes look into mine, they grow lighter.

A dear face is in front of me.

"Mother? Is that you?"

I can see her. She's standing at the gate. Her arms are open, but her face is sad. The leaves in the arch above her hang heavy with raindrop diamonds. Rose blooms shed their petals in a scarlet shower.

"Come back, my dear. Come home." Her voice is low and soft. "You've done enough."

"I want to come mother. I want to, but I must do my duty. I am a soldier of God. I must follow His will."

I call to her, she fades – in her place the old lady stands and stares. Now I know. Now I understand.

"Get thee behind me, Satan!" I hold up my hand and push the taunting demon away.

A man stops and turns back.

"You alright there, miss?" He looks at me oddly. Surely he wouldn't recognize me. Perhaps he is a policeman out of uniform? I take a deep breath and smile. I look at him in what I hope is a demure manner.

"Yes, I'm fine, fine, but thank you. The weather ... so hot ... and she was so close."

"She's just an old gypsy, she don't mean anything by it. Just trying to make a few pennies, aren't you, granny?"

The creature stares. Quietly she mutters words at me in a tongue I do not understand. A demonic spell? A curse? I don't know, but it unsettles me. For a moment I doubt the very reason I am here, but no, she is just a stupid old woman. I must not falter.

"It's alright old love." The man tries to sooth the ranting bundle. "I'll give you something." The old woman shrugs him off. He too is alarmed at the strange goings-on. I can tell that he now regrets his intervention. I retreat behind him.

He turns to me. "These diddies, they do take on so. You've really upset the old girl."

Do not make a fuss. I cannot draw attention to myself. Most of all I cannot think of she who waits for me. If I see her face, hear her voice calling me home, I will not be able to do what I must.

A long deep breath. I collect myself and watch as the man turns back to the old woman and fishes in his front pocket, pulling out a couple of coins. "Here, take this ... ."

But she has gone. I take the opportunity to slip away too. I drift through the crowds, light and invisible, back to my spot. It is busier than ever, louder, rowdier. But I walk through them easily and take my place. Thank you, God. Not long now. I know I can bear it.

I look at the racecard again. Number 1. Royal colours. Purple and red. Remember the purple and red. There's Mary selling her newspapers. Does she know? I doubt it, but pretend not to see her. I settle myself and look out across the racecourse, over the top of the crowd, to the hills beyond. "God's in His heaven, all's right with the world." I think of the Cause, the headlines tomorrow. They'll probably lock me up again, if I am still here, but it will be worth it. Under the King's very nose.

Shouts go up in the distance. The noise of the crowd, the deep shaking of the ground; they tell me that it is time. I hold my racecard up to against the sky to better see the horses approach. I peer over the railings and up the slope. Purple and red. Purple and red. They are coming. How calm I feel. I let the first ones go. I smile to myself; it's time, I'm ready, and my body will not fail me. Go. Go now.

I dip under the white rail, quietly. I see the purple and the red. Two horses come at me from nowhere, steaming engines bearing down; not them, avoid them. "Yea, though I walk through the valley of the shadow of death, I will fear no evil."

I run to the purple and the red as fast as I can. Run now, quickly. They see me. Surprise in their eyes, and then fear. Too fast. I stand in front and my hand goes out for the bridle. I try to call out but the words won't come. I look up into the face of the man. A crack. I am flying. I see her. "Mother, I love you."

Bertie felt the thud in his chest, then his head, and the spinning. Darkness was all around. A shadow of light. A tall, thin woman, almost floating, was before him. He knew her face from a hundred nightmares, but her features were now still and composed. She looked like a schoolteacher about to take the lesson and she stared right at him.

That's all I remember, but I walk here a lot. I would like to go home to Morpeth, but I stay. So here I am, Mr Jones. Standing here before you. It was never my intention to hurt anyone, but you see, there was no other way, sometimes there is no other way. I knew that this would make them sit up and take note. We have to make sacrifices for our beliefs, otherwise what are we?

"Send her to the light, Bertie," Tildy called to him, but he couldn't see her. "Send her in peace to the light."

Bertie repeated the words until the image of the woman faded.

"Who's there?" a man called through the dark.

The voice startled Bertie. The tick of a bicycle wheel slowed to nothing. Torchlight lit up the posts and the contours of the grass. How dark it was now, thought Bertie as he turned and stared into the beam. Caught by its glare, it took a while to make out the shape behind the blinding light.

"Mr Jones? Bertie? Bless you, what are you doing out here?" The voice had lost its menace.

Bertie stood still, one arm shielding his face.

"Mr Jones, it's me, it's Sam. Oh, you gave me a fright at first. Thought it was, well, you know, trouble. We're on a high alert. Good to see you here though, wasn't sure you'd ever come back after that terrible business. Expect you're inspecting the course, that's it, eh Bertie? Early bird and all that."

"Where's Tildy?" Bertie looked round.

"Who?"

"You know, Tildy, the fortune-teller."

"Oh, you mean the old diddy? Hasn't anyone told you? She died a couple of months back. They burned her vardo on the Common. Caused no end of commotion at the time, they thought it was another of those suffragette attacks."

∪ ∪ ∪

Bertie walked the course with the Guv'nor and Walter, thinking it might help to steady him. It was as busy as ever; the sunshine had brought people out in droves. More buses and motorcars appeared. A stream of brightly dressed people poured out from the station, all happy to escape the city heat. Without Tildy, though, it was all empty and without heart.

There were uniformed guards everywhere, and particularly along the line of the course itself. It made everyone nervous. Groups huddled and looked about them, keeping a wary eye on their neighbours. There were some who recognized him, Bertie could tell by their sideways glances, but they moved away and left him in peace.

As they walked along, Bertie strained to hear the Guv'nor above the background babble of the crowd. The murmur of voices was drowned by vehicles driving past, even more occasionally a skylark could be heard calling overhead.

The sharp crack of gunshot echoed from the hill. Everyone stopped. Bertie jumped. Six bullets, one after the other, exploded in the air. There was complete silence for an instant. Then men called out. Women and children screamed.

Police whistles sounded and more uniformed men rushed to the spot. A black, windowless van crawled through the gibbering mass.

"Please get back to the enclosure now, Mr Jones," a policeman ushered him along.

"Not again." Bertie felt his legs go weak. "Surely not again. Will this never stop?"

"I'm afraid, sir, this is only the beginning." The policemen saw him safely to the jockeys' room.

∪ ∪ ∪

The big race was up next. Bertie put on his silks. His hands shook as he tried to tie the scarf. Five attempts it took before he felt happy. The Guv'nor had said that if he didn't want to come to Epsom at all that year, let alone run in the Derby, it was perfectly understandable. But Bertie couldn't hide away all his life.

Danny came and sat next to him on the bench. He was ready for the next race and about to go to the weighing room. "Everyone thinks you're very brave to come back."

"No one else has stayed away. Why should I?"

"But no one else was pulled over by some mad old bird."

"Don't say that, Danny. It's no joking matter."

"Sorry, Bertie. I didn't mean to be flippant, but I was being honest."

Bertie sighed. "You know, we heard shots earlier, out on the hill."

"That's nothing to worry about, it's alright," said Danny. "I mean I heard what happened. They were blanks. Some woman had been given the gun by her husband, and you'll love this, to be used in case she was molested. Anyway, she unloaded the thing into this copper. I gather the Metropolitan Police are not too amused, but she's not a protestor, or anything like that."

"Well, that's something, I suppose."

Some of the other jockeys were chattering and laughing. They fell silent as they went by.

"Have you heard from Lily lately?" Danny asked.

"She's still staying with Flora. Jess goes down a lot and we met for tea a couple of weeks back. She is getting better."

Danny fiddled with his gloves. "Back at Ascot, you said that you'd never trusted me. What can I do to put that right?"

"You've already done it, Danny." Bertie looked him straight in the eye. "You've been a true friend through all this, more than, well, more than others I thought I could rely on."

"Do me a favour, Bertie, would you? Give yourself a bit of a break, eh? You're always so hard on yourself." Danny winked at him and tap-danced out to the weighing room.

Bertie sat quietly for a few moments. The last year weighed heavily on him. Maybe Snowy had been right to get out of riding.

Sam came rushing across the room to him. He was waving a brown paper package. "Bertie, this was left for you. I'm sorry, I forgot all about it, if truth be told." Sam paused to mop his brow. "Come to think of it, that old gypsy you were asking about last night, she left it. It's been here a while, we weren't sure whether to send it on, but she said to wait until you came back. And you always do come back."

Alone in the corner of the room, Bertie took off the paper. Underneath was a blanket and inside was the carved dove from Tildy's vardo. Bertie held it. Under the gold paint, the shape of the bird felt so real that there should be a heartbeat. The soft wood felt almost like down, plump and warm; each wing held itself ready to expand into flight. Tildy's presence surrounded him and he heard her voice, remember the souls of our dear ones are always with us, even if they are far away, even if they are in heaven. Taking a deep breath, Bertie pulled on his boots and got himself ready for the race.

U U U

Bertie left the weighing room. Outside it was yellow. Yellow sunshine, yellow grass, yellow parasols. Bertie scanned the crowds. Yellow became gold, the auburn hair of Percy. There he was with Clar on one side, and Jack and Mark on the other.

"Hello, Bert." Percy waved. "You look surprised to see us."

"Alarmed is probably more the case, Percy my darling, but Bertie is too polite to say so," Clar gave Bertie a kiss. "Hello, brother Bertie. I've brought these three reprobates along but made them promise to behave."

"Well as long as you don't go leaving us abruptly like last year," joked Percy.

Clar dug him in the ribs.

"For heaven's sake, Perce," muttered Jack.

"But Bertie doesn't mind. I'm just trying to put a lighter view on things, to cheer him up," protested Percy.

"I'll do my best," Bertie tried to smile.

"Well, Bertie, we'll push off. But remember we're here and cheering for you," said Clar.

"Good luck! See you later." They called and waved as Bertie carried on to the paddock. He didn't look back.

U U U

Bertie led the field out on to the course. His horse shivered despite the bright sun. A small boy squinted up at him, stretching out his hand to try and touch them. Bertie tipped his cap. The boy gasped and, standing as straight as a soldier, saluted with a serious face.

Tapping the horse lightly with his boots, Bertie cantered down to the start line. He kept his eyes straight ahead. He knew she was watching. He knew she would always be watching.

Postscript

EMMELINE PANKHURST, THE FOUNDER of the suffragette movement, died in 1928. Bertie Jones attended the funeral, travelling
to London and laying a wreath. On the wreath was written:

"To do honour to the memory of Mrs Pankhurst
and Miss Emily Davison."

Author's note

Although *The King's Jockey* was inspired by real people and actual events, it is a work of fiction. Events, characters, timelines and situations have been changed. Certain characters are composites or entirely fictitious.

A big thank you to all the lovely people who have given me such help and support while I have been working on this book. Thanks go in particular to: Elise Valmorbida as it was her evening class at Central Saint Martin's that inspired me to write fiction again and it was while doing this that I "found" Bertie; Jill Dawson and the brilliant Gold Dust programme put me on the right track with my first draft; and Richard Beard and Rena Brennan of the National Academy of Writing who helped me get to a final draft.

I would also like to thank Ermyn Lodge Racing Stables and Stud in Epsom, owned by Lesley & Tony Smith, and especially to Pat Phelan the trainer who was kind enough to take the time to show me round their fabulous stables. Thanks also to Angela and David Marshall, as well as Alan Knights, for arranging the trip to the stables and listening to me blather on. Any errors in horsemanship and racing are due entirely to me and not to any information I received.

While working on this book, I have been lucky enough to meet many talented writers, many of whom I am proud to call my friends: Taiwo Dayo-Payne, the Corpus Christi group, and the NAW class of 2011.

Many thanks are due to Charlotte and Val for their incisive editorial input and devilish red pens. I would also like to thank all at Solis Press for their patience and belief in this project. Last, but certainly not least, thank you my dear family and, above all, Rob, who is always my guiding star.

Printed in Great Britain
by Amazon.co.uk, Ltd.,
Marston Gate.